MAY✲BIRD

and the Ever After

BOOK ONE

MAY ❧ BIRD

and the Ever After

BOOK ONE

JODI LYNN ANDERSON

Illustrations by Leonid Gore

Atheneum Books for Young Readers

New York London Toronto Sydney

Atheneum Books for Young Readers

An imprint of Simon & Schuster Children's Publishing Division

1230 Avenue of the Americas

New York, New York 10020

Text copyright © 2005 by Jodi Lynn Anderson

Illustrations copyright © 2005 by Leonid Gore

Map on pp. x–xi by Peter Ferguson

Manufactured in the United States of America

First Edition

10 9 8 7 6 5 4 3

Library of Congress Cataloging-in-Publication Data

Anderson, Jodi Lynn.

May Bird and the Ever After / by Jodi Lynn Anderson.

p. cm.

Summary: Lonely and shy, ten-year-old May Ellen Bird has no idea what awaits her when she falls into the lake and enters the Ever After, home of ghosts and the Bogeyman.

ISBN-13: 978-0-689-86923-5

ISBN-10: 0-689-86923-1

[1. Fantasy.] I. Title.

PZ7.A53675Mayb 2005

[Fic]—dc22   2004017829

For

My Mom and Dad

❦ CONTENTS ❦

A Thank-you to the Dearly Beloved

Herein lies Jen Weiss, an editor who was nice; and

Herein sleeps Sarah Burnes, who helped me to earn.

Zhenya Fomin was my boyfriend; may he now rest in peace.

Erika Loftman lent brilliance, so off her plot, please.

Liesa Abrams gave heart, but then *it* gave out.

Ginee Seo pitched in, but soon came down with gout.

Lexy James rose to aid me, but fell out of a tree.

He went down with a fight, but I must thank Chong Lee.

Jeannie Ng's graceful pen sadly held poison ink.

Leonid Gore was de-limbed, I think.

Ben Cawood flew off, but his insights were shared.

Winter took Pony Boy, who never had hair.

And here for your view is a family of six,

Plus nieces, one nephew, and others I've missed.

My family trees are what gave me the woods,

And the woods helped me write this and

Think that I could.

PLATTE OF DESPAIR AND UNKNOWN LANDS
SNIFFING PHANTOM
Ether
Southern Territories
DEAD SEA
Nine Knaves Grotto
Party of Ghouls
Catacomb Cliffs
GHOUL
Belle Morte
BOGEY

MAY BIRD
and the Ever After

PROLOGUE

ay Ellen Bird was born on a Saturday, in the east wing of the third floor of White Moss Manor. Tiny and squishy and curious, she balled her little fists and noticed many things: the spider snoozing in its nest in the window, the thick smell of the woods crouching outside the house, and the shadowy figure that hovered over her crib when no one else was around.

Just a simple baby, she didn't know she had any reason to be afraid. She didn't know that Briery Swamp, West Virginia, had lost seventeen people to mysterious causes.

In 1897 one Bertha "Bad Breath" Brettwaller, age 83, hobbled into the woods to forage for wild garlic. She didn't come back. When the townspeople searched her house for clues about where she'd gone off to, they found nothing curious, except that she did not own a toothbrush.

Three nuns moved into a cottage on Droopy View Hill in 1902 to live a quiet, holy life and teach a small group of Appalachian children to spell "Appalachia" and other words. One April morning the three, up to shenanigans on their day off, skipped into the woods for freeze tag and a cool dip. They were never heard from again.

At a lake deep in the shelter of the trees, a mother duck was sunbathing blissfully when her seven ducklings waddled off for a swim. They floated out onto the water, happily quacking the latest duckling gossip to one another, when there was a splash. They vanished completely. Their mother waddled forlornly along the water's edge for three days before quacking her sad way south. Being just a simple duck, she could not report the incident.

The biggest and most shocking tragedy to hit Briery Swamp came in 1927. That was when twelve fur trappers, meeting for a trappers' convention at that same lake in the hills, went in to bathe under three feet of water and didn't come up again. Nobody in town knew of anything amiss for three days. They didn't know the trappers or even that they were in the area. Nobody ever *would* have known if it hadn't been for Elmo Peterson.

Elmo was the thirteenth trapper. He straggled onto Main Street that third day, tired, hungry, and smellier than any skunk Briery Swamp had seen since Tickles, the stuffed skunk that hung on the wall of the old post office. Jada Lincoln Tully, a reporter for *The Briery Inquirer*, never did get the story, because Elmo Peterson had gone stark raving mad. He took to wearing footy pajamas and jogging circles around the town at midnight. The bodies of his friends were never found.

After that, people started to move away.

Judge Fineas McCreely said that he'd developed allergies to the West Virginia jasmine that bloomed nightly, and moved his family to Montana. A whole slew of lawyers and their families left with him.

Alligator Jasper, who was named for the teeth scars he'd

obtained as a toddler on a visit to Louisiana, got his seventeen cousins, who made up half the town, to go on safari with him in Africa. They were trampled by a rhinoceros.

Aida Peterson, the town beauty who married crazy Elmo Peterson, because of his fame as sole survivor of the tragedy, claimed they were moving to be near her ailing aunt in Tampa. But everybody knew Aida Peterson didn't have any kin still living.

The truth was, everyone was afraid. After a while the only residents left in Briery Swamp were the postmaster and Tickles, the stuffed skunk.

Soon a drought came to the town, and the swamps dried up—all but for one lake in the mountains, back behind skunkweed and sinkholes and brambleberry bushes, where no one bothered to go.

Eventually the postmaster died. The post office saw its last letter come in 1951, nearly a year later. The mailman who delivered it wandered off his route into the woods that same afternoon and disappeared.

The letter sat in the post office for many years after that, unread. Fifty years later a young woman, with the last name of Bird, moved into the old Brettwaller place, and had a child. Briery Swamp slept. And May Ellen Bird, only a baby after all, who did not know the strange history of her town or even the name of it yet, was blissfully unaware that it slept with one eye open.

PART ONE

Into the Woods

CHAPTER ONE

A Sack of Beans

May Ellen Bird, age ten, occasionally glanced at the brochure her mom had taped to her door that afternoon, and scowled. SAINT AGATHA'S BOARDING SCHOOL FOR GIRLS WITH HIGH SOCKS. A few minutes ago May had taken her black marker and written the word "socks" over what had originally been the last word of the headline. Judging by the photos of girls in stiff plaid uniforms plastering the brochure, girls with "high prospects" was not nearly as accurate.

The woods watched silently through the farthest east window of White Moss Manor as May tried to concentrate on her work. And sometimes, looking up from the curious project strewn across her desk, chewing on a pencil, May watched them back.

Skinny and straight, with short black bobbed hair and big brown eyes, May ran her fingers over the objects before her—a clump of black fur, a lightbulb, a jar, a book titled *Secrets of the Egyptian Mummies,* and some wire. Occasionally May swiveled to gaze at Somber Kitty, who laid across her bed like a discarded piece of laundry. His belly faced the ceiling and he eyed her lazily.

Neither May nor Somber Kitty knew it, but passing squirrels and chipmunks thought the cat was decidedly ugly. He had huge pointy ears and a skinny tail, and he was mostly bald, with just a little bit of fuzz covering his soft skin. His mouth was turned down in a thoughtful frown—an expression he had been wearing ever since May had gotten him three years before, on her seventh birthday.

May had disliked him immediately.

"He's bald," she'd said.

"He's a hairless Rex," her mom had replied. "He's interesting."

"He looks depressed."

"He's *somber.*"

May's mom had then explained that "somber" meant "sad," which also meant "melancholy." So that was the one thing they both agreed on. The cat was most definitely sad. It was almost as if, from the moment he had set his tilty green eyes on May, he had sensed her disappointment in him, and sympathized.

May had not wanted him, of course. Her first cat, Legume, had died when May was six, and she had resigned herself to a life of grief. She knew there could never be another Legume, which, by the way, is another word for *peanut.* She'd insisted on wearing black ever since.

But her mom had insisted on another pet. "You spend too much time alone," she had said with big, brown, worried eyes, even bigger and browner than May's. Mrs. Bird had long ago given up trying to get May to bring home friends from school.

"Why don't you invite Maribeth over?"

"She has the chicken pox."

"Claire?"

"She's only allowed out on President's Day."

"Mariruth?"

"Leprosy. It's so sad."

Finally one afternoon May had stood in her mom's doorway, crossed her arms, and announced that she would accept a cat as long as it was a black tiger.

She got stuck with Somber Kitty.

Noticing her watching him now, Somber Kitty opened his mouth and asked, "Mew? Meow? Meay?"

"That's my name, don't wear it out," May replied.

Knock knock knock.

May's mom poked her head into the room.

"So what do you think?" she asked hopefully, smiling. "It looks like a great school, doesn't it?"

May crossed her arms over her waist and looked toward her bed. "Maybe if you're a nun," she offered thoughtfully.

The smile on Mrs. Bird's face dropped, and May felt her heart drop too.

"Maybe it's okay," May added. She looked at Somber Kitty who looked at her. Their traded glance said Somber Kitty understood, even if Mrs. Bird didn't: May could never be happy at a school like Saint Agatha's, wearing high socks and stuck in New York City without the woods.

"Well, it's something to think about," Mrs. Bird said hopefully, biting her lip. "I think the structure would be good for you. I'd live right nearby. And we could tour the city on the weekends."

Mrs. Bird ducked into the room, stooped down, and made her way to May's desk. From the ceiling hung a number of objects: a dragonfly wind chime, a clothes hanger strung with old sumac

leaves, old dry strands of ivy. At the window sat a pair of binoculars to watch for insects and critters, and a telescope aimed at the
sky for looking at the stars.

The walls were so covered in pictures that you couldn't see the
old calico wallpaper. They were drawings of Legume, of Mrs. Bird,
of the woods, and of imaginary places and friends and creatures:
some with wings and purple hair, black capes and horns, and one
particularly spooky one with a lopsided head. There were none of
Somber Kitty, who often followed Mrs. Bird's eyes to the wall with
hurt curiosity, searching for a likeness of himself.

Studying the spookier, darker pictures, Mrs. Bird's eyes sometimes got big and worried again. "You don't want people to think
you're eccentric," she'd say, looking more somber than a certain
cat.

"You ready for the picnic?" Mrs. Bird asked, walking up behind
May and hugging her tight.

May nodded, tugging at the tassels of the sari she'd wrapped
around her body like a dress. Because Briery Swamp was too
small and empty to have a Day, May and Mrs. Bird always
attended the annual Hog Wallow Day Extravaganza and Picnic.
It was two towns away, but it involved a parade and games and
seeing all the kids from school. "Yep," she replied, trying to
sound bright.

Mrs. Bird kissed the top of May's head, her jasmine perfume
sinking into May's sari.

"Your classmates will be happy to see you."

May blushed. She doubted it.

May didn't mention that since school let out, she had made
improvements—*in secret*—getting ready for this exact day. She

had gained two pounds, eating sesame-and-peanut-butter balls two at a time, so she wasn't *quite* so skinny. Her knees didn't look as knobby as they had. And she had worked on her smile in the mirror. Usually May's smile looked like a grimace. But she'd gotten it to look halfway normal, she thought. Girls with nice smiles made friends. Mrs. Bird liked to remind May of this when she came to volunteer on hot-dog days and saw how May sat at the end of the fifth-grade table, curled over her carrots.

"I don't know how to make friends," May would say, embarrassed.

"Well, actually, you don't really *make* friends," Mrs. Bird always replied. "You just have to let them happen."

May didn't think that was very helpful.

"What are you making now?" Mrs. Bird asked.

May surveyed the pieces in front of her. "A materializer. It makes things you imagine real. Like if you imagine a pair of emerald earrings, it makes the earrings appear."

Mrs. Bird crouched, moved back toward the door, then turned a thoughtful gaze on May. "Maybe you should be a lawyer someday—then you can make enough money to get me those earrings *for real*." May glanced at the materializer. It was *supposed* to be for real.

"You'd better get a quick bath. I'll run the water."

May lounged on her bed, picturing what it would be like if she went to the picnic today, and her classmates couldn't recognize her with the extra two pounds and the big, real-looking smile pasted on her face.

Who's that girl? one of the boys, Finny Elway, would say. *She reminds me of May.*

"They'd see the best me," May said aloud to Somber Kitty.

"Meow," the cat replied with interest.

A few minutes later Mrs. Bird's footsteps sounded on the stairs again, then came the squeak of the spigot being turned off, and the footsteps retreating. May stripped off her sari and walked out into the hall for her bath. Just outside the bathroom door, she paused. Inside she could hear the splish splash of the water being swirled around the tub.

May grasped the ceramic door handle and twisted it, opening on an empty room. In the middle sat a white tub with claw feet, with water gently waving back and forth. Leaning over, she inspected it, then climbed in. May was used to strange things like this. Her mom had always said all sorts of quirks came with a house as old as theirs. May used to insist it was ghosts. But Mrs. Bird had long ago given her one too many stern looks on the topic. So May simply sank beneath the water and let bubbles drift out of her of nose.

When she stepped out of the bathroom in a towel a half an hour later, the steam poured out behind her, engulfing the tiny figure of Somber Kitty, who waited in the doorway, licking his paws one by one. With the cat at her heels, May walked into her room and pulled on the turquoise tank top and shorts her mom had laid out instead of the usual black clothes.

Last summer May had built a tiny shelf that snaked its way around the whole room, way up high. Along the sill was the collection of quartz rocks she'd carefully picked from the woods. Her mom swore they were worthless, but they seemed as dazzling and precious as diamonds to May. There was also a complete zoo of lopsided animals she'd made out of paper clips, a perfect heart-shaped pinecone she and Somber Kitty had found together in town, and an onyx brooch left behind by the lady who'd once lived here before them—a lady by the name of Bertha.

The quartz rocks stared at her as if they, too, wanted to go wherever she was headed. Once she was dressed she pulled the smallest one off the shelf and let it hitch a ride in her pocket, for luck.

The picnic was a disaster.

Sweaty and red-faced, May Bird spent much of the afternoon pedaling around the lawn of Hog Wallow Town Hall on a bike with tassels flapping from the handlebars and a stowaway Rex cat who'd insisted on coming tucked into her backpack. She'd spotted a gaggle of classmates across the grass, talking and laughing.

May kept herself busy, scaring crickets out of the grass, then sat against a tree near the picnic table where mothers had gathered, working on her smile.

She overheard the parents talking. "Thank you, we love the house. We're always getting offers," Mrs. Bird was saying, adjusting her hat in a familiar way. She had always said the sun on her face gave her wrinkles. "But I think May needs to be somewhere more . . . average." May's mom looked down at her hands while she said this.

Unseen, May blushed. She knew that the reason her mom wanted to move was because she thought *May* needed to be more average. At that moment, Mrs. Bird's eyes drifted toward May's direction and widened, embarrassed.

May pretended she hadn't noticed, plucked grass between her

fingers, and then stood up. Without looking up she made her way toward the other kids.

Pollen blew across the grass, and Somber Kitty nipped at her heels. She lifted him up, frowning at him. "I'm going to hang out with the humans," she said. "Go play." He kissed her, his tiny pink tongue darting out to tickle her chin, making her wince before she placed him on the grass and gave him a pat on the butt to shoo him away. She nervously straightened out her clothes and made her way against the breeze to where the children had huddled into a tight group. There she tacked herself to the circle awkwardly, like a losing try at pin the tail on the donkey.

Claire Arneson stood at the center of the group of kids. Instead of being pulled into the usual pigtails, her hair was down and combed across her back, shimmery as mountain water. Two bright, pink-ribboned barrettes held back her bangs. May had always wondered why she couldn't be more like Claire, when Claire made being herself seem so easy. She always had something funny to say. She never looked big-eyed and serious. And she had a million friends, none of whom were bald cats.

"I'm only allowed to have eight people," Claire was saying, "Maribeth's coming, and Colleen. . . . Finny, can you come?"

May smiled big as Claire singled out the kids that would attend her annual Kites and Katydids birthday party. Maybe they hadn't even recognized her yet. Maybe Claire would invite her to the party, thinking she was inviting a mysterious stranger.

"Hey, May . . ."

May brightened and nodded as Claire turned to her, her heart doing a jig in her chest. "Isn't that your dancing cat?" Claire pointed one perfect finger across the lawn and all eyes followed.

Oh. Disappointment. "Yes." May tried her nongrimace smile again. It felt like the old one—grimacelike.

The whole class remembered Somber Kitty because May had brought him in for her "How To" report in February. Everyone else had done their reports on things like "How to Make a Bologna Sandwich" and "How to Sew a Pillow." May had done hers on "How to Teach Your Cat to Dance." It was one of the few times May's classmates had actually noticed she was alive in a good way. (They'd noticed her in a bad way many times.) It had also sort of been cheating, because Somber Kitty, despite his general sadness, loved to dance and had known how since he was a kitten.

"That was so cool!" Finny Elway said.

May cleared her throat, her disappointment fading. They thought she had a cool cat.

"Yeah," Elmore Smith said. "But the best was when May tried to fly off the roof of her mom's car with that bunch of balloons, remember?" Everyone burst into giggles. May's heart sank. She tried to smile, as if she was in on the joke. She rubbed at the scar on her knee from that incident, which had happened at last year's picnic. Ever since then she'd been afraid of heights.

"Hey, remember May Bird, Warrior Princess?" Maribeth asked. Now the laughter exploded, and May began to really and truly blush, remembering the day the photo had fallen out of her social studies textbook onto the floor. It had been a shot of her and Somber Kitty pretending to be Amazon warriors hiding in the trees. In it, May had on her black sparkly bathing suit that made her feel like she was wearing the night sky, and a belt wrapped around her shoulder with long sticks tucked beneath the strap for arrows. Mrs. Bird had said May shouldn't dress like a half-naked wild thing, but she had stuck the photo into one of May's note-books to surprise her and make her smile. It *had* surprised her by falling out. It *hadn't* made her smile. It had made her want to sink into the gold and green tiles of the school floor.

"Remember when May forgot to lock the bathroom door on the bus trip, and it swung open?"

May shifted from foot to foot, looking at the ground to hide her flaming face. She gazed toward the adults' table helplessly, want-ing to make sure her mom couldn't see. Luckily Mrs. Bird was still busy talking with the other grown-ups.

It was the three-legged race that saved her. The mayor of Hog Wallow announced that everyone was to line up across the lawn by the pink flag.

No sooner had he said it than, shouting and laughing, the children went tearing across the grass. Dazed, May dragged her-self after them, her long skinny legs straggling. Races were her favorite. She was deadly fast.

But you needed a partner for a three-legged race. And everyone paired up without her.

"Mew? Meow? Meay?" Somber Kitty asked, appearing out of nowhere and rubbing against her shins.

"Cats can't race," May said with a sigh. They watched the racers line up, and then the starting bell went off, and Claire and Maribeth pulled out in front. They were way slower than May would have been. But May would have traded her speed for a partner to race with.

She turned around and walked back to her bike, far away from the crowd, and plopped down next to it in the grass.

"I think if I could go somewhere else, I could be someone

else," she whispered to her cat. She picked a puffy white dandelion out of the grass between her sandals and blew at the seeds.

Somber Kitty, who always seemed to know May had no one else to tell her feelings to, mewed in agreement, though he had no idea what she was saying.

"But that doesn't mean I want to move to New York," she quickly added.

Then she slumped. She felt as heavy as a sack of beans. But then, a sack of beans never got embarrassed or did stupid balloon tricks in front of other sacks of beans or forgot to lock the bathroom door. Come to think of it, life was probably easy for all the beans of the world. Being a sack of them wouldn't be so bad.

May picked another dandelion and blew on it. "Maybe I'd rather be a sack of beans," she told the fuzzy white floaters. Somber Kitty meowed disapprovingly.

"Don't worry, Kitty. I'm not going anywhere."

Somber Kitty rolled himself into a ball and continued to stare at her. He didn't look so sure.

"Unless you know something I don't."

At the edge of the grass, the trees watched her.

They knew better.

CHAPTER TWO

A Letter From Before

"Y ou can drop me off here."

Mrs. Bird looked at May, then at the dirt road ahead of them, then back at May, who sat with her back straight the way her mom always asked her to. Mrs. Bird ran her free hand through her wavy brown hair as she brought the car to a stop.

"You sure you don't want to just come home, pumpkin?"

May nodded.

"I wish you wouldn't spend so much time in the woods. I worry about snakes."

May opened the car door, but felt her mom's hand on her back. She turned. "I love you, pumpkin," Mrs. Bird said.

"You too."

"Wait, May?"

May was halfway out of the car when she ducked back down to meet her mom's eyes. "You know I wouldn't trade you for any-body in the world, right?"

May smiled. Mrs. Bird seemed to breathe a sigh of relief before May went around to the back of the car to get her bike and her backpack. Somber Kitty jumped out of the back too, just before May closed the door and the car pulled away.

"Thank gosh," May said. She looked around the dilapidated and deserted main square of Briery Swamp. Except for being dry and dead, it looked like any other town in the state of West Virginia.

May Bird had always thought that if states were like people, West Virginia would be the shy relative of, say, Texas. Texas was big and bad and sprawled out flat, saying "Look at me, I'm Texas!" West Virginia was mysterious and it liked to keep to itself. It hid in the folds of mountains, resting in the cool shade. It was sweet, beautiful, and bashful. Its woods held its secrets, or at least it seemed that way to May.

Briery Swamp wasn't much of a town anymore. The houses that had once stood in a sociable gaggle at the town square had crumbled into crooked piles of bricks, overgrown with weeds. A possum, four snakes, and a hundred thousand three hundred and six earthworms had moved into what used to be the mayor's graceful mansion. The postmaster's old cottage was the centipedes' favorite place for hatching long crawly babies.

The only building in town that still looked like a building at all was the post office itself. It stood up from the weeds like a snaggle tooth, three of its walls mostly collapsed and pouring onto the grass like a waterfall.

May laid her bike on its side and stared around. There wasn't much to do except meander around the square with Somber Kitty and tell him made-up stories about the people who'd lived here, and why they'd moved away. Since there had been a drought in Briery Swamp for as long as she could remember, her favorite theory was that the rain had retired to Florida, and all the people of Briery Swamp had followed it there.

"Meow," Somber Kitty said, which May interpreted to mean "At least we have each other." The pair spent an hour or more kicking rocks up and down the road, until Somber Kitty ran off into the woods chasing a moth. Then, for the millionth time, May ducked in through the hole in the old post office wall and began digging through the rocks for treasures. Once she'd found a stuffed skunk mounted on a plaque. She'd also found three old rubber stamps saying "First Class," "Second Class," and "Third Class."

Now she thrust her hands into a pile of rubble against the back wall, sifting out the larger rocks from the smaller ones, hoping to find maybe another stamp, or an old letter. She was just digging in with one last thrust when her fingers lit on something that felt distinctly different from rubble. It felt like paper. May pinched with her thumb and forefinger and gently extracted it, watching a corner of molded white emerge from the pile. It slid out with a little scratch.

It *was* a letter. A huge find. May couldn't believe her luck.

"Meay?"

"Oh, you scared me," May said, her heart racing as she met Somber Kitty's tilty green eyes. "Look at this."

May held the letter up for the cat to see. "Somebody didn't get their mail." She ran her tongue against the inside of her bottom lip, thinking. "Maybe it's some private stuff," she whispered breathlessly to the cat, who had already gotten bored of the letter and started licking his black paws.

The envelope was clearly very old—yellowed with age. One

corner was folded back so that the stamp and postmark were visible. Though it was faded, May could just make out the date: June 11, 1951.

"I hope they weren't holding their breath," May said with a small, curious smile. A slant of light found its way through the hole in the wall and striped her face, making her look like two halves of herself. Where the flap of the envelope ended in a point there was a faded stamp of a tree surrounded by snowflakes and, when May looked closer, the face of an old woman, peering through the leaves. May stared at the stamp for a long time, a knot of unease gathering beneath her ribs. It was one of the prettiest pictures she'd ever seen, but her gut didn't like it. She had to think for a minute to figure out why, but then she had it. The thing about it was that you couldn't tell if the person who'd drawn it had meant for the lady to be a nice, old woman, inviting you into the tree, or someone not so nice, waiting to pounce on you like . . . a tiger.

Letting out her breath, she turned the letter over, rubbed at the dust and mold covering the address, and froze. She blinked twice. She read the words in front of her three times, her eyes as wide as cereal bowls.

The envelope, in blue, loopy letters, read:

Miss May Ellen Bird
White Moss Manor
Briery Swamp, WV

"Meay?" May jolted, her eyes shooting to Somber Kitty, who'd snuck up beside her.

"Shh, Kitty."

She patted the cat's head absently, then returned her gaze to the letter. She looked at the seal on the back, then turned it over again to look at the address. *Her* address. She felt like a firefly was lighting her up from the inside out. She stood up and looked around, then sat down again.

It had to be a different May Bird.

But then, there was her address.

May chewed on a finger, thinking hard.

The date had to be wrong. Nineteen fifty-one. May didn't even think her *mom* had been born then.

But if the date was wrong, and the letter was sent recently, then how did it end up buried under all the old bricks of the post office?

May turned the letter over again and again and again, trying to make sure she was really seeing it.

"Well, Kitty," she whispered, "what do you think we should do?"

May bit her lip, then raised a pinky to her mouth and began nibbling just the tip. She lowered her fingers to the slit in the back of the envelope to open it, then changed her mind and stopped, then started again. Once she started, she ripped it open with lightning speed.

There was nothing strange about the letter itself, except what was written on it. It was a single sheet of yellowed paper, just like an old letter should be, mottled with blue swirls and waves where the paper had gotten wet, making the ink bleed and blur. May pulled it out gingerly, worried it might disintegrate. She unfolded it.

Dear Miss Bird,

The Lady of North Farm had asked us to send you this map to Briery Swamp Lake, just in case. She thought you might be having trouble finding it on your own, and she is expecting you to be prompt. We are very sorry for the danger you will endure, but we eagerly await your arrival should you survive it, as we are in great need of your help. The Lady joins me in sending you good luck and best wishes.

Sincerely,

Ms. H. Kari Kagaki

T. E. A. Travel

May let out a sigh of relief. That settled it. She didn't know Kari Kagaki or any North Farm. They had the wrong person. She sank back, feeling like a casserole dish full of Jell-O. She looked at the envelope and the picture again. It brought back that uneasy knot.

May's fingers stretched toward the map, and she looked at it sideways, trying to pretend that she wasn't looking at all. She immediately recognized a few things. There was the town square. There—the knot got worse—was White Moss Manor, and there were the woods. The map even showed a dark smudge, where the giant gathering of briers—the Endless Briers, May called them, because she'd never managed to cross them—wound their way thickly along the east side of May's woods.

And beyond them, there was a lake.

Almost as much as the letter itself, this couldn't be believed. There were no lakes in Briery Swamp. Not even a puddle. The squirrels and chipmunks, May had always supposed, went to the next town over to get their water. If the lake had been there in 1951, it wasn't there now.

May crumpled up the letter and dropped it on the ground. But as soon as she stood up, she swept down and picked it up. Turning red, she flattened the letter out, folded it, and tucked it into her knapsack. She caught Somber Kitty looking at her thoughtfully.

"I don't want to litter," she said, knowing there wasn't a thing in the world that would get her to go looking for that lake. But Somber Kitty didn't appear to be convinced. May sighed. "Really."

The truth was, nobody had ever said they needed her.

"Mew," was all she got in reply from someone who needed her very much. If a cat-to-English dictionary had been handy, and May had looked up "mew," it would have translated into something like "curiosity killed the cat."

May climbed onto her bike, held her knapsack down for the cat to crawl into, and together they headed home.

CHAPTER THREE

Beyond the Endless Briers

L ate the next morning May put on her favorite black tank
top and black denim overalls and walked out onto the front
porch. She sank into the rocker, balancing a bowl of oatmeal and a glass of orange juice in her hands. Somber Kitty
appeared just behind her, slipping his way through the crack in
the screen door and perching by her feet.

She yawned, her mouth gaping like a bat cave. Last night her
mom had gotten her out of bed to watch a meteor shower. They'd
laid on a sleeping bag on the back porch and competed over how
many racing, fiery balls they could each point out.

Things had started nicely enough, but
soon May had started trying to steal
her mom's meteors, and vice versa.
After that they'd started poking
each other to cause distractions.

"You care more about winning
than about me!" May had shouted,
laughing.

Mrs. Bird had laughed too.

"That's not true. I care about you more than all the meteors. Even more than most of the smaller comets."

"Ha-ha." May had rolled her eyes.

They'd stayed up until long past midnight.

But even though May was tired this morning, she wasn't *sleepy*. It was the kind of day where the world seemed full of promise. The dragonflies were humming, and the sun beating on the porch made the wood smell woodsy. It felt like it was a Day that Meant Something.

May thrust her hand into her pocket and felt the map. She wanted to think it had jumped into her pocket on its own. But she knew that wasn't quite true.

She drank and ate quickly. If it was a Day that Meant Something, she wanted to find out what that Something was.

In the breeze Somber Kitty stretched his body long and thin as a rubber band, and then leaped up onto her lap. He licked her chin, thumping his paw down on her chest to hold her in place.

"Yuck." May scrunched up her face. She stood up and brushed him off with the slightest move of her wrist, though he struggled to stay on. He clung to the waistband of her short overalls, dangling like a set of keys on the school custodian.

"Mew? Meow? Meay?"

"C'mon, Kitty, off."

Somber Kitty let go, bounced back onto his rubbery hind legs, and watched her walk to the edge of the deck, then down into the grass of the front yard. He jumped down behind her and lifted his paws gingerly. Already the sun had scorched the grass so that it was brown and dry.

"Mom, I'm going in the woods," May called in through the screen door.

"Don't go too far, baby," her mother's voice called back.

May pulled out the map, looked at it once more, and tucked it in her pocket. Her bike was lying right there on the grass in front of the stairs. She picked up the tasseled handlebars and set the bike to moving, straddling it and standing on the pedals. A pinwheel she'd stuck into the rim at the back of her seat spun and glinted in the July sun. She bumped along the grass to the edge of the woods, where a dirt trail zigzagged its way into the trees.

May was flying, leaves tickling her bare arms on either side as she flashed and bumped and jostled past the trees. Somber Kitty raced behind her, stopping only to clean his paws occasionally, or bite a gnat out of his fuzzy coat before racing to catch up. When May skidded to a halt right in front of the fallen tree that marked where the bike track ended, he skidded too, leaping at the last minute to avoid a collision and wobbling through the air to land on his feet on the other side. May slid off her bike as she laid it down and stepped over the tree, slapping at the mosquitoes on her legs. The mosquitoes, she'd always assumed, got their water from the blood of the squirrels that got *their* water in Hog Wallow.

Two bobwhites were introducing themselves to each other somewhere in the shade of the trees.

"Bobwhite?" asked one, its chirp sounding almost human, the way bobwhite chirps did.

"Bobwhite?" the other replied politely.

May took a deep breath and started walking.

An hour or so later she stopped, parted her bangs like curtains so that the breeze could blow on her forehead, and surveyed the area around her. This part of the woods was full of large, old trees—oaks and maples and sumacs that stood a mannerly distance apart from one another. May knew that if she walked forward and to the left, she'd meet a sloping hill where the trees grew smaller and closer together. She knew if she walked ahead and turned right, she'd run into a dried creek bed and a collection of giant, flat boulders that had served, in the past, as ships, forts, and stages for Somber Kitty's dance routines.

Immediately to the right, and just through a little rise of pines, were the Endless Briers. May had tried many times to find her way through the prickly plants, always winding up stranded and itchy a few feet in, and gloomily plucking her way back out again. She pulled out the map. There was no way she could go around them and get home by dark.

May shrugged.

She walked to the edge where the thick of it began, a few smaller plants catching against the fabric of her sneakers.

"Nasty prickers," she said, high-stepping.

"Meayy."

May looked over her shoulder. "You should go home, Kitty." Kitty was standing a few feet behind her, staring at her curiously. He looked over his shoulder, then back to her as if to say, *Are you kidding? Things are just getting good.* She watched him skillfully picking his way through the same small plants she just had. May rolled her eyes and stepped farther into the briers, feeling the sting of them on her legs and her bare ankles. Slowly she made her way, treading on fallen logs and scattered rocks to stay as far above the ground as possible. Within ten or fifteen minutes she'd made it so far into the patch that she couldn't see where the briers ended in any direction. Somber Kitty shot out in front of her, leaping from log to log, darting ahead, ducking under low branches playfully. They backtracked several times, running into impossible walls of plants and turning back to find an easier way.

It seemed to take forever. Fifteen minutes later the briers still stretched as far as May could see in every direction. Another fifteen and it was the same, and the knot in her ribs from yesterday started gathering again. She wondered if maybe just crossing the briers was dangerous. What if she couldn't make her way out?

Somber Kitty, finding it all terribly easy and starting to get bored, now turned back to watch her struggle through the densest patch she'd run into yet.

"Kitty, maybe we should turn around." May peered up at the sky. The sun was getting lower. She'd started too late. Somber Kitty, tilting his big ears downward in sympathy, turned and started walking back toward her.

"Wait." May stuck a fingernail into her mouth and nibbled on it. There was a small, clear patch a few feet away. If she leaped just right, she could make it. She bent her knees, jumped, and landed hard on both feet. She looked behind her. It didn't make much sense to turn back now.

A few minutes later the briers began to spread themselves out, getting farther and farther apart, until May hardly had to slow down at all to pick the odd one off her sneaker. The ground, she noticed, began to change almost immediately. Instead of the hard, dry dirt back near her house, the ground here was softer, a tiny bit mushy, almost *wet*. The knot tightened. Looking back to the wall of stickers she'd come across, she felt so far from home. In fact, May felt too far.

Somber Kitty trotted on ahead, glancing over his shoulder occasionally to encourage May to catch up. He crested the top of a hill and disappeared. The next second, May heard a strange growl up ahead.

"Kitty?"

May crested the rise in a rush, ready to defend her cat, and at the same time she realized two things. First, that the growl was coming from Somber Kitty. And second, that they had reached the lake.

Kitty's tail stood pencil straight, his pointy ears trembled, and the growl seemed to come from deep in his throat.

"What is it?" She followed his gaze to the small, black body of water in front of them, disbelieving. It was only a small lake, which took the form of a misshapen *O* in the clearing. But it was bigger than anything May would have dreamed she would find. Nothing, not even a lily pad or a spare leaf, floated on the dark, glossy surface of the water. It rippled just slightly at the edges, where it touched the rocks of the shore, and mirrored the thin, white clouds circling overhead. This lake was full and deep and thriving. It was as if May was standing in the rain forest instead of the dry hills of Briery Swamp. It couldn't be as deep as it looked.

May took a step forward and tripped, righting herself again. She turned around to see what had tangled her feet.

Just behind her, lying on its side, was a bear trap with a jagged slit down the middle and rusted metal hinges. It was connected to a little chain and a rusted metal post lying flat on the ground.

May wondered how old the trap was and who had left it there.

Thinking that it might still be dangerous, she bent over, picked it up by the chain, and tossed it in the lake. It landed with a splash, sending out tiny black waves. She felt, suddenly, like she shouldn't have done it. She looked around, checking the woods. Up above, the clouds had started to drift away, as if startled. May swallowed.

She looked around again. There was no sign of a house or a farm. No lady.

"Meow? Meay? Meeeaayyy?" Somber Kitty moaned, pacing back and forth toward the edge of the woods, as if he wanted May to follow him home.

"It's just water, Kitty."

May walked to the wet tip of the lake and leaned over the edge to look at her own reflection. There she was, her short flat bangs parted to the sides, her black top and overalls, her knobby arms and legs. And there was something else: a tiny shimmering light.

Standing up straight again, May looked at the sky. There was the sun, up behind the filmy clouds that were darting away. She looked down at the water, then up again. But the sun's reflection was in a whole other place entirely. This light almost looked like it was in the water. May leaned a little bit farther, squinting. The light moved, quick, like a fish.

May sucked in her breath. She knew she'd lost her balance the moment it happened. She swung her arms out at her sides to right herself, but it was too late. She toppled forward and hit the water with a splash.

May's arms splayed out in front of her, and for a moment she stayed motionless, feeling the cold sting of the water and swallowing a mouthful of it before she started flapping her limbs.

She paddled up and took two strokes toward the edge of the lake, breaking the surface and reaching for the shore.

And then she felt it. It felt like a set of very strong fingers, grasping her ankle. They rested there for a moment, tightening, and then *yank!*

May went under. She scooped out her arms and flapped them wildly, much harder than before, feeling the fingers still around her ankle. With all the energy she had she yanked both knees forward, and the hand went slipping off with a jerk. May lunged for the shore again, Somber Kitty's high-pitched, panicked meow ringing in her ears. She felt just the slightest brush against her calves as she pulled herself up onto the dirt, and whatever it was slipped off again, giving May a chance to scramble up onto dry land, panting and heaving.

She turned to face the water and crawled backward, just as Somber Kitty jumped in front of her like a lion defending his pride.

May reached, grabbed him, and yanked him back to her chest. They both watched the water, waiting for whatever it was to surface.

It didn't.

May stood up and started to back away, slowly, carefully.

If she had been paying attention to anything but the pounding of her heart, she would have noticed that every creature in that part of the woods had gone quiet. She didn't look up to see that even the filmy white clouds were gone completely.

At the top of the rise, she turned her back on the lake and started to run.

Mrs. Bird was on the phone in the kitchen when May, soaked and sore, her legs nicked in several places from the briers, snuck through the back door and up the back staircase toward her room.

The staircase ran up behind the kitchen, and above her own heavy breathing she could hear her mom's muffled voice. "We're not sure yet, Sister Christina, but we're seriously thinking about it. Yes . . . Latin . . . really . . . and French? I'm not sure May wants to speak French. Well, she's very into art class at her school . . . Oh, I see. Well, I think she'd miss it . . . Well, that's true . . ."

May tiptoed up to her room and changed out of her wet clothes into her softest silk pajamas and wrapped herself in the covers of her bed like a larva, shivering. Somber Kitty leaped up beside her, patting the crown of her head with his paw until she opened the top of the covers and let him come in too. He snuggled up against her and licked her wet cheek several times. They stayed like that for more than an hour.

Finally her mother appeared at the door. "Honey," she said. "I didn't hear you come in. Are you feeling okay?"

May stayed covered, biting her lip.

Mrs. Bird came and sat on the edge of the bed. "I was just about to make dinner." Somber Kitty's head perked its way out of the covers at the word "dinner." May slowly perked her head out too.

"Did you take a bath?"

May remembered her wet hair. "Um, yes."

"Honey, what is it?" Mrs. Bird said, leaning forward with concern at the sight of May's face.

May sat up and scurried into her mom's arms, hugging her tight. "There's something bad in the woods," she whispered.

Mrs. Bird's grip tightened, and she pushed May to an arm's length, so she could look in her eyes. "Did you see someone in the woods?"

May looked at her and shook her head. "No. I didn't see it. It's . . ." May took a deep breath. "It's in the lake."

"The lake?"

The warm, worried look on Mrs. Bird's face slid away to make room for a suspicious one.

May snapped her mouth shut. She knew she'd made a mistake. There wasn't a lake anywhere she was allowed to go to. May plucked at the threads of her quilt, and her mom rubbed her forehead with one hand.

Mrs. Bird sounded tired when she spoke again. "May, did you see someone in the woods?"

"No. It was just . . ." A monster? What could May say? Her mom looked too brokenhearted to hear a story she wouldn't believe. May looked at her desk, then traced her favorite quilted flower with her pointer finger.

"May, why do you make things so hard? I don't understand."

May didn't reply. She pulled her lips together tight and tucked her chin.

"I just can't help but think . . . in boarding school, with all those other girls, you'd . . ." Mrs. Bird eyed her for another second, then felt her forehead. "You're warm. I'll get you some aspirin. And you're grounded from going to the woods."

May smiled weakly to show she understood, but she knew it came out as a grimace. It didn't matter anyway. Her mom was already moving into the hallway.

May burrowed back under the covers. The fear was still crouched under her ribs, but after the talk of Saint Agatha's, she wasn't sure the thing in the lake was the only thing making the fear burn.

And though she thought it would never let her get to sleep, she fell into slumber, much like a rock sinking into deep water.

Somber Kitty, a spider, and a ladybug were sitting beside the stone path in the backyard just after midnight, listening to the crickets, catching flies drawn by the Birds' porch lights, and nibbling on a blade of grass, in that order, when a figure emerged from the edge of the woods.

All three creatures stopped what they were doing to stare as the figure moved forward, drifting along the stone path that led up to the back entrance of White Moss Manor.

As it floated through the door, Somber Kitty merely gazed at it lazily. He was used to the creatures that drifted around the house at night. Watching the figure disappear up the back stairway, he merely lifted a lazy paw and licked between the soft pink paw pads. They tasted like summer grass. His favorite.

CHAPTER FOUR

A Stranger Arrives

May was in the middle of a dream. She had fallen into a great, black sea. A set of long fingers was holding on to her ankles. When she yanked her legs away, the hand held out a moldy old letter with her name on it. The fingers tapped on the paper of the letter. Tap tap tap.

Tap tap tap.

Tap tap tap.

Hours after she had fallen asleep, May sat straight up in bed. She pushed her palms down on the bed to make sure she was really there and not still dreaming. *Thank goodness.* She breathed deeply and looked around her room, noticing her familiar objects in the shadows. Her mom had never come to her with the aspirin, or had she?

She climbed out of her bed and dug her balled-up, wet shorts out of the closet, prying her waterlogged letter out of the pocket. She walked to the window and held it up by the light of the moon.

Tap tap tap. May froze. The noise had come from just outside her door.

May looked out her window to check the moon—it was high in the dark sky. That meant it was midnight or a little later. She laid her letter on the windowsill, trying not to creak as she crossed the floor to her door. She paused at the threshold for a moment to listen. The sound outside the door was very gentle, like a twig beating against a window. Or fingernails. She reached out and grasped the handle, opened it, and looked. There was nothing but the dark.

Tap tap tap. The sound started again, but now it was farther away, up ahead of her in the darkness. May tiptoed toward it, pausing halfway—at the top of the back stairs—to look down toward the second floor. Nothing. She continued on to her mother's bedroom door. The sound had stopped. She listened hard, to the chirping of crickets and the dry leaves rubbing against one another outside. And tapping again. Behind her.

May swallowed. Her chest began to flicker hotly.

She turned slowly and quietly. The sound was now coming from her room at the end of the hall. And there was something else coming from there too. A pale blue glow, like someone had left a television on.

There wasn't a television in all of White Moss Manor.

May's limbs zinged.

"Hello?" May whispered, her breath barely coming out. "Mom?"

The tapping stopped for a moment, and then started again.

"Hello?" she whispered, but very low this time.

She looked back at her mom's door, torn. Her mom had looked so tired. The last thing May wanted to do was to wake her. Especially for something that was probably nothing. May tried to think like her mom would: It *was* nothing. It was her imagination getting away. The light was probably coming from the moon.

Quietly May padded down the hallway. She stopped just short of her door. Her breath, which had been on its way to her mouth, changed its mind and froze in her throat.

There, sitting on her bed, with its back to her, was a figure. Stretched out to one side, its long, white fingers drummed against the windowsill, while the other hand seemed to be tucked up in front of it, as if it was supporting its chin. Its body was long and skinny, covered by a long, ragged shirt and a pair of ripped pants, and its head, from what May could see of it, was enormous and round like a pumpkin, with a tuft of hair up top. Through the figure's body, the round orb of the moon and the trees below were completely visible. He was like a piece of light. . . .

May couldn't move. She couldn't breathe. She opened her mouth to scream, but only a squeak came out.

At the noise, the creature perked its head to the left, and then swiveled to look at her.

The thing was nothing close to human. Its mouth was a giant, jagged gash. Its nose, two holes in powder white skin. Its eyes were long and droopy, the sockets hanging around horrible black eyeballs. Looking at May, they widened in surprise, and then squinted in concentration. Finally the mouth split open and stretched from cheek to cheek in a wicked smile—revealing crooked, broken teeth.

May's voice finally found its way to her lips. She screamed.

"Moooommm!"

The smile on the creature in front of her descended into a

deep, horrible frown. It shot up from the bed, rushing toward her. At the same moment, the sound of footsteps hitting wood echoed at the end of the hall. May jumped back and flattened herself against the wall, still screaming.

The creature sailed through the doorway, its face a mask of ugliness. May threw her arms up in front of her, but instead of lunging for her, it sailed right past her, disappearing around the corner and down the stairs just as Mrs. Bird's door flew open.

"May, what is it?" Mrs. Bird cried, running to her daughter and grabbing her shoulders. "Shhhhhhh. Shhhhhhh."

For several agonizing seconds May couldn't catch her breath to say anything. She flung her arm in the direction of the stairs, and the word finally came out. "Ghost!"

Mrs. Bird frowned. "A ghost?"

May nodded, thrusting her hand toward the stairs again and panting. "He went down there."

Mrs. Bird looked at her for another moment, then walked into the stairway and disappeared. She was gone long enough for May to worry she'd sent her to her doom. But to her relief, she reappeared a few minutes later. May was standing against the wall, nibbling hard on her fingers.

"Did you see it?" May asked, looking over her mother's shoulder.

Mrs. Bird shook her head, her eyes heavy-lidded, her mouth set in a droopy, tired line. She sighed. "No, honey. There's nothing down there. Come on." Putting one hand on May's back, she ushered her down the hall and into her bedroom.

"But, Mom, it was there, I swear." A few taps on the stairs and in the hallway, and Somber Kitty appeared, rubbing against May's shins.

"It was just a dream, baby."

"But, Mom—"

"C'mon, hop in." Mrs Bird had pulled down the top of the covers into a triangle, and rubbed the sheets to indicate where May should hop. May stared at her, disbelieving. "Hop in."

"But . . ."

Mrs. Bird sighed, running a hand through her soft, fuzzy brown hair. "Please, honey, I'm tired."

May stared for a second longer, then crawled up under her mom's arm, into the space provided.

"But, Mom."

"Honey, I promise you, it was just a dream."

"Can I sleep with you?"

Mrs. Bird shook her head. "May, you're ten years old."

May tugged at her nails, frustrated. She and Somber Kitty exchanged looks. Somber Kitty let out a long sigh, and then hopped off the bed and pranced back into the hallway, his footsteps sounding on the stairs, and then May heard the swinging of the cat door to the front.

"Mom?" May searched the space behind her mother in the hallway with her eyes.

Mrs. Bird turned, tugging at the hem of her pink nightshirt drowsily.

"Will you look out the window? What if it's in the yard?"

Mrs. Bird frowned, then knelt on the bed and looked outside. She turned to May. "Nothing."

"Okay. Will you check the back too?"

Mrs. Bird nodded wearily and made her way to the door.

❁ ❁ ❁

After her mom had gone, May sat in her bed, her arms wrapped around her knees, eyeing the corners of her room. Finally, once she got the courage to move, she sidled up to her window.

May leaned forward and gazed out onto the lawn. There was Somber Kitty, out on the stone walkway, playing with his tail. And there, in the glow of the moon, standing on the grass, with the bush behind him visible through his skinny, see-through legs, was the horrible creature with the pumpkin head, watching her.

Meeting her eyes, he quickly turned, floating across the grass and into the woods.

CHAPTER FIVE

What Lives in the Lake?

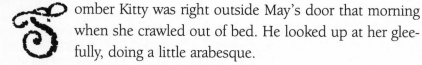

omber Kitty was right outside May's door that morning when she crawled out of bed. He looked up at her gleefully, doing a little arabesque.

"Some guard cat you are," May muttered.

"Meay?"

The two made their way down the stairs, one staggering, the other trotting, to the breakfast table. May slumped over her oatmeal, watching her mom putter around the kitchen. Occasionally Mrs. Bird watched her in return, the two doe-eyeing each other thoughtfully. But neither of them said anything.

"I'm going outside," May finally muttered.

"Remember, no woods," Mrs. Bird said, wiping the counter.

May walked down the hall and outside, looked around to make sure there was no one standing in the grass, and planted herself on the stairs. She had been up most of the night, hiding under the covers and watching her door, knowing that at any moment the ghost would come through it. He hadn't. At dawn she'd dared to look out her window again, but he hadn't come back. She sat for several minutes, restless, eyeing the line of trees across the lawn. Then she got up and went down onto the grass. Now, walking under the sun to the edge of the woods, she felt like a dark blotch, moving across the ground.

At the edge of the trees she paused. Something fuzzy knocked into her calves, making her jump.

"Kitty, you scared me." She crouched and picked him up, his body stretching out underneath him like a piece of chewed gum. Together they stared into the darkness beneath the trees. May searched the branches above, as if the creature from last night would actually appear up there, swinging by his knees.

"What lives in the lake?" she asked Somber Kitty.

"Meay."

"Do you think it's a ghost?"

"Mew."

"Do you think it's coming after me?" she whispered low.

"Meow."

She didn't know whether that was a yes or no. She took it as a maybe, and hurried back into the house.

That afternoon May sank down at her desk, moved her materializer to the floor, and wrote down notes from *The Ghost Hunter's Guide to the Paranormal*, which she had found in the crooked-floored, crooked-shelved recesses of White Moss Manor's dusty library that afternoon. As she wrote, she leaned her head on her free hand and let out the occasional yawn. Her notes read:

Come after dark
Scared of: iron, obsidian, silver, periwinkle, horseshoes,
   spitting, salt
When one is around, the temperature drops.

Upon copying this last line, May stood up and made a beeline down to the thermometer that hung outside the back door, then carried it back to her room and hooked it to the wall next to her bed.

A few seconds later she was back to reading again, and her eyelids were getting heavy. She began to droop farther and farther down on her desk, her elbows sliding, and her head finally resting on her hands. Somber Kitty, who'd curled up on the floor by her chair, listened to the steady noise of her breathing and watched the sun droop outside the window, below the horizon, until darkness slowly crept up from the trees.

May only stirred once, to turn her head to the side. And then she jerked up, suddenly wide awake.

There on the wall in front of her, among the many imaginary creatures May had drawn over the years, was one she had done when she was only three or four. The creature in the drawing had a round, lopsided head, like a pumpkin that had grown on its side, and a gash of a mouth. He was wearing a long, ripped shirt, a jacket, and a pair of trousers rolled up at the bottom. A tuft of yellow hair sprang from the top of his head.

May sat, her mouth hanging open, for several minutes. There was no mistaking him.

It wasn't possible.

As she tried to make sense of it, May's eyes drifted to her letter on the windowsill. She stood up and grabbed it, pulled it out of the envelope. Amazingly it was still legible, though even more blurred than before. She read bits of it: "the danger you will endure" and then "great need of your help."

She looked at the envelope itself, and sighed.

The tree, and the woman's face hidden in its leaves, was gone.

May stuck her thumbnail between her teeth.

"Mew?" Somber Kitty inquired.

"Shhh," May hissed, concentrating. One question after another started racing through her head.

Was the creature in her room the danger she had to endure?

Was it the creature from the lake? Were they the same?

What did it have to do with this Lady?

May looked out the window, pressing her nose against the glass. She could only see the shadow of the trees. She felt like a prisoner.

Are you out there? she thought, trying to picture the Lady from her letter. She squinted, trying to see her eyes in the trees. *Do you need me?* It was hard to imagine. May knew she wasn't much good for anything, not much that was useful. Wasn't that why her mom thought she needed Saint Agatha's?

A few minutes later, a chill slid across her and roused her from her thoughts.

"Honey, why don't you take a bath?" her mom called from downstairs.

May sat on her bed and peeled off her black shorts and black slippers, not noticing that the mercury in the thermometer by her bed had dropped. She walked into the bathroom, smoothing her bangs away from her forehead and turning on the spigot. She had just turned to close the door when the bath water splashed behind her. The hairs stood up on the back of her neck.

She turned.

A woman with long black hair and pale white skin and hollow, dark-circled eyes sat in the bathtub. She was completely translucent. And she was wearing a shower cap.

May felt a scream rise up in her throat, and clamped down on it, hard.

Slowly, pretending she didn't notice, she backed out through the bathroom door and tiptoed to her mom's room, where she found Mrs. Bird sitting in front of her computer.

She stopped on the edge of the room, squeaking to a halt and trembling.

Her mom looked up. "What's wrong?"

May's breath fluttered in her throat. Visions of Saint Agatha's suddenly danced in her head. "Um." She looked back over her shoulder, toward the bottom of the stairs.

"May?"

May hesitated. She didn't move. "Can you come, um, check the, um . . ." What could she say? "I think I saw a spider in the bathroom."

Mrs. Bird eyed her quizzically. "A spider? May, can't you squish it?"

"Um, I don't squish spiders." She paused, then whispered, "I think it's a tarantula."

"Oh, May." Mrs. Bird looked longingly at her laptop, then slowly stood up. The old floors creaking as she walked, Mrs. Bird led the way down the hall.

They passed the stairs.

Somber Kitty was sitting about halfway down, looking at the banister, clearly wondering if he should jump onto it and slide, which he sometimes liked to do.

As Mrs. Bird turned the corner into the bathroom, May waited for her to shriek or leap backward, but none of that happened. When May turned the corner, her mom was just pulling back from the bath, where the woman still sat.

"The water's spider-free, May. It's fine." She bent down to turn off the spigot.

The woman in the tub looked at May, her big, dark eyes mournful and horrible. May looked from her, back to her mom, and back to the woman. Somber Kitty entered the room and leaped up onto the sink, trying to catch the drips from the tap.

Both her mother and her cat were relaxed and carefree.

May was on her own.

CHAPTER SIX

The Hauntings

I t looked like life at White Moss Manor would never be normal again.

It was not so much that the house seemed to be flooding with ghosts as much as it seemed that ghosts had been in the house the whole time, and May simply hadn't seen them. This impression was created because, from that day forward, whenever she saw a ghost, it appeared to be right at home.

The night after the ghost in the bathtub, May came face-to-face with a woman dangling by a rope from the rafters of the back stairway, her neck tilted at a horrible angle. May threw both hands over her mouth and sprinted down the stairs, hiding under the high bed in Bertha Brettwaller's old guest room. When she investigated an hour later, the woman was gone.

In the kitchen for a late-night snack that night (she hadn't eaten all day), May found six men in football uniforms, sitting at the table, moving their mouths but making no sound. May's mom sat in the one seat not occupied by a ghost, working on her laptop. Only Somber Kitty looked at the men from time to time as he lapped at his water dish.

The next evening Mrs. Bird found May, hiding behind the couch in the dusty, rarely used second parlor, where she'd just seen a pair of small, glowing children with missing hands, playing hide-and-seek. When Mrs. Bird questioned her, May said she'd been catching dust bunnies.

Strangely the creature with the round, lopsided head was the only one who appeared more than once. While the others never showed up a second night in a row, he returned night after night, appearing in the strangest of places at the most unexpected times. May opened her closet to get her pajamas, and there he was, dangling from a clothes hanger, a wicked smile plastered across his face. May walked down to the study to grab a book, and he was lying on the chaise lounge, one hand lazily draped behind his head while he looked out the window at the fireflies that had come out to light up the backyard like dancing stars. She sat at her desk, and she would find him in her doorway, watching her, and she'd crawl under her bed until he went away.

For five nights in a row May stayed up each night, most of the night, with her eyes on her bedroom door for ghostly intruders. And every morning just before dawn, she watched through her bedroom window as the ghosts trickled down the front walkway and into the woods in what seemed to be the direction of the lake. It was only when the last ghost disappeared into the trees that she ever fell asleep.

Dark circles formed under May's and her mother's eyes. Though May tried her best to hide the situation, it would have been hard for anyone not to notice her spitting and throwing salt wherever she went. She'd started wearing every piece of silver she could find. She'd tied a four-piece set of silverware around her waist like a skirt, and pinned the onyx brooch from her shelf onto her shirt.

She collected all the food she could fit in her arms, filled her favorite canteen with water, and built a tepee in the most protected corner of her room. It was filled with her small collection of silver dollars and dried periwinkle from one of her mother's wreaths. She posted a NO TRESPASSING sign on the entrance. It became her nightly hiding place, where she curled against the back wall and watched for ghosts.

But life at the manor had changed in another way, too. A host of papers, catalogs, and brochures had begun pouring in from Saint Agatha's, landing on the kitchen table in a heap as they tumbled out of Mrs. Bird's arms. While May stayed as far away from them as possible, Mrs. Bird pored over them in earnest, clutching her tea mug in one hand and turning the pages with the other.

"May, they even have seminars on making good first impressions. Isn't that great? Wouldn't you like to make good first impressions?"

May had become afraid of going outside. So at times like these, May avoided her mom by drifting from room to room of the manor—the two parlors, the library, the five unused bedrooms, and the attic, which had the highest window in the house.

She didn't know what she was looking for. But it seemed that if she looked hard enough, she'd find a way to save herself from Saint Agatha's. She pressed her forehead to the windowpane, staring toward the woods, Somber Kitty tripping along at her heels until he'd get bored and zip away.

She wondered about the Lady of North Farm. The way her mom looked at her, like she'd grown a second head, made it seem very important that somewhere, somebody said they needed her. Even if that seemed impossible. It was enticing to think that someone thought she was good enough to be needed.

It made her long to see the lake again, a feeling so strange, it made May feel like she had grown *three* heads.

About half an hour after midnight, May was huddled in her tepee, reading the *Encyclopedia of the Supernatural* while cuddling Somber Kitty under one arm. She was just turning the page, when she heard her door creak open. She froze, not even daring to turn her head.

A shadow approached the tepee, looming large against the walls, and May felt her body going cold. A shadow hand reached out and closed around the blanket.

May couldn't hold back. She screamed and rolled sideways, knocking the tepee over. It fell around her as she howled, getting more and more tangled in the blankets. A moment later, hands yanked the blanket off. There was her mother, her brown eyes wide. There was no sign of a ghost anywhere.

"We're packing your things first thing in the morning," Mrs. Bird said stiffly. "We'll stay at a hotel and make plans for New York." She paused, shook her head, and rubbed at her eyelids. "I can't do this anymore, May."

May sank onto her back, tears crawling out of the sides of her eyes and winding down her cheeks. Her mom merely tightened her lips and left the room.

It was a half hour or more before May wiped her eyes, stood up, and tiptoed into the hallway. Her mother's door at the other end of the hall was closed, and the light was out. Letting out a ragged sigh, May crept up the stairs to the attic, keeping an eye out for ghosts.

May looked out the east window, pressing her face against it and getting new tears on the glass. The woods stared back at her like an old friend. New York City seemed like a million miles away. It seemed like the moon.

"Mew?" Even Somber Kitty seemed to know he should whisper. May picked him up and held him tight. They both peered into the night.

"What do we do?" she murmured, touching cheek to whiskers.

Just faintly she could see a blue glow beyond the trees, flickering.

"Meow," Somber Kitty replied, which meant "I don't know."

"I'm not feeling very brave," May sighed quietly.

Then she put her cat on the floor and tiptoed down to her room to sleep.

At the foot of May's bed Somber Kitty slept soundly, curled in a Cheez Doodle shape, dreaming of a field full of moths to catch. His paws twitched contentedly, swiping at this and that fluttering insect, putting them in his mouth to chew on. May, on the other hand, lay in her favorite black silky pajama top with her eyes wide open, staring at the dragonfly wind chimes above her bed. She flopped back and forth on the bed, her legs splaying one way and her arms another, the sweat gathering at the backs of her knees and the crease above her lips. In her hand she clutched her letter.

Quietly, so she wouldn't wake the cat, May rose. She went to her drawer and pulled out her black sparkly bathing suit. If she was going to face what was in the lake, she was going like a warrior.

Once she was dressed, May reached up to her shelf and plucked a quartz rock from the group, slipping it into her pocket for luck. She grabbed a flashlight from its hook beside her binoculars. She grabbed all of her ghost supplies: her silver and onyx and salt. Finally, she tucked her mysterious letter into her pocket.

Outside, the stars were shining in full force. May stopped on the lawn and looked at her house. In the light of the moon, it seemed to glow. Its crooked lines and sinking roof and the additions tacked on at every angle showed up extra bright. She had the sick, belly-aching feeling she'd never see it again.

"Don't be silly," she said under her breath.

She turned and continued across the grass.

The trees were black slashes standing up from the ground until May was standing close to them, at the edge of the woods. Peering in, she could see the occasional lightning bug, up past bedtime, looking for a mate.

Before she stepped into the line of the trees, she took one last look toward home and sucked in a breath.

❧

CHAPTER SEVEN

Light Underwater

The lake was a glossy black hole, completely still. May stood just at the edge of the clearing, shining her flashlight on its surface, then on the surrounding area, looking for signs of movement. Navigating the briers had been easier tonight, knowing what was at the end of them, but her legs still itched from where she'd pricked herself. She bent down and rubbed at her calves gently.

Suddenly there was a rustle in the bushes behind her, and she swiveled around, pointing her light at a group of shrubs that shook back and forth.

A small figure emerged from behind them.

"Kitty!"

Somber Kitty waddled up to her and rubbed against her shins. May lifted him up, walked him to the bushes, and dropped him in. She pointed over his head, and he followed the line of her finger with his eyes. "Go home. Home."

"Meow."

"Don't play dumb with me." She stomped her foot. "You're gonna get hurt. Home."

But Somber Kitty wouldn't budge. "Fine," she said. "But you stay there."

May turned and started toward the lake.

"Ouch!" She leaped into the air, grabbing onto her foot with one hand and jumping up and down. Her flashlight went tumbling. "Kitty!"

She sank onto the ground and stared at her foot, disbelieving. Two twin lines of blood dripped down the back of her heel.

"What'd you do that for?!"

Somber Kitty sat down beside her and meowed pitifully. But he also tilted his chin up in the air defiantly. "Meow. Meay."

"Go home!" May yelled. She leaped to her feet and took a few running steps at the cat, sending him scuttling backward. But he turned around at the bushes and started to creep back toward her. "Meow?"

"Leave me alone, Somber Kitty! Go home!" She waved both arms at him as if she meant to hit him. Finally he went zipping back into the briers, disappearing down the path.

May crossed her arms and waited for him to come back, her foot aching.

Nothing.

"Go home!" she hollered again, but it didn't seem to be any use. Somber Kitty had gone.

"Kitty?"

May chewed on her thumbnail. She hoped he would find his way home okay. She picked up her flashlight from where it had landed, to look for her ghost items, which she'd dropped in the fray. But just when she did, the light died.

May shook it furiously a few times. "No," she moaned, her

heart drumming. How would she ever find her way back home?

She turned and looked back toward the lake. Now in the dark, and with Somber Kitty gone, she felt very alone. She ought to try to catch up with him. But now when she turned to face home, she could see a very dim glow coming toward her through the woods.

She backed toward the lake, panting, until she was just on the edge of the water. Her heels touched the liquid coolness. *Click.*

May turned. With a sound like a giant light switch being turned on, the lake had come completely aglow.

Mesmerized, May took a few steps sideways, then stood at the edge of the water, looking down. She forgot about what might be behind her. Looking down was like watching a giant television. Way down in the water, someone—or something—was swimming. The figure got larger and larger, as if it was coming from somewhere very deep, toward the surface.

Something in May told her she should get away, but her feet stayed rooted to the spot. The figure looked to be a woman, now that she was closer. A beautiful woman with hair down to her toes that swirled in all directions as she stroked upward. She flipped and twisted as gracefully as a water dancer.

When she was only a few feet away, her eyes met May's, and she smiled. The woman came right up to the surface of the water, resting just below it. She beamed at May for a moment more, the most gorgeous vision May had ever seen. May herself had never felt so beautiful, or so lit up, or so happy. The woman's smile seemed to say, *I see you. I understand you. I know.*

And then her body began to widen and grow. As May watched, dazzled, it stretched into eight glowing points. Her eyes still locked on May's, the woman's smile widened, revealing not teeth, but fangs. A hot arrow of fear shot down May's back. She started to pull away. But not before one arm shot out of the water, grabbed her by the leg, and yanked her in.

As she was dragged farther and farther downward, May's lungs felt like they were going to burst. She could still feel the woman's hands around her legs, but she couldn't see her shape anymore. She was just a glow as bright as the sun, pulling her down, down, down, down, down. Down farther than May thought any lake could go. It felt like she was being pulled to the center of the Earth.

Then her vision started to go black, and her lungs relaxed, and May let go of the hope of reaching the world above. She stopped struggling. Her arms floated up in surrender. The light started to fade away.

And then she saw it—another tiny glow, way above her. As it got closer, she could see it was coming from the horrible ghost with the lopsided head. He was plunging toward her, his long bony hands reaching out to grab her.

Just as he reached her, May's vision went black.

CHAPTER EIGHT

The Beginning

Way back in the woods, behind a patch of briers that stretched almost a mile wide in each direction, the only lake in Briery Swamp glowed and flashed like lightning. Around it, not a single critter could be seen. The fireflies had swarmed off. The insects, the night birds, the snakes, and the lizards had crawled or flown or scurried to other safer parts. The only movement came from a skinny, hairless cat who was slowly creeping out from underneath the thorn bushes.

Keeping low to the ground, mewing softly and sadly, Somber Kitty squiggled himself like a snake, up to the edge of the water.

"Meay?" he asked softly in a whisper. Nothing came back from the water except for the eerie twinkling light. Somber Kitty gingerly touched one paw to the water, then snatched it back, shaking off the wetness. He looked behind him, back to the path that led out of the briers.

Somber Kitty appeared to be caught in an argument with himself. Finally he tilted his chin down stubbornly, raised his ears and tail so that they shook with warlike energy, bared his teeth, crouched, and—snapping like a rubber band Finny Elway would have shot at Claire Arneson—went splashing into the water. He came up once, paddling madly. And then he disappeared beneath the surface.

Behind Somber Kitty, Briery Swamp remained silent. The lights of the lake flickered out. An owl landed on a nearby tree and let out a hoot. Critters trickled back to the sound of nibbling leaves.

In the woods of the swamp, all appeared to be normal. There was no one to notice what had been lost.

PART TWO

The Ever After

CHAPTER NINE

A Faraway Shore

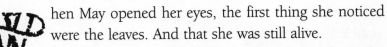hen May opened her eyes, the first thing she noticed
were the leaves. And that she was still alive.

"Ouch," she whispered, rubbing at her face. She
sat up and squinted at the brightness around her, fearful and
dazed as she tried to focus on the leafy branch above her, which
seemed to be waving at her for attention. Beyond it a pair of
eyes—or were they just spots of sky showing through?—were
watching her. May squinted harder, but in another moment the
leaves rearranged themselves in the breeze, then nothing.

That's when May finally noticed where she was. She was on the
shore of the lake. It all came back to her.

"That's weird," she whispered. She remembered falling in. She
didn't remember swimming *out* of the water and crawling onto
the shore. All she remembered was the cold, strong hands around
her legs and at the last minute, the ghost—from her house—
reaching out to grab her. She shuddered. Had she imagined it?

May stood slowly, her bones aching. Her body felt flattened and
doughy, like it had been stuck in a waffle iron. Why was it so light
out? Had she slept all night? Her stomach turned over. "Mom."

She searched behind her for the trampled brush that would mark the way she'd come in, but no path presented itself. May nibbled on her fingers. Her mom would be furious. She took a step closer to the woods and . . .

"Ah!"

Someone—or something—was crouching in the bushes in front of her. May stumbled back into the clearing just as the ghost from White Moss Manor rose and drifted forward.

He put one finger up in front of his jagged white lips and shook his transparent head. He was shaking slightly.

May held out her hands in a stop motion, fear making her legs tremble like kite strings. "Leave me alone."

The creature bit on a finger, then looked around. "Shhhh. Oh, my. Don't get too close to that water. Sh-Sh-She'll come back for you."

May blinked at him for a moment in shock that he had spoken, then recovered herself. "Leave me alone!"

The creature flinched, then widened his sad, droopy eyes at her. "Please. You're going to get us into trouble. There's s-s-something even worse. They may be on their way already. . . ."

May didn't bother waiting around to hear the rest. She darted across the clearing and burst into the trees. A moment later she emerged onto the clearing. She came to a dead stop, sucking in her breath. The lake lay before her, glossy and still. The woods she had just run into lay in front of her. The creature stood where she'd left him, peering into the woods all around them nervously. "It won't work. You'll never get out that way. Now come with . . ." He drifted in her direction.

May shook her head. "Stay away!"

She scrambled around the side of the lake and across the clearing toward the trees again, pushing into the underbrush. She just needed to get home. Once she got home . . .

And there she was again. Right back at the clearing.

May shook her head hard, then started toward a giant elm and a stand of pine trees. She put her arms out in front of her to move the low branches aside, this time going a bit more slowly. A few more branches pushed aside and . . . there was the lake.

May's lips started to quiver. Something was wrong. Something was very horribly wrong.

All the while the creature watched her, his great head tilted to one side, his fingers digging into his chin.

"You've got to come with me," he said. "Th-Th-This is a dangerous place."

"No!"

May tried to run into the woods three more times, each time her heart thudding a little bit faster, each time returning to the lake. "It's impossible," she whispered. Tears trembled on her eyelashes.

The creature floated toward her again, reaching out his long skinny arms. "Please don't cry. Crying always sets off the detector."

"Why won't you leave me alone?"

He frowned, his horrible gash of a mouth turning downward. "Ohhh, maybe we should start over. I'm Pumpkin. I'm trying to help you!"

May backed away a step, wondering if maybe she was dreaming.

A sound made the creature called Pumpkin stop and look toward the trees on the opposite side of the lake. May thought she heard it too. It sounded like dogs barking.

"The Black Shucks," Pumpkin hissed, his droopy eyes widening in terror. "Oh, my. The Bogey's coming for you!" His whole body began to shake, his feet hovering above the ground unevenly. "Come on!"

Pumpkin reached out a long arm again, his fingers outstretched toward her. May gazed around at the trees. It was definitely the sound of dogs, but snarling, growling dogs, like dogs closing in on their prey. And something else that made May's blood run cold. A *crack crack crack,* like the sound of a whip. Every hair on her body stood up on end.

She looked back at Pumpkin.

"Come where?" She crossed her arms over her chest.

"Through the door. Ohhh. We've got to hurry."

"I don't see a door."

Pumpkin rolled his eyeballs around. "That's why ones like you never make it out. Come on!"

Pumpkin zipped to the edge of the woods, pulled some branches aside and revealed, to May's amazement, a black door. It seemed to stand on nothing, and to lead nowhere, except that there was a small gap across the top, emitting a bluish light. Across the middle, it read in big, red letters ALL DEAD THIS WAY.

May gasped. Beyond the trees the sound of dogs had gotten louder.

Pumpkin raised his hand to the door, then lowered it to his lips for a moment, muttering to himself: "Knockitty knock? Knockitty knockitty?" He raised his fist back to the door and knocked out a strange rhythm.

The door creaked open, revealing not the forest behind it but a big, dark, empty space. A faint shimmer of light came from the inside, like the flicker of a television screen.

"I'm not going in there," May said, backing up and shaking her head. "And I'm not going with you. I'm going home."

There was a loud yelp off in the distance. Pumpkin snapped his head to look, then he looked back at May, his eyes huge. "This is the *only* way! Hurry!"

The sound had gotten so loud that May's ears started to hurt. "Wh-What's coming?" she yelled above the din.

The Pumpkin creature put his hand up to his ear. "What?" he shouted.

"Who is it that's coming?!"

Crack crack crack. Way back in the woods, May could hear the sound of wood splintering and trees falling. The barking and yelping continued to grow louder. She found herself sidling closer to Pumpkin until she bumped into him with a cold shock, then swiveled toward him. She didn't want to be too close to him, but she also didn't want to be near whatever was coming through the woods.

"Why should I trust you?" she cried.

Pumpkin shifted back and forth, drifting this way and that, wringing his hands. "You have to."

An ear-splitting crash drew her attention back to the woods. Several of the farthest trees she could see were falling to the left and right, as if something huge and vicious were plowing through them. May and Pumpkin flinched as the trees fell. Whatever it was was making its way straight toward the clearing. May's knobby knees began to falter underneath her.

And then a set of cold white hands were around her arm,

sending zaps like electricity running up and down her body. May lost her breath. In an instant she was being yanked through the door as it slammed shut behind her.

Beyond the edge of the trees, the crashing came to an abrupt halt. Loud sniffs and growls shook the leaves on the trees, but no creature appeared on the shore of the lake. There was a moment of listening, sniffing silence, and then whatever it had been, retreated slowly through the woods, sending the smaller trees toppling like toothpicks behind it.

CHAPTER TEN

"Make the Most of Your Eternity!"

n the clearing, for a moment it was hard to tell whether the rippling on the lake had been made by the echoes of falling trees, or something unseen underneath the surface. But as the seconds passed, the ripples grew larger, and a dark form took shape as it drifted upward and burst into the open air with a splutter.

The creature sneezed and spat and paddled its way to the shore, dragging its long skinny body along the ground and collapsing there like a piece of gum that had seen one too many chews. Its face was strikingly sad and melancholy, but this was not unusual.

Somber Kitty was limp and half-dead. His big pointy ears lay flat and his skinny tail sagged on the dirt like the top of a deflated exclamation mark. He lay between life and death for several seconds. And then his nose began to twitch.

Pushing himself up onto wobbly legs, Somber Kitty sniffed harder. He stumbled several times as he followed May's path— across the dirt, into the trees, and up to a closed door.

He reached out one gentle paw and scratched at the door. He

sniffed it again, then scratched again. He stood on his hind legs and sniffed higher and with more urgency.

Behind him the lake began to bubble. But Somber Kitty didn't notice. He was too sure that May was getting farther and farther away.

May turned to look at the door she had just come through, but it was no longer there. All that remained was a small gap with a sign below it reading: VIEW OF THE WATER DEMON IN ITS NATURAL HABITAT. She gulped and swiveled around, blinking while her eyes adjusted to the darkness. They were in a dark, flickering hallway. Pumpkin still had his cold, trembling hand around her arm, zapping her with tiny shocks of electricity. May yanked herself free.

His giant eyes drooped a look at her, and his white cheeks flushed pink. "Sorry." He stuck a finger in his mouth and looked down the hall. "We're safe now. They'll think the demon's gotten you, after all. Come back to finish the job." Pumpkin shivered. Before May could ask who the "they" was, he spoke again. "I think the only way out is there," he whispered. "It's very important no one sees you. Come on." He drifted down the hall and stopped at a door on the right. The blue light she had noticed seemed to be coming from the room that lay beyond it, flashing patterns on Pumpkin's ghastly face. He looked back at her expectantly.

May stayed where she was, rooted to the spot. Her heart, which was still beating hard, told her to wait. He floated back toward her.

"If you stay here, May, you'll be caught."

May checked behind her one last time, then pushed on the wall. It didn't budge. At a loss she followed Pumpkin back down the hall, and they both peered through the flickering doorway.

They were at the entrance of an old-fashioned movie theater, complete with a squeaky projector that cast a long thread of light out over rows of seats filled with figures May couldn't quite make out in the dark. The whole place smelled dusty, as if it hadn't been used in a hundred years.

May shrunk to the left of the door, eyeing her companion sideways. He kept his gaze locked forward, his whole body trembling. She let her attention move to the movie in front of them.

Up on-screen a thin man in a butler's suit was in the middle of saying something. His face was horribly pale, and his eyes were sunken and dark, his whole body as transparent as Pumpkin's. May looked around her again, trying to make out the others in their seats, and then back at the screen. She shivered.

"Please look carefully at this list of items that are not allowed into the Ever After. If you are carrying any of these, please hand them over to the nearest greeter."

A series of pictures flashed on the screen, showing horseshoes, bags of salt, brooms, then a giant picture of all sorts of animals standing in a group, surrounded by a red circle with a slash across the middle.

"Please note that all animals are strictly prohibited. If you and your pet died together, please have that pet out for confiscation when you leave the theater."

"You'll notice there are four exits from the theater." The man in the butler's suit moved his hands to indicate where they were. His voice was like crushed ice. "At the front and on either side. All evildoers—rogues; scoundrels; nasty pieces of work; baddies; and menaces, including masked ones—please exit through the front so that you can be moved to the proper area. All others please exit through the side doors where you will be aided by one of our greeters. They will help you choose from a wide array of regions." The man smiled. "Also, please don't forget to take one of the brochures provided for you at the gates." The camera panned back to take in the man's full body, revealing a knife handle sticking out of his shirt. He bowed.

The movie ended with a great flapping sound as the film in the projector ran out. The screen went black, but the glow remained. The whole *room* stayed full of soft blue light. And it seemed to be coming from the audience members. As they stood up and began moving toward the exits, May noticed that they all drifted a few inches above the ground. She bit her lip. Tears snuck out to the corners of her eyeballs. What was this place? Was she? . . . May didn't dare to finish the thought.

"Oooooh, come on," Pumpkin groaned, continuing on down the hall to a door marked ALLEY. Beside it, a bony hand stuck out of the wall, holding a fistful of scrolled-up papers. Above the hand a sign read TAKE ONE! May did. The hand readjusted itself, tightening around the remaining papers.

Pumpkin opened the door a crack, peered outside, and then waved May forward. She followed him, and they emerged onto a tiny brick alleyway.

"Oh, I knew I should have stayed in bed this morning. I'm not cut out for this. We've got to get onto a boat," Pumpkin said, floating ahead. He stopped just where the alleyway ended, and waited for May to catch up. When she did, and looked at what lay ahead of them, her stomach lurched, and her hands flew up to her mouth.

Before them was a wide beach, its sandy fingers reaching into a vast and oozing river that glowed bright green. Up above, the dusky sky was filled with zooming points of light, like millions of shooting stars. And all over the beach, gathered into lines and milling around, were ghosts, like the ones May had seen at her house. Like the one standing beside her.

There were thousands of them—their feet hovering just slightly above the ground, their bodies transparent so that you could look at one and see three more behind him, all giving off a soft blue glow. Some were missing limbs. Others were thin and gaunt, their eyes sunken in their heads. A woman floating up ahead paused, seemed to remember something, and then turned back to pick up her foot, which had stopped in the sand a few feet behind her. They were all gathering into groups and lines up near the water, where several large, bright blinking signs lined the shore: SOUTHERN TERRITORIES, NOTHING PLATTE AND THE FAR WEST, DEATH KNELLS, NEW EGYPT, PIT OF DESPAIR AMUSEMENT PARK. Beyond the signs, boats drifted around on the water. Some were empty, docked just before the signs, and some were full of passengers and floating away.

May started backing up. She didn't care. She'd take her chances with whatever was back at the lake. She turned to run.

"Meay?"

Somber Kitty crouched at the base of the door in the woods, staring straight up at the top of it. Stubbornly he had already leaped against it many times, hoping that his brute strength would open it. This was a rare tactic for Somber Kitty, more doglike than a cat would care to admit, and now he licked his shoulders and back in an ashamed and embarrassed way. Then he meowed desperately at the gap above, hoping May would hear him.

Though he was too distraught to notice it, the lake had begun to glow behind him and a figure—stretched out into eight points—was visible just below the surface, watching him. It seemed to be waiting for the right moment to strike.

Bubble. Bubble.

Somber Kitty's ears perked up, and he straightened his whiskers, though he did not look behind him. He stared at the door in a deceptively calm manner as his muscles began to coil. Behind him something else was coiling too, ready to launch itself out of the water.

Somber Kitty leaped at the same time the water demon did, its long wet arm whipping at the ground where, a second before, the cat had crouched. With a yowl Somber Kitty went hurtling through the gap above the door, scraping his belly and dragging his legs as he came tumbling down on the other side.

When he landed, he was in a dark hallway.

He was also on all fours.

May took a few running steps and crashed into solid brick wall.

"Ow." She threw a hand to her aching forehead and backed up, staring at the graffiti-covered bricks that had appeared before her.

Glowing spray paint scrawled words across the wall: BO CLEEVIL IS WATCHING, ANTONY LOVES CLEO. Across the top, up several stories above May's head, in giant, glowing blue letters, a sign read SPECTROPLEX. May pushed on the bricks, then pounded on them.

"No," May cried, the tears finally spilling onto her cheeks. "I don't want to be dead, I don't want to be dead."

"Oh, don't do that! You're being too loud!" Pumpkin grabbed her by the waist, sending another cold zap through her. He looked over his shoulder at a group of skeletons that lingered by the edge of the water, guiding people into the boats. They all wore exactly the same long robe and each held a staff. It was too much. May's head swam.

"Here," Pumpkin slid out of his jacket and placed it over her shoulders. "M-M-Maybe it'll tone you down. We have to get out of here." The jacket felt light as air, and when May tried to touch it, her hands went right through it. But it stayed on and gave her a glow that was, she noticed, pretty flimsy compared to the other spirits on the beach. "Oh, thank goodness. There's a boat over there, see?" May looked. On a deserted stretch of beach far to the left, a tiny boat clung to the edge of the sand, lifting gently with the ripples of the water. "Um, you should probably keep your head down and stay next to me." Pumpkin froze, flinging his hands up over his eyes. "Oh no, I can't do it."

He shrank back against the wall. "This is just too much to ask of one spirit. If Arista was here . . ."

May sucked in breaths, wiping her eyes. "Who's Arista?"

"It doesn't matter. We're doomed for sure. I think . . . oh, yes . . . I'm having an asthma attack." Pumpkin started wheezing.

"Ghosts have asthma?" May asked doubtfully.

Pumpkin looked at her, startled, and the wheezing came to an abrupt stop. "Good point." He crouched deeper against the wall and chewed on his fingers.

May looked out across the sand at the boat and slumped against the bricks. She turned to rest her head against the wall, but seeing something there, she backed up.

It was only one word, and the paint looked so old and faded that it could have been there forever. It simply read: HELP.

May dipped into her pocket, and her hands closed around the soggy ball of her letter. It was still there. If this was all real, then her letter was real too. *Help.* She traced the word on the bricks with her fingers, her stomach tingling, wondering if it was somehow meant for her.

May didn't think she could help anyone. She needed too much help herself. Crossing her arms tightly across her chest, she turned to watch Pumpkin. He was a horrible sight. His mouth zigzagged up either sides of his face. His body—straight as a rake-jutted out at harsh angles. She remembered his terrifying appearances in her room—the sight of him diving at her in the lake, grabbing at her; his arms dragging her here, zapping her . . .

She waited until Pumpkin was looking in the other direction, then took a few faltering steps forward, out onto the open sand.

"Oh, dear." Pumpkin caught up with her, clutching her arm as he kept his eyes on the cloaked creatures at the water's edge. May shrank from him, but he held on tight. "You're going to get yourself destroyed," he whispered, trembling again. "I'm trying to help you."

May looked around as they moved across the sand, wondering who it was that was trying to destroy her.

After a few agonizing minutes, they were standing next to the boat.

"Hurry. Hop in."

May hesitated. She could see the water through the transparent bottom of the craft, and it looked like if she tried to step inside, she would fall right through. A cold nudge hit her from behind, and her feet went stumbling in anyway. It sank slightly under her weight.

She looked down the beach, wondering if she should call for help—most of the figures on the beach looked much more human than Pumpkin did. But she gave up that thought when she saw that one of the skeletal characters in black was gazing in their direction. He walked over to another robed skeleton and leaned toward him, his jaw bones opening and closing. Then they both looked in May's direction.

Pumpkin climbed down into the boat beside her and sat down, folding his hands tightly on his lap.

The boat stayed where it was.

"It's your weight in the boat. Get down," Pumpkin whispered, gazing at the two skeletons down the beach, who had started to move toward them. "Oh, no. Oh, no no no." He seemed not to notice that, now that they were in the boat, they needed to set it to moving.

May, huddling tightly, started to feel panicked too. Her gaze shifted from Pumpkin, to the robed creatures, to Pumpkin. "Shouldn't we push off?" she finally asked.

Pumpkin's lips trembled. "Yes, yes, you're absolutely right."

He jumped back out of the boat onto the shore, sneaking another look at the two figures that were now advancing quite quickly down the beach. Then he seemed to gauge the direction in which he wanted to push the boat. "Southern Territories, Southern Territories," he muttered. Finally he gave the boat a hard diagonal shove and tried to jump in. Instead only half of him made it. The other half splashed into the water, his long legs flailing.

May stared, not knowing what to do. With one tiny push, she could shove Pumpkin off the boat and escape. But where would she go? Who would she go to? And what if the skeletons caught him?

Her hands shot out to grab him, her fingers turning to ice as she helped to drag him onto the boat.

He smiled at her crookedly. "Thanks."

May merely gazed at him in reply, then toward the shore, then peered around, unsure as to whether she had made the right choice. "How do we paddle?" she finally asked.

"We don't," he breathed. "We just have to hope I pushed us in the right direction. The greeters are experts. They don't miss. But one time I did this wrong and ended up at the Pit of Despair Amusement Park, clear on the other side of the realm. It took me a year to get home."

Sure enough, the boat kept moving on its own. By the time the cloaked figures reached the part of the beach Pumpkin and May had launched from, they were far out into the water. The two skeletons stared after the boat for a moment, then one of them shrugged its bones, and the other patted him on the spinal column. They turned and drifted back along the sand.

Pumpkin and May drifted far and fast, until all of the figures on the beach became small. May could just make out the dark opening of the alley they'd hidden in and a tiny, black speck standing in its shadow, moving its tail. It made a tingling start at the base of her neck. She shook it off and turned to look over her shoulder.

The boat indeed seemed to be steering itself. Up ahead, May could make out several places where the river branched off. Their boat slowly made its way into one of the branches, which looked like it went on forever, though it was no wider than two of the boats put together. A strip of beach lined it on either side, and poking out of the sand just by the mouth was a sign that read: SOUTHERN TERRITORIES.

"Oh, thank goodness." Pumpkin breathed. Looking back, they could see other boats heading in the same direction, drifting lazily behind them.

Back on the beach the spirits outside the southeastern portal, Spectroplex, weren't paying much attention to much of anything but themselves. If they had been, they may have noticed the tiny, black nose that occasionally peeped out from a certain alley. They may have even heard the tiny, plaintive sound of a meow or two, drifting out on the breeze. But most of the specters were busy coming to terms with their recent deaths.

Somber Kitty's slitted green eyes scanned the beach, but May was nowhere to be seen. He had curled up around her freshest footprint just at the edge of the alley, sniffing it thoughtfully several times. He longed to follow her tracks, where they led across the sand, but his instincts told him to beware. His gaze kept drifting to the bony fellows in robes.

Finally he couldn't wait any longer. He pressed his ears back, watched a lady drift close by, and darted forward into the folds of her dress.

Keeping his paws tightly in rhythm with her movements and ignoring the bewildering cold zaps of her clothes, he scurried from spirit to spirit, following May's scent like a checker zigzagging its way to kinghood. At the water just beside a newly beached boat, he froze. Here the scent disappeared.

Somber Kitty's eyes rolled, and he let out a low, plaintive mew, which drew a few stares. Spirits began tugging one another's sleeves and pointing at him until a loud howl erupted from one of the robed creatures several yards away. And then the crowd flew apart as several of the creatures began zipping toward him, all howling.

Somber Kitty arched his back and hissed, leaping sideways and waggling in the air toward the boat. In a maneuver of amazing skill he teetered on his two side paws as they hit the bow, then shifted his weight into the boat, setting the craft in motion.

The cat trembled under the frontmost bench seat for several minutes. Eventually his desire to look for May overcame him. He snuck his eyes and nose up over the rim to gaze at the shore as it drifted away. Several robed creatures now stood there, pointing and waving toward him. He darted under the seat again, his tremble becoming a shake.

If he had remained aft, he would have seen the sign marking the path his boat drifted into, though he could not have read it.

The sign, crooked and glowing, leaning as if it might fall into the water, announced Somber Kitty's destination in bright green letters: PIT OF DESPAIR AMUSEMENT PARK.

☙ ☙ ☙

All had gone quiet now. Pumpkin and May stayed quiet too for a few moments, May gazing at the zooming stars above, still not quite believing them.

"Am I dead?" she finally croaked.

"Oh, I really don't think so."

"Then what am I doing here? What is this place?"

Pumpkin turned his sad, droopy eyes to her and grimaced, his mouth stretching extra wide. "I'm not the best spirit to ask. Arista is. He's very smart."

"Where's Arista?"

"Back home."

"Home?" May asked hopefully.

"Back home in Belle Morte," Pumpkin said, nibbling a finger.

"Belle Morte? But what about my mom? What about Briery Swamp?"

Pumpkin shook his head. "Oh, my." He eyed her sadly. "You should really ask Arista."

"But when do we see him? How far to Belle Morte?"

Pumpkin seemed to consider, his eyebrows scrunching. "I'm not sure. I'm just a house spirit, you know. The next sign should tell us."

A few minutes later they drifted past a gnarled tree that curved over the water. A sign hung from it that read: FIERY FORK, 48 MILES, BELLE MORTE, 1,300,017 MILES.

May gasped. She couldn't even imagine how far that really was. "How long will that take?"

Pumpkin sighed, flinging his arms behind his head dramatically. "Ages. Most of the night probably. You should rest."

She sank down in her seat, staying as far away from Pumpkin as possible. There was no way she was going to sleep. She stared up at the zipping stars that spread out over the dusky sky. An hour later it hadn't gotten an ounce darker, and Pumpkin was snoring gently, his huge head lolling on his skinny neck, his wide mouth open and drooling.

May tugged at the top of her black sparkly bathing suit nervously, then shoved her hands into the pockets of her shorts. Her hands closed on a piece of paper, and she pulled out the scroll she'd picked up at the movie theater.

In red, drippy letters, the front of the brochure read: I'M DEAD, SO NOW WHAT? As May watched, the letters dripped down off the page onto her hands. May lifted up her fingers to see if it was ink, but there was nothing on them.

She opened to the next page, dazed. It was blank for a moment, and then a glowing green picture of a skinny man with a hangman's noose around his neck appeared. He lifted his hands in the air questioningly, his shoulders shrugging. More drippy writing scrawled itself beneath him. "Don't panic. The Afterlife can be scary! But that doesn't mean it can't be enjoyable, too. Talk to your local Undertaker about ways to make the most of your Eternity. All visits are confidential!"

May turned the page. Again it stayed blank for a moment, before a glowing blob oozed across the page. It formed itself into a jellylike mass, from which suddenly sprouted two big round eyeballs and a pair of horns. The creature smiled at May. She flinched.

"The Ever After is filled with lots of strange spirits, some you won't recognize from your life on Earth. Don't panic. Only a few are truly evil." The blob creature moved its head to look behind itself, then its eyes widened in terror, as if something were chasing it. It went blobbing off the page. From the far right side of the paper, a dripping, dark, manlike creature appeared, with long gangly arms and a hunched back. His face was deformed into a mask of hatred, and he was dripping with slime. He drooled, rubbed at his nose with his forearm, and loped off the page.

May's blood ran cold. She quickly turned the page. What appeared there scared her even more. Two red eyes appeared on the page. "Remember, Bo Cleevil is watching you!" The eyes flared brighter red, and then disappeared, replaced by the line "Have a pleasant stay!"

May closed the brochure. It vanished from her hands immediately.

Pumpkin rolled over onto his side loudly, mumbling and snoring and flinging his cool arm across May's shins. May stared at him. He was, without a doubt, the ugliest thing she had ever seen. She wondered what he had looked like when he was alive. She wondered what had happened to him to make him look the way he did now. She gently pulled her feet out from under him.

She laid back and watched the stars zooming overhead. It reminded her of the night she and her mom had watched the meteors, and that planted a seed in her throat that grew into a lump.

The lump grew as she thought of how mean she'd been to Somber Kitty the last time she'd seen him. She might never see him again.

That was her last thought before she fell into a sleep so sound, she didn't notice when someone had carried her off the boat.

❧ ❧ ❧

That evening news traveled quickly along the Styx Streamway System about a fugitive cat who had been spotted leaving the southeast portal, heading toward the Pit of Despair Amusement Park. Several Dark Spirits were dispatched with nets, daggers, and spears. But one creature and his slew of dogs, to the surprise of many, stayed away.

CHAPTER ELEVEN

Beehive House

zzzzzzzzz."

May was lying on a bed, in a room with a low, rounded ceiling. She sat up, feeling like she'd had a long, vivid nightmare.

"Bzzzzzzzzz."

The noise was coming from beyond a door that was rounded at the top, like the ceiling.

"Bzzzz. You didn't dream at all last night, my dear," she heard from the other room. "Slept like the dead. Come have some soup, zzzzz."

The voice tapered into a series of long, soft buzzes. May slowly slid out of bed, tiptoed up to the doorway, and put her hands against the wood. She gave it a tiny nudge.

From the sliver of room that revealed itself, May could make out a small, sloped space, and a man in the middle of it with his back turned. He was a very tiny, very old man—only a little taller than May—in a long cloak that was interrupted every six inches with a yellow stripe, or a black one. He reminded May of—

"A bee. Yes, I get that all the time. Only natural, I suppose. My great-great-grandmother was part bee. She was also part goblin. Lord knows how that happened. But I assure you, I don't favor the goblin side. Come on out, won't you?"

The man turned and smiled warmly. May gasped.

"Oh come, dear, no need to be so dramatic." He frowned as he waved a hand in the air in a come hither gesture. "You've been around Pumpkin for way too long already."

His eyes were completely shut—but what had made May gasp was that they had no way of opening. There were no eyelashes, no lids, just skin where his eyes should have been. Two antennae twitched on top of his head. His chin was adorned by a pointy, triangular white beard.

Was he—

"Blind? Certainly am. Have been my whole life."

Oh. Was he reading her mind? And *who* was he? He wasn't like the ghosts she'd seen last night. Like Pumpkin, he didn't look like a person at all. And where was Pumpkin?

"That's a tough one. I'm one of a kind, as we all are, of course. I'm a spirit first and foremost, but . . ."

The man shrugged indifferently, turning his back to her again and throwing around this and that pot. "It's hard to explain to a Live One."

May ran a hand down her arms and pinched the skin inside her elbow. Her skin was slick with sweat. "Pumpkin's in the back with the bees, by the way."

"Um." Her voice came out rusty, like it needed to be oiled. "Sir? Where am I?"

The man didn't seem to notice that she'd finally used her real voice.

"Beehive House, Belle Morte. The most frequented vacation spot in the southeast. Belle Morte, that is, not Beehive House. I like my privacy, actually. I'm Arista." The man turned again, and his hand shot toward May truly as an arrow, as if he could see perfectly well after all. His antennae stood stiffly, proudly. "And you are May. Pumpkin told me. Do you have a last name?"

May faltered for a second, surprised. "May Bird. Sir, I thought—"

Arista nodded. "I can't read what you're not thinking," he said, in answer to the question she hadn't asked. "You weren't thinking your name, so I couldn't see it."

"See it?" May shook her head. "But what I—"

"See the words. You know how these things go. It's a bee thing."

May blinked at him.

"Didn't you know bees are psychic? Oh, of course not. Live Ones don't know much of anything, of course. Now, let's see . . ."

Arista ducked into a cupboard, his antennae drooping to accommodate him, and pulled out a large wheel of white cheese that seemed to be jiggling slightly. He laid it on a plate that was half its size. "I haven't entertained a Live One in at least two hundred years, so you'll just tell me if I don't put out enough. These are offerings from the Glastonbury Tor in England. Only a couple of years old. Very nice." He opened a jar and began to dip out something that looked like honey, laying it down on another plate. "My last living guest was a Russian magician, quite more frightful-looking than you, I assure you, and he wasn't a big eater, you understand. Of course, people don't leave offerings for us like they used to, so it was probably for the best. I barely have enough soul cakes to make three solid meals. . . ."

May opened her mouth to ask the questions she'd asked Pumpkin last night. Was she alive, or dead? Where was she? How could she get home to Briery Swamp and her cozy room and her kitty?

But what Arista did next made her mouth clamp shut. With the snap of his fingers a cupboard flew open and a skeleton-shaped loaf of bread came out of it as if it was on rollers. It rolled down to the counter, where Arista lifted it, revealing thousands of tiny spiders that had carried it along the way. May gasped.

"So you and Pumpkin finally introduced yourselves to each other. That's nice. He's been talking about you for so long." Arista closed the jam jar and dug into the cupboard again, his antennae twitching this way and that energetically. "I'm sure it was the thrill of his life. He showed real promise yesterday, going to get you. Has troubles, Pumpkin, you understand. In ways he doesn't . . . but, yes . . ." Arista seemed to lose himself in his thoughts. On the table the cheese continued to jiggle.

"There you are. Have a seat."

A table stood in the middle of the room. One of its legs was missing, and it was covered in dust and cobwebs. Arista brushed a few of them aside, again moving as deftly as if he could really see them, and laid the plates down in front of an empty chair.

The chair, too, was covered in silky, gossamer webbing. On the floor a brigade of spiders had gathered around its legs and were slowly pulling it out for her. Some were spinning more webs across the seat. May gasped.

And then she realized it wasn't the cheese jiggling, it was something *in* the cheese, squirming. In fact, it was the maggots coming out of the cheese. There must have been hundreds of them. Her hands flew to her mouth.

"You don't like the helper spiders? Really, they're quite reliable. . . ." Arista patted her with one limp hand. Then he sat himself in the chair opposite May's. She steeled herself and sat too. "I haven't seen a Live One in so long, I forget how disorienting it can be." He pushed the plate toward her. "Try some honey. I raise the bees myself—"

A door slammed behind them, and suddenly Pumpkin walked into the room. A blue, dusky glow followed him through the doorway.

"Pumpkin, May has awoken. She's every bit as lovely as you said. Not at all ghastly, like most of them."

Pumpkin appeared to be speechless. He walked over to a lounge chair in the corner of the room and sat on it, then pulled his knees up to his face.

"Moody fellow," Arista muttered to May, "but I must admit, it's not every day a ghost goes to . . . well . . ."

Goes to Earth to kidnap children? May scowled at Pumpkin. Above his knees Pumpkin blushed all the way to the roots of his yellow tuft of hair.

"It's hot in here, Pumpkin. Can you cool us off a bit?"

Pumpkin sighed deeply. He poked his mouth out above his knees. "I'm exhausted." Then he ducked back behind them.

"Pumpkin, really, you are the laziest servant I've ever had."

His mouth appeared again. "Fine." Pumpkin sucked in a breath, and then let it out, the air coming out of his mouth frosty. The whole room seemed to get cooler. He huddled back down against his legs.

"Better." Arista cut a chunk of cheese for himself and began nibbling tiny bits off and chewing them very slowly, indolently, wiping a maggot from the corner of his lips and tucking it into his mouth.

May cleared her throat. "Won't he eat?"

Pumpkin's eyes widened, and he shook his head furiously a few times.

"Zzzzz, Pumpkin doesn't eat or drink. Most ghosts don't, though a lot do like honey and honey alone," Arista said matter-of-factly, lifting his own cup and sipping from it daintily. "Specters are often big eaters, but only for the idea of it. They cling to the past so. Poor dears."

May blinked in confusion.

"*Specters,* my dear," Arista raised his voice as if she was going deaf. "You don't know the difference?"

May shook her head solemnly. "Oh, my. I forget how much you wouldn't know, being a Live One. Specters have lived. Ghosts haven't. Simple as that. Get it?"

May stared.

"For instance, I doubt you've ever seen a living person with antennae on his head?"

May shook her head.

Arista nodded, satisfied. "Exactly. You'll find you like ghosts much better than specters. Their kind can be so . . . yes, they're quite conceited. 'I've lived and you haven't' and all that. You know . . ."

May blinked.

"Very like Live Ones in that way. 'I exist, but ghosts couldn't possibly,' all that nonsense." Arista had begun to frown disdainfully.

May shifted in her seat, feeling they were getting away from the point. "Excuse me?" May squeaked. "Arista? How did I get here? Did Pumpkin make this happen? Am I dead?"

"Oh, dear," Arista said, frowning. "Zzzzz, you *are* impatient, aren't you?"

She nodded in Pumpkin's direction. "He said I'm not dead, but—"

"My dear Miss Bird," Arista said plainly, "have a look at yourself over there, won't you? Then I'll be able to see you properly, through your own eyes." He pointed to a tall, floor-length mirror across the room. May did as she was told, walking over to the mirror and staring at her disheveled form.

"You see? You are very much alive. Look at you. You're still solid, you don't float, you're very colorful. I quite like looking at you, actually—it's a nice change."

May turned back from the mirror. "But"—May thought hard—"the first time I fell in the lake, I started seeing ghosts. Maybe . . ." May lit on an idea. "Maybe I was half dead? And now—"

"You weren't half dead. Who ever heard of such nonsense. You simply got your sight back, that's all. Live Ones are born with it, and then they quickly lose it. You got yours back."

May pondered this, still confused.

Arista tapped his forehead in a gesture of impatience. Apparently the answer was too obvious to say. "Really, with your extraordinary imagination, and you didn't even guess. I'd expect more from you, according to what Pumpkin tells me."

May looked at Pumpkin. An idea was hopping around her brain. If people were born with sight . . .

"When I was little, I think I drew you."

Pumpkin nodded, letting his knees fall slightly to reveal a hopeful little smile.

"Oh, dear, you really take the cake, don't you. My dear, Pumpkin is your, ehhh, *house spirit*. If Live Ones paid any attention at all, you would know that. Every house has one. Pumpkin is my manservant during the day—he helps me with house chores and raising the bees. At midnight he comes to you. He's known you your *entire* life." There was a hint of pride in the smile that Pumpkin gave the two of them now.

May frowned back at him.

"Another house spirit might have left you for dead."

May stared at Arista. "I don't understand," she murmured.

"Of course," Arista sighed, "*not* being dead is maybe the worst curse that could possibly befall you."

"What do you mean?"

Arista chewed on another chunk of cheese and spoke with his mouth full. "Being alive will cause you great trouble."

"What do you mean?"

"Live Ones are no longer welcome in the Ever After." Arista stood from the table. "You must get out of the realm. That is your only hope."

"I don't understand," May said, a stone sinking in her gut.

"I mean, if they catch you here, you *will* be dead. Worse than dead. And they *will* catch you eventually. There are spies everywhere."

May stared in shocked silence at Arista's face.

He motioned at her, his antennae drooping somberly. "This is only scratching the surface, zzzz. I understand why it might be confusing. Come with me."

🦂 🦂 🦂

May followed Arista through an arched doorway on the side of the room into another, dimmer area, its curved walls lined with shelves of books, all the spines of which were blank until May focused on them and words began to blur themselves onto the paper. In one corner of the room was an old television set. Above it hung a gleaming silver clock with tiny skeleton hands for hands. And on a wide wooden desk sat a gleaming white skull and what looked like a glass globe, only it was blank—with no continents or oceans mapped out along its curving surface.

Arista reached out his hands and laid them on the globe. Suddenly it came alight.

"Ohhh," May breathed. Arista smiled.

"Nice, isn't it, dear? Zzzz, Christmas present from Pumpkin. He bought it at an estate sale. Copernicus has a company that makes them, have you heard of him?"

May nodded.

"Poor fellow got summoned to the northeast last year and never came back. Too rebellious a mind, I suspect. That happens these dark days. Here . . ."

The glow within the globe had begun to separate itself into thousands of tiny points of light. The glass surface disappeared completely.

Inside the globe May recognized the spiraling Milky Way from fifth-grade science, the same class where she'd learned about Copernicus. "There's yours," he said, pointing to one of the millions of dots. A little square of light loomed up where he'd touched, and formed a miniature vapor Earth, complete with swirling clouds. Words appeared beside it.

Earth
Population: 6,087,983,408
Portal Type: Water
Portal Count: 4
Please look both ways when haunting.

Arista wetted his thumb with his puckered, wrinkled mouth, spun the globe, and then with his crooked old pointer finger, staked out a dot in the swirling mass—a star, one that looked just like all the other stars, tucked deep in a spiral cloud on the other side of the globe. It lit up extra bright when Arista touched it. Tiny writing appeared above it, with a miniature May beside it, complete with knobby knees and straight short bangs, and wearing a black sparkly bathing suit and shorts. Next to her stood a miniature Arista. *You are here*, it read.

May almost choked.

"But, but Earth . . . it's so far away!"

Beside it a box had popped up like the one for Earth, and this read:

The Ever After
Population
  Dark Spirits: 11,103
  Ghosts: 16,874,939,004
  Specters: 8,783, 208,965
  Live Ones: 111

Arista seemed not to have heard her. "You see, we're a tiny realm, and we orbit very fast. That's why the stars go by us so quickly. I believe on Earth they appear more still, isn't that so?"

"How will I ever get home?" she asked, ignoring his question.

Arista's antennae twitched thoughtfully. "Oh, that's quite impossible. Live Ones can't get out of the Ever After once they get in."

"But you just said that's what I need to do."

"Yes."

"But you're saying it's impossible."

"Yes." Arista frowned.

"But you're saying I'll be killed if I stay."

"That's true." Arista seemed confused.

"But what should I do?"

Arista considered. "My dear, I hate to tell you, but I simply don't know. Zzzz, Bo Cleevil will make sure you're found, that's certain."

May remembered the eyes that had appeared in her brochure and shivered. "Arista, I don't understand."

Arista looked at her and shook his head. "Why don't you sit, my dear?"

May sank onto an overstuffed black velvet chair, and Arista sank onto the seat by his desk.

"Bo Cleevil is our most powerful spirit. *Horrible* spirit." Arista's antennae swayed and drooped. "How horrible I don't think anyone really knows. He rules the realm."

May swallowed.

"You see, the realm is made up of four corners." Arista pulled a faded piece of parchment out of a drawer and lifted a quill pen out of its inkwell at the corner of his desk. In bloodred ink he traced out a four-cornered sketch, then divided it into four parts, then tapped his quill onto the paper. May scrunched her nose, queasy. Was it really blood?

"Oh, don't get caught up in trifles, dear. Here." He tapped again, on the lower-right corner of the drawing. "You and I are far down in the southeast and not far from the Dead Sea. Bo Cleevil lives here, in the northeast." Arista pointed toward the upper-right corner. "And the Northern Spirits live here, in the northwest." He pointed to the upper-left-hand corner. "I won't concern you with the west. It's very empty but for the desert and some ancient settlements. They're trying to draw more tourists out with the Pit of Despair Amusement Park. The City of Ether lies at the very center." He pointed to where the four lines intersected in the middle of the paper. "And South Place lies deep beneath all of it."

"Now as you can see there are four kinds of inhabitants in the realm. Ghosts, Specters, Live Ones like yourself, and Dark Spirits. The Dark Spirits—poltergeists and goblins, ghouls, demons, that sort—live in South Place. They're not allowed in the Upper Realm, but they sneak up from time to time. And when they do, you can be sure it is to serve Bo Cleevil. And then, of course, the Bogey. That's who came after you with the dogs."

Even Arista seemed fearful for a moment. He tugged at his antennae, agitated. "He helps to clean out the territories. Gets rid of all the spirits Bo Cleevil sees as troublemakers. Only ever visits Earth in children's nightmares."

"But"—May looked at the globe again—"There aren't many Dark Spirits compared to the ghosts and specters. Can't everyone stop him?"

"Well, zzz, everyone is too afraid. And many just don't think about it. Spirits don't like to use their heads. Especially the ones who've lost them in horrible accidents, or beheadings. Too lazy to think.

"Plus, zzz, Bo Cleevil's filled spirits's minds with all sorts of notions—that specters are better than ghosts, convincing ghosts that specters are conceited." Arista sniffed. "Which they are, I must admit. And then there's you. Zzz, most spirits believe you Live Ones only care about one thing: exorcism. That's why you must never, ever show yourself to any but a select few. We believe you are spirit killers."

"But that's not true. I . . ."

"You don't need to convince *me,* dear. I don't buy into all that poppycock. *I* am not too lazy to think." Arista waved at his shelves of books. "There are good and bad Live Ones, the same way there are good and bad spirits. But Bo Cleevil, I'm afraid, is above all, a liar. Anything that makes spirits more afraid, makes his power grow. And as long as spirits are afraid of other things, they won't think too much about him."

"But what does he want?"

"Zzz, I have no idea, dear. Nor do I know what he looks like. Bo Cleevil himself never leaves his fortress in the northeast, beyond the Platte of Despair. It's very treacherous there, and few who ever go come back. Those that do have been struck dumb by fear and can't describe what they saw."

"You should do something," May urged. For the moment it didn't seem so strange to be having a discussion in a study on a star billions of miles away from home. Her imagination painted a picture of Bo Cleevil that was too big to ignore.

"I think there's not much to be done," Arista said cheerfully.

"It's too much bother to go against the flow. From what Pumpkin tells me, you should know something about that, May."

"But that's no excuse." May stared, frustrated, and then blushed. Recently she had tried with all her might to go *with* the flow. She just hadn't figured out how to do it.

May looked at the distance on the globe, longing with a throbbing in her heart for home. Then she remembered her letter. She dug into her pocket and pulled it out.

"Arista, I got this . . ." She held it out to him, smoothing the soggy paper out with both hands. As she did she noticed with a gasp that the picture of the lady in the trees had reappeared on the envelope. At the same moment Arista recoiled.

"Oh, my."

May looked up at him. "What's wrong?"

"Zzzz. Oh, my. Please put that away. Zzzzz. I had *no* idea."

May looked at her letter, then tucked it back into her pocket. She stared at Arista, befuddled. "It says there's a Lady on a Farm. It says she needs my help. And back at the Spectroplex I saw . . ."

Arista's antennae described a wild circle, like the propellers of a helicopter. "Don't show that to just *anyone*."

They stared at each other for a moment in silence. Then Arista's antennae perked up straight and still. "Yes. We'll call the Undertaker. We must. You can show it to her."

"The who?"

"The Undertaker. She'll know what to do."

"Can she help me get home?"

But Arista wasn't paying attention. He was already leaning over his desk, toward the skull that rested on the corner.

The mouth of the skull opened, a green glow emanating

from inside. A low, crackling groan arose from the mouth, then a few more groans, and then a moment of silence.

May studied the globe while they waited, thinking tearfully of her mother and her cat. It took her a moment to notice that the globe was blinking very oddly, and the population number was rising one, falling one. Rising one, falling one.

"Arista, what's . . ."

"Well, I say," Arista muttered, reading her mind and putting his hands on the globe. "That's odd, I've never . . ."

"You have reached the office of the Undertaker," the skullophone boomed. "If you have recently died and are looking for employment, please press your skullophone's right molar. If you are worried that you might be exorcised, please press your skullophone's right front tooth. If you would like to speak to a dead operator, press your skullophone's left front tooth."

Arista sighed and pressed the left front tooth.

"Hellooooo," a spine-chilling voice rasped.

Arista cleared his throat. "I'd like an appointment."

"Let'ssss ssssee. We have a sssseven a.m. availablllllle . . . ," the voice hissed.

"Dear sir, you don't have any later?"

The line went dead.

Arista shook his head. He smiled weakly at May's confusion. "Zzzzzz. The Undertaker's assistants always think they're better than everyone else. Their bosses are very vain, and I suppose it rubs off. All that power over death. I'll handle this."

Arista waved May out of the room.

May trailed back into the kitchen, where Pumpkin was busy making hand shadows on the surface of the cupboard. "I'm a water demon" he growled, the shadow he made really resembling the horrible woman in the lake. "I'm not scared of you," he said in another voice, his hands fluttering into the shape of himself. May watched, confused.

A second later Arista emerged. "We have an appointment for seven in the morning."

Pumpkin turned, saw May, and blushed.

"Now we just have to figure out how to get you into town, unseen, on one of the biggest vacation days of the year."

As May slept that night in her tiny nook of a room, the globe in Arista's study continued to blink oddly. Something had entered the Ever After that it did not know what to do with, a creature it hadn't processed in more than two hundred years.

One million, three hundred thousand, seventeen miles away, the cause of the confusion was curled under the bench seat of a small boat as he drifted down the Styx Streamway.

Somber Kitty was only a few miles from the Pit of Despair Boat Basin, sound asleep, when his nose began to twitch. He sat up with a start, his large ears rotating like satellite dishes.

A scent he recognized was drifting up the river toward him, and it made his back arch and his fuzzy coat stand on end.

The cat planted his front paws on the side of the boat and stared downstream. There was nothing to see but the gentle curves of the water through sand and low beach brush. Still a low growl emanated from Somber Kitty's throat. The air was full of the smell of danger.

His slitted eyes darted to the shore on either side of the boat, calculating the distance. It was several feet away, an impossible jump for a person to make. But Somber Kitty didn't think twice. The muscles of his hind legs coiled like bedsprings, and he sailed forward, hurtling onto the sand.

He landed on all fours with a small breeze blowing at his back, gave his shoulders a few much-needed licks, then looked around furtively. He was on a scrubby beach dotted with scrawny bushes and large quartz boulders. He looked right, left, and up for the moon, but saw only zooming stars. He leaped onto a rock to get a better view. And then he crouched backward and hissed.

There before him, traced in the sand at the base of the rock, were the eyes of a lady, her face hidden in the sand-traced leaves of an enormous tree. Above her, one hand extended upward, with one finger pointed along the sand.

Somber Kitty's eyes followed the direction of the finger, then darted back to the lady. But the tiny breeze scattered the sand, and the face disappeared.

"Meay?" Somber Kitty asked the sand. But there was no answer. Not knowing what else to do, he followed where the hand had pointed.

CHAPTER TWELVE

Belle Morte

The television, which Arista called the Holo-Vision, showed nothing but ads. That morning May, Pumpkin, and Arista sat on the couch in front of the glowing three-dimensional screen, waiting for a cab to arrive. Arista had called at ten past six.

At the moment they were watching a commercial for something called Crook-Be-Gone cologne. A man in a black-and-white-striped prison suit sat in an electric chair, holding a bottle straight toward them so that it came out of the set, his hair standing on end. "When the smell of thievery keeps you from entering your favorite city," the man said, "Crook-Be-Gone will have you smelling like a normal, law-abiding citizen. Proven to fool sniffing phantoms nine times out of ten."

They'd already seen an ad for getting rid of annoying exorcists, one for the freshest soul cakes in Belle Morte, and another featuring a psychic who could tell you who had murdered you (in the case of a poisoning or other mysterious death). May had been confused by all of them. What were sniffing phantoms? And why did smelling like a crook keep you out of your favorite cities? And what did crooks smell like, anyway?

Another commercial was just coming on. This one was a spine-chilling group of words popping out of the screen, warning the public against the danger of Live Ones. May nibbled her nails as she read, "If you see a suspiciously lively looking spirit lurking in your town, don't hesitate to blow your Bogey whistle."

Pumpkin was glued to the set, his eyes big. Arista shook his head. "What a bunch of nonsense. Pumpkin, isn't May proof that it's all . . ."

A bloodcurdling scream shattered the room.

May leaped in her chair and looked around frantically.

Arista merely sat up and said, "The cab."

May followed him and Pumpkin into the kitchen and did as Arista had told her to the night before. She crawled into the big basket of dirty clothes Arista had left by the door, letting them pile the clothes on top of her head—thickly enough so that she couldn't be seen through the filmy garments. She peered out through the cracks between the fabrics.

The first thing she noticed when they opened the door was that, though it was morning, it was barely lighter out than it had been the night before. The doorbell sounded again, rattling the walls.

"We're already here, good man," Arista said irritably, then muttered under his breath, "You'd think they'd hire drivers with heads. But no. The tourists want a headless horseman, zzzzz. Nine times out of ten."

May heard the sound of a door opening, and then felt herself being hoisted into the cab.

"The Undertaker's, please," Arista said, low. The carriage started.

"You can come out and have a look, my dear. We have trick windows in the deluxe cabs."

May climbed out of the basket and sat beside Arista, across from Pumpkin.

Arista pointed to a dial on the ceiling. "We can set it to look like one of these things to those on the outside—just a novelty really, but good for privacy. Each cab has a different set of options. . . ." The glowing words next to the dial read: KING ARTHUR AND QUEEN GUINEVERE AT GAME OF PINOCHLE, SLEEPING SKELETON, BIGFOOT, and UNICORN DISCUSSING SOMETHING SERIOUS. Arista turned the dial to the first option.

May stared out the window. It seemed like a normal window to her. Through it she could see that they were on a sandy road with nothing on either side of it but desert. The sky was still filled with flashing stars.

"No. No need to worry about being seen in a deluxe cab."

May sat back. "Arista, what happens if I do get seen?"

Pumpkin and Arista looked at each other.

"Then the Bogeyman comes, my dear."

"Who . . . who is the Bogeyman?" May ventured to ask.

"Zzzzz. He and his Black Shuck dogs scour the realm looking for Live Ones, patrolling the portals for strays and answering any distress calls."

"Distress calls?"

"If anyone sees a Live One, a call goes out to let him know. Each spirit has one of these. They were talking about them on TV, remember?" Arista and Pumpkin both reached into their shirts and pulled out a long, gleaming cylinder hung from a chain.

"Each spirit has a Bogey whistle?" May asked, disbelieving.

"You blow on it and the sound that comes out is very high pitched. Only his dogs can hear it—from any part of the realm. And they travel with lightning speed. The Bogey himself is mostly blind. They are his eyes and ears."

May shivered, remembering the sound of the dogs back at the portal. "Can he read minds too?"

"Oh, no." Arista nodded. "He's not like me. He's not completely blind either, he's just blind to pure goodness. He simply can't recognize it. The dogs help him with that."

"Wh-What does he do to people when he catches them?"

Pumpkin whimpered and held his hands up to his ears.

"Oh, really, Pumpkin." Arista's antennae drooped sadly as he turned back to May. "The worst fate that can befall a ghost. He sucks you up into nothingness."

May tried to imagine becoming nothing. It made her stomach ache. Her lips began to tremble. "But why?"

"Who can say, dear? He works for Bo Cleevil. That's enough of a reason for evil."

May scratched her chin. "Mom used to say that if I stayed up too late, the Bogeyman would get me."

"Oh?"

"Well, actually, I always thought it was the boogeyman." May remembered with an ache in her heart, staying up in bed, imagining what the Bogeyman was like. Usually he was very scary, and he liked to dance. And then she'd run into her mom's room and curl up under her covers with her.

"Well, actually, that's how he started out—dancing. Before he came up to this realm he used to throw big parties, apparently, for all the Dark Spirits, in South Place."

"Hm." May rested against the window, too overwhelmed to ask any more questions. She didn't think she wanted to know, anyway. For a few minutes all she could see was the endless stretching sand in either direction. A few tumbleweeds started to bounce into sight and roll past them.

May peered through the little slot at the front of the cab that gave a tiny view of the driver's seat. She could see the back of the horseman, who was indeed headless, his hands outstretched and holding a pair of reins that were connected to nothing but the empty space out in front of them. There were no horses. And just inside the front of the carriage, there was a little box with two sets of blinking numbers. One was marked PRICE and the other was marked MILES. The miles number clicked past 100, 150, 200, 250, 300.

"Are those really the miles?" May asked, and Arista nodded. "But we're not going that fast."

"Things here are not like they are in the living world," Arista said simply.

May moved back to the window just in time to see a woman in a bathing suit ride by on a rusty bicycle. Her skin was completely blue, like she'd stayed underwater too long.

And then Belle Morte proper came into view.

The town of Belle Morte crouched at the base of a set of enormous cliffs that curled out above it like giant black waves. May shrank back, hating the look of them immediately. But then curiosity overcame her, and she leaned forward again. The town itself was made of the same slate gray color as the cliffs. It rose in points, its roofs puckered triangles, reminding May of a bunch of lopsided ice-cream cones—like houses that were a little bit melted, with irregular rectangular windows that shrank together at the top, blue glows emanating from inside.

Ahead May could see the main street that cut through town, festooned with blue lights on invisible strings. At the very end of it was a glowing blue box that looked like a phone booth and said TELEPORT on top.

"The Boulevard," Arista said with a hint of pride in his voice. "Pretty, isn't it? Carved from rock from the cliffs. They brought the Easter Island people in to design them about thirty years ago. Of course, Easter Island was their minimalist phase. Dear, I can't tell you what it's done for tourism. Prettiest town in all of South Ever After."

As they rolled into the edge of town, they passed a very tall building, at least seven stories tall, with flames leaping out its windows. A sign along the double doors read TOWERING INFERNO HOTEL. As May tried to peer through the front doors, a person plummeted past her window, letting out a horrible scream and landing on the road with a thud. Another person followed, and then another.

"Arista!" May cried. "Help!"

Arista chuckled, but he didn't bother to move. "Makes ghosts feel like they're in an actual fire. Very pleasing. Zzzz, very popular with specters who died in volcanic eruptions."

May pressed her face to the window, amazed. The three figures lying on the road sat up slowly, their faces and bodies blackened and burned. They were all wearing togas. They stood and brushed themselves off, then started laughing and patting one another on the back.

"You see," Arista went on, "that's the Pompeii crew. Very friendly for specters. Wish I spoke more Latin."

The figures turned around and raced back into the hotel. A few seconds later came another set of screams, and May looked out the back of the carriage to see them lying in the road once again.

"But . . . why would they want to do that?"

"Like I said earlier. Specters. Stuck in the past. Spirits don't change, generally. They don't get older, they don't get smarter, or braver. Unlike you, zzz, spirits have no hope of growing inside or out. Specters are no exception. Anyway, it's a great hotel. Pumpkin loves the pool."

"I like the slide," Pumpkin added, blushing.

"Zzzz. Quiet now. We're getting into traffic soon."

Just as he said it, a carriage like the one they were in zoomed past, and then another—neither of them pulled by horses. And then they got to the crowds. May held her breath, amazed. This wasn't like the crowd back at the Spectroplex, where everyone had been human-looking. These ghosts were all shapes and sizes.

A woman as gooey and soft as caramel, with long drippy eyes and a frown that hung down off her chin, sifted through a bag slung over her hunched, tiny shoulders. A moment later she pulled a length of long metal chain out of the sack and held it next to her ear, giving it a good solid rattle. A large white tag dangled from it on which were scrawled the words I'D RATHER BE IN BELLE MORTE. For a moment her frown lifted above the line of her chin, in an expression that May could only assume was a smile, and she stuffed the chain back into her sack and moved on.

"Lots of people in town on account of Lost Souls Day," Arista said. "Most of them traveling here from up north. Lots of money coming in."

A bald man with devilish horns walked by carrying a knapsack, and then three clowns whispering to one another. One of them laughed at what another had said, revealing two rows of razor-sharp teeth. And then a carriage, racing from behind and coming out of nowhere, ran over him. May watched, stunned, as the other two clowns grabbed their knees, laughing. The third one stood up, his head completely flattened now, looking annoyed.

It was like every character from every nightmare May might have had, thrown together onto one street, shopping.

They passed a shop with a sign across the front door that said SILK LADIES' FASHIONS FOR ALL ERAS. In the window stood several mannequins, each hunched over or deformed in some way. One was missing an arm. Another had a hangman's rope dangling from her hand. One female mannequin wore a look on her face of pure terror while another stood beside her, her arms raised as if to startle the first, a snarl across her features. May shuddered.

"Why do those ladies look so mean?" she whispered.

"Oh, the Silkies," Pumpkin whispered, widening his eyes. "They're murderesses."

May shuddered.

"There's a group of them in town who like to have tea at the Public House," Arista added. "They don't do anyone much harm, just like to talk and whisper to one another about the people they killed when they were alive. Compare notes, that sort of thing."

"You couldn't pay me to get near one," Pumpkin said.

"You couldn't pay Pumpkin to get near much of anything," Arista replied, annoyed.

They pulled to a stop a few minutes later, in front of a large window full of shattered glass. "Okay, my dear, hop in." Arista indicated the laundry basket—May obeyed, pulling the clothes over her head, but still leaving a few little cracks to breathe and see.

They climbed out of the cab, Pumpkin and Arista holding either side of the basket. There was the sound of jangling as Arista paid the driver. Then the sound of the door closing. Through the cracks of the basket, May got just a glimpse of the carriage as it drove away. In the window, to her amazement, were a bearded man and a beautiful woman, both wearing crowns, playing a game of cards.

"Pumpkin," Arista said, "do stop looking so petrified, will you? You'll give us away. And watch where you're going."

"Arista!" someone shouted. May sank farther into the clothes. She could just make out the outline of a figure hurrying up beside them. "Laundry day, huh? I've just got a new shipment of bees in from the west. Thought you might want to take a look at them, do you think . . ."

Staying as still as she possibly could, her heart racing, May held her breath. Through the crack she could see that the man was standing just off to the side of Arista, in front of the large window full of broken glass. Above it a sign read: THE MOLDY PAGE: PURVEYORS OF FINE USED BOOKS SINCE THE WRITTEN LANGUAGE WAS INVENTED.

The shelves behind the glass were filled with all sorts of books, many so yellowed and decayed that they'd crumbled in half, splitting apart at their seams. A few piles of dust looked like they might have been books in a past life. None of them had anything written on them. But then, as May stared at each one, words began to form themselves in green letters on the covers: *Life after the Guillotine: The True Story of My Two Hundred Years in the Western Territories* by Marie Antoinette; *I'm Dead, You're Dead* by Dr. Franco Smiley; *The Real Ghost's Guide to Runes* by Ra.

In the center of the display, on a special shelf all its own, another stood out: *I've Got Spirits, How 'Bout You: The Unauthorized Biography of the Ever After's Most Infamous Spirit, Bo Cleevil.*

As she stared, something else began to form on the cover. May felt the hairs on the back of her neck go up again. Two eyes, red and angry—the same as from the brochure—appeared. They glowed a deep, dark red.

Another line of words began to write itself on the bottom of the cover, beaneath the eyes. *I . . . s . . . e . . .*

"Bring them by tomorrow, then," Arista was saying. May felt herself being lifted again. She kept her eyes on the book.

e . . . y . . . o . . .

She could feel herself being carried toward a doorway, and the bookstore fell out of sight. But not before May had made out what the words spelled, her heart pounding.

I see you.

CHAPTER THIRTEEN

The Undertaker

We have an appointment."

Though May was still piled under the clothes, she could tell they'd come into a dark hallway. A few moments ago she'd heard a door creak open and slam shut. And then she felt the cool air blowing on her sweaty face.

Now she could just make out the legs of a desk. And then a pair of feet hovering before her.

"Right this waaaaay . . ."

May was jostled along, and then they came to another stop.

"You will be called in shoooooortly."

Another creaking door sound, and then the clothes over her head were pulled out of the way, and Pumpkin smiled down at her. "How are you?"

"Okay, I guess."

"You can come out, my dear," Arista said.

May climbed out of the basket and looked around. They were in a pitch-black room. She couldn't see anything but Pumpkin and Arista sitting next to each other, and a glowing sign that read 2,007,998 SOULS SERVED.

"Arista," May whispered, "back at the bookstore—"

Ding, ding, ding.

A list unrolled before them in the dark:

RULES OF THE UNDERTAKER

- Please extinguish any burning body parts before entering.
- Please, no cameras. The Undertaker, while extremely good-looking, will not show up in photographs.
- Under the psychic privacy act, views of your past, present, and future are protected.
- No talking in the waiting room!

ANYONE NOT FOLLOWING THESE RULES WILL BE SUBJECT TO POSSIBLE MUTILATION AND A FINE.

Looking back and forth between Arista, who sat calmly and gravely, and Pumpkin, who no longer seemed afraid but curious—swinging his legs and looking around the room as if they were at a picnic—May said, "But that book—"

"Silence!" The voice that came out was so loud it made the walls shake. Pumpkin shook with them. He sat on his hands.

They all stared at one another, May bursting with the news of what she'd seen.

Just then, ahead of them, the darkness began to open up, one section at a time, like puzzle pieces of light being put together. The pieces formed a childlike shape, with skinny legs and a bob haircut. It was the shape of May, glowing blue before them. The sign above it announcing the number of served souls dinged to 2,007,999.

May looked from Pumpkin to Arista, who nodded to her, then back to the cutout May in the darkness.

She walked up to the opening and squeezed through. It was a perfect fit.

May was in sunlight. All around her were white, fluffy clouds. Her feet appeared to be standing on nothing.

A red velvet couch sat a few feet away, and on it, a figure in a long black robe, a black hood obscuring its face in an oval of darkness, its hands gently stroking a sharp, gleaming scythe.

May shrunk back just as the figure sat up and reached for its hood. She took a few more steps backward, but her feet began to sink into the clouds beneath her, and she moved forward again. The hood fell back, revealing a beautiful woman with long glossy black hair, alabaster skin, and ruby red lips. She smiled at May as she splayed her feet out in front of her and filed her nails against her scythe. There were wings on her ankles.

The woman squinted for a moment. "You're alive."

May nodded.

"What's your name?" The woman arched her perfect black eyebrows in a question mark.

"May Bird, ma'am."

"Born in?"

"Briery Swamp."

"May Bird. May Bird." The woman put her manicured pointer finger to her chin and tapped it thoughtfully. Her fingernails were decorated with tiny painted earthworms. She laid down her scythe, pulled a tiny black book out of her cloak, and flipped through it. "Ah, yes. Yes, May Ellen Bird. From West Virginia. You're early."

May swallowed. "Arista made an appointment—"

"You shouldn't be dead for eighty-three more years."

"But—"

"And to show up here alive, at a time when it couldn't be more dangerous." The woman shook her head. May shrunk under her disapproval. "What are we going to do with you?"

She swept off the couch and sashayed across the clouds at their feet, a few snakes unfurling themselves in a trail behind her. "Do you mind if I take a look at your past, present, and future? You have the right to refuse. And the privacy clause keeps me from seeing too many personal details."

May nodded, dazed.

The woman crouched and looked into May's eyes, squinting thoughtfully. "Ah, yes, the portal. Interesting . . . you seem so timid, but . . . hmmm."

May couldn't stop marveling at how beautiful the woman was, and then at her cloak and her scythe.

The Undertaker smiled at her obvious curiosity.

"Are you the Grim Reaper?" May asked boldly, surprising herself.

"And I already saw that you're exceptionally curious. Which helps to feed your exceptional imagination. I see that very well." She pulled back, then shook her head a little. "'Grim Reaper' is what Live Ones call me sometimes. The Living can be so dramatic. I much prefer 'Undertaker.'"

May shrank back. "But Grim Reapers . . . You . . . kill people!"

"No no no. Most people get that wrong. We Undertakers are actually psychopomps."

May looked at her blankly. The Undertaker didn't *look* like a psycho, but May suddenly felt too shy to say it.

"A guide. I just help people out when they're dead. With things like finding the right house and the right place to haunt, getting a job." The Undertaker waggled her hands casually. "Actually, there are several of us, all siblings. We're very powerful, you know. Very unique. All the Undertakers are. And very speedy. We have so many dead coming in that we have to be." She indicated the wings on her heels. "But I'm probably the best-looking. Don't you agree?"

"Um, yes?"

The Undertaker nodded, satisfied. "We're here to help. The Ever After can be a dangerous place, especially nowadays. And especially for you, my dear. Even more than most Live Ones, I'd say."

A wave of frustration ran through May. She didn't think she could take more bad news. She clenched her fists.

The woman squinted into her eyes again. "There are powerful spirits around you. Who are they?"

May shrugged, feeling on the spot and nervous. The Undertaker frowned more deeply. And then May remembered.

"I . . . I got a letter." May reached into her pocket to pull it out, but the Undertaker held her hand in a stop motion.

"I see it in your file. Hold on."

Then she tossed her head back, letting her long black hair swish out behind her. She looked at May for a long time. Now that May was staring into her eyeballs, she could see motion in them. She gasped. There was May, a horrible black dog lunging at her, and shattering glass, and a boy surrounded in light.

The Undertaker grew very grave and held out her hand for the letter, then read it a few times. Finally she folded it up solemnly.

"May, this is very big. It means you are attached to a powerful spirit."

"Wh-What kind of spirit?"

The Undertaker ran a hand along her scythe again, thoughtfully.

"Nobody knows much about the Far North or the spirits who live there. But it's the seat of the old ways. All of the old rules come from there. And the Lady of the North Farm is the oldest, and the most powerful, of its spirits. She's a great mystery. To say that she needs you, well . . . I don't understand it. It means you are surrounded by power, certainly, but I'm afraid it also means you are surrounded by great danger."

"The Lady is dangerous?"

The Undertaker took May's hand.

"I couldn't say. It's not that simple, and I really don't know. But her enemies certainly are. Keep the letter secret. Whatever it means, you don't have a choice. You have to go."

May looked at the floor, guilty. At home it had been easy to want to help a mysterious person in trouble. It had sounded nice to be needed.

But the reality was very different.

"I don't want to anymore."

The Undertaker sighed. "You won't be able to help it. She is more powerful than you can guess."

"I just want to go home."

The Undertaker frowned again. Her eyes flashed through scenes too quickly for May to make them out. "Your future profile is very confusing. I see great fear. You fear too many things. You even fear yourself. Why?"

May stared at her blankly.

"Oh, yes. You don't believe in your heart. You doubt yourself. It's a great failing." The Undertaker gazed at her solemnly. "But there's also great courage."

May looked at her feet. She was the least courageous person she knew. "Maybe I can help the Lady from home. Maybe I can be courageous there."

The Undertaker sighed. "No Live One has ever left the Ever After."

"Arista said I came through a portal. I can go back through." May crossed her arms.

The Undertaker smiled indulgently, then tucked one hand into the neck of her cloak and pulled out a necklace with an Earth-shaped pendant. It was divided into four corners.

"There is one portal in each corner of your globe that connects to each one of the corners of our realm. There's one in a hot spring in Japan, in the ocean near Bermuda, one in Europe, and one in the mountains in West Virginia."

May nodded.

"The portals have been there since ancient times, created by the natural order of things for the spirits of the dead to pass through, you see. And they only go one way."

The Undertaker looked at May for emphasis here. "It's been that way since Earth and the Ever After have existed. Now, in the old days *others* occasionally slipped through. Live Ones, like you.

"But things have changed since then. A couple of hundred years ago Bo Cleevil—you've heard of him?"

May nodded.

"He decided that Live Ones were dangerous. Some say he did so after reading the Book . . ."

"The Book?"

"I will get to that. But first, he placed water demons at the four portals. Their job was to guard the entrance into the Ever After, so that no living souls could make their way through. The few that did, the Bogey got them.

"That was about the same time that animals were banished from the Ever After—all of them except for the Black Shucks. Those that were found afterward were sent to the animal realm, except for cats, of course."

May swallowed. "What happened to cats?"

"Oh, Bo Cleevil *hates* cats. All the cats were destroyed."

May thought of Somber Kitty and how she'd sent him away from the lake. Maybe it had been the right thing to do. She didn't want to think about what the water demon would have done to him. Much less Bo Cleevil.

"Are you paying attention, dear? The point is water demons get very mischievous. Sometimes they snatch people just to play with for a while, and then they eat them."

May gulped. The Undertaker patted her hand. "I don't blame you for getting caught. The water demons have been killing people for years. Your town has no doubt lost many to the lake. And, of course, you must have a lot of spectral traffic coming through your home on account of the portal. But that's beside the point.

"The demons are very beautiful *and* very crafty. They *entice* their victims. They're good at it."

"So . . ." May cleared her throat. "So the lake in Briery Swamp is a portal, and the water demon pulled me in?"

"Yes."

"But . . . I lived."

"Somebody must have helped you."

May thought back to the moment before she'd gone black. "Pumpkin," she said quietly.

The Undertaker shrugged. "Any that make it through are destroyed by the Bogey. All portals are equipped with Life Detectors, though usually the water demon finishes what it starts, even if the Live One makes it that far."

May stared. "But Arista's globe said there are Live Ones here?"

The Undertaker did not answer at first. "There are some. Hiding out in the Northern Territories perhaps. But they don't have long. Bo Cleevil's power is growing. Most spirits don't know it yet, but they suspect it, they *feel* it. Even your Arista feels it."

"Arista says there's nothing that can be done."

The Undertaker frowned. "Arista is a very intelligent spirit. If that is his attitude, then we are certainly in bad shape."

May felt the tears trembling. "But I've got to get home. My mom . . ."

The Undertaker patted May's hands gently. "I know."

She pulled May onto the couch. "There is one possibility. I was just getting to it."

May sat up. "What?"

"Well, I don't recommend going against the Lady's will. But if you feel you must . . ."

The Undertaker seemed unsure whether to continue, and tapped one earthworm-bedecked fingernail against her bloodred lip before continuing. "*The Book of the Dead* lies in a vault in the City of Ether, in the Eternal Edifice. It was written by the Spirits in the North. In fact, many believe the Spirits of the North also built the Edifice, which is very old. The Book holds the answers to all questions for both the living and the dead. It can tell you much more than I can."

"Do you think it'll tell me how to get home?"

"If there's any thing that would, it would be that book. But, May, you must beware. You may notice spirits can twist themselves to drift through small spaces—cracks and such. But the Edifice itself is airtight. And among the few who have made it to the book, even fewer have been able to open it. It chooses those who can read it. I, myself, tried to open it once, to find out my own future. It didn't let me. And now Bo Cleevil has control of the Edifice."

They stared at each other. "He may already know of your arrival. If the Lady of the North Farm is watching you . . . I don't know. I can only see shadows."

"I saw a book in the shop window, outside. It said 'I see you.'"

The Undertaker shrugged. "A parlor trick, most likely. It probably does that to everyone. Helps to keep spirits fearful. But be wary."

The Undertaker sighed. "If you do choose the dangerous path to the Edifice, you'll need help. There is a spirit by the name of John the Jibber, in a town called Nine Knaves Grotto. If it is indeed possible to get to the Book, he's your specter." She surveyed May doubtfully as if she were about to act against her better judgment. "Here . . ."

The Undertaker reached into her cloak and pulled out a handful of dust. She blew on the sand, and it scattered out in front of her, separating into various mounds and dips and curves. A tiny set of black cliffs formed alongside a big, black spot. A tiny road wove along the other side of the cliffs, and tiny towns popped up along it. Each town had one little house marked with a tiny cloaked person.

She traced a path with a jagged fingernail. "This is the way, via the road. But if you choose to do this, you must stay away from the towns. Most spirits have learned to fear Live Ones, and they'll call on the Bogey if they so much as set eyes on you. You were very lucky at the Spectroplex, because you were surrounded by the newly dead. But the road is full of danger and is not an option."

She pointed to the miniature slate gray cliffs that rose above the road. "The cliffs are faster, but they hold many villages, on account of the view being so nice. It's prime real estate and will leave you almost as exposed as the roads." She paused thoughtfully. Her pointy finger drifted along a stretch of thin shore beside a strange black blotch.

"Yes, the best way is along the beach. But you should stay within the shadow of the cliffs so that no one will see you from above. The cliffs are filled with caves—the Catacombs—and some of these would lead you to the grotto as well. But do not be tempted into taking them. Avoid them at all costs."

"Wh-Why?" May asked.

"We don't know what lurks inside, but I fear whatever it is is treacherous. I haven't found an Undertaker yet who is willing to investigate."

May nodded. Everything in the Ever After seemed treacherous. She was beginning to feel dizzy. Each word the Undertaker said made getting home sound more and more impossible.

The Undertaker continued tracing the path along the beach with her finger to a dip where the cliffs pulled away from the sea.

Then she grew grave again. "May, I must tell you again that if the Spirits of North Farm want you, I don't believe you will able to resist them. So I need to warn you. I hear things have changed a lot up beyond the city. It could be that things with your Northern Spirits have changed too. I can't make it out—all I see are shadows—but I hear strange reports. It could have to do with Bo Cleevil. I see dark things ahead for all of us."

The Undertaker was very grave, shaking her head. "And I see danger all around you. I can't see details very far ahead. There will be heartache. You will lose friends. I'm sorry."

"But I don't have friends . . . ," May whispered, ashamed.

"You have more than you think."

Tears trembled on the edges of May's eyes. She surveyed the map, the vastness of it. She had never felt more alone. "I can't do it. I'll never be able to do it. There's got to be something easier."

The Undertaker only stared at her with beautiful, sympathetic eyes.

A bell sounded through the clouds. The Undertaker, under a heavy mood, patted her shoulder. "I'm sorry. But your time is up." She stood up, stretching her arm toward the May-shaped hole, which had opened up again.

The tears began to dribble down May's cheeks. "I can't. Please."

"May." The Undertaker touched her chin and lifted her face, staring deeply into her eyes. "Do you remember?" She held up her hand, and in it appeared the photo of May and Somber Kitty in the woods—the one that had fallen out of May's book and caused her so much humiliation what seemed like a hundred years ago. Somber Kitty stood beside her protectively, like a bold, hairless lion. May reached out and touched the picture. It was real.

"Take it. It's a gift."

May did. She held it tight.

"You were a warrior, remember? This is to remind you that you *are* that girl. You are braver than you know. Please remember that. Only when you forget it will you be lost."

May nodded her head decidedly as the Undertaker leaned down and kissed her on the cheek, then pulled the hood back over her head. Her face disappeared into darkness.

And then May was standing all alone.

CHAPTER FOURTEEN

The Bogey Arrives

May followed the exit signs into a dark alley, where Pumpkin and Arista were waiting with the laundry basket. May couldn't look Pumpkin in the eye, now that she knew he'd saved her and she'd been so mean to him. She hunched her shoulders as she passed him and crawled inside the basket.

"What did the Undertaker say?" Arista asked.

"I have to go to the City of Ether."

"Oh. Oh, my," Pumpkin said, nibbling on his fingers.

Arista frowned. "How on Earth does she expect you to do that? The city is probably the most dangerous place in the Ever After you could be!"

"I have to find something there." May wrapped her arms around herself.

"What in heaven's name could be good enough to justify going to the city?"

"*The Book of the Dead.*"

"'*The Book of the Dead.*' Never heard of it."

"She said I need to go to Nine Knaves Grotto first." May added quietly, unsure now, and already losing her nerve. "There's a man there who'll help me."

"Nine Knaves Grotto! Indeed! Well, you'll certainly never make it up there alone. You'll *never* make it, period. You don't know anything about the spirit realm. Even if you did, Nine Knaves Grotto can be deadly enough on its own—to any being."

Arista and Pumpkin hoisted the basket up and moved down the alley, Arista buzzing thoughtfully.

"I'm of a mind to say someone should go with you." He buzzed twice more. "Pumpkin, you must escort May."

"But, I—"

"No *buts.*"

"But . . . can't you do it?"

"I certainly can't do it. I've got bees to raise."

"But I'm scared of the city. And I think what happened at the lake really took it out of me. . . ." Pumpkin began to fake a cough. "I think I have a sinus infection too."

"Pumpkin, you don't *have* sinuses! Zzzzz. You're going. You can come back as soon as you've helped her get to the Book. Now, zzzz, let's stop talking about it or someone will notice."

May ducked farther into the basket as they got to the end of the alley and emerged onto the boulevard. She could feel Pumpkin's side of the basket shaking.

"Now really, Pumpkin. Get ahold of yourself. You're drawing all sorts of attention to us."

Pumpkin's hands continued to shake. "Yes, sir."

May could see through cracks in the clothes that they were making their way through the town square. Around them on all sides, the spirits hustled and bustled.

"You there, horseman," Arista's voice called. They stopped, and then started moving in another direction, toward a waiting black carriage. May could just make out the wheels, and then—

"Watch where you're going, Pum—"

On her right Pumpkin slammed into something hard. The basket went tumbling forward, and May went tumbling out of it, onto the street, landing on the ground with a thud. She quickly jumped up, looking around.

In the square you could have heard a pin drop. In every direction, all the spirits had come to a standstill. All eyes were squarely trained on one spot. May started to back up to where the basket had fallen, as if she could crawl back in and everyone could forget the whole thing.

Suddenly a scream rang out from one lady in a dark gray dress. And chaos broke loose.

Spirits started screaming, moaning, groaning, screeching, and wailing. Everywhere they were knocking into one another, banging into carriages and walls, scurrying through the doors of buildings to hide, while others hung out of the windows above to see what all the ruckus was about. The awnings over the shop windows began slamming down all over the place, the carriages peeled off and down the rock road, and one souvenir vendor lifted the whistle from around his neck and, meeting May's eyes, blew on it, then crawled under his booth.

"Oh, we'd better hurry," Arista said, grabbing the basket and zipping forward, then freezing in midair to turn back and look at May and Pumpkin. "Well, what are you waiting for? Run!"

As May tried to keep up, Pumpkin and Arista zipped along in front of her, a trail of clothes spilling out behind them. Arista shoved the basket into Pumpkin's arms and fished through his pockets. "I always keep one teletoken on me, just in case," he was saying. "If I can just—"

"There," he said, interrupting himself and motioning to the glowing blue phone box May had noticed on the way in. They turned toward it now, Arista digging at himself frantically as he floated. They stopped outside the booth.

"What are you looking for?"

Arista ignored her, but Pumpkin stuttered, "We c-can't make it home on f-foot. We have to t-teleport."

"But. How do—"

May's voice caught right in her throat at a faint sound in the distance. She and Pumpkin looked at each other.

"Oh, dear. Oh, dear, it's the Bogey. Of all the times to misplace it . . ." Arista clasped at himself.

Sure enough, the sound got louder and more pronounced, separating itself into faint barks and yelps. May and Pumpkin looked out across the hundreds of miles of sand at the edge of town. There, in the distance, and so small it almost seemed like she could be imagining it, the tiniest cloud of sand rose up above the horizon.

"Get in!" The force of Arista's hands pushing her through the door of the booth knocked the wind right out of May. Pumpkin squeezed in behind her, then Arista.

"Oh, these things are always too small," he said, still digging frantically in his pockets. "Oh." He looked out at the desert, his antennae twitching wildly. May peered out through the window of the booth and across the sand. The Bogey had to be moving fast. Already May could now clearly see the cloud of sand looming larger and larger.

"Drat!" Arista reopened the door of the booth and squeezed out. "I think it was in my other robes!"

He started following the long trail of laundry that stretched across the sand into town, frantically yanking up this and that robe and rifling through its pockets.

Crack crack crack. May moved to the door of the booth and leaned out. She could now clearly make out several dark spots on the horizon.

"Arista, hurry!" May looked over her shoulder and watched him pick up another robe, then another, and another. She looked through the door of the booth, leaning over Pumpkin, who had curled into a ball.

Beyond him, the Bogey approached. The specks had enlarged into dogs. Though they were still probably a mile away, May could tell they were humongous—the size of horses, with red gleaming eyes and huge teeth dripping with drool. But somehow they weren't nearly as frightening as the figure riding on the sled behind them, cracking a long black whip. He wore a dark suit and a top hat. A fireball of fear shot into May's stomach.

"Found it!" Arista cried, floating back toward them, then freezing at the sensation of the Bogey and his dogs. His antennae twitched wildly. Then he started moving again, floating toward them at top speed and slamming into May with a shock. The whole booth shook. It began to fall to the side.

May could see the Bogey clearly now, the sand flying out behind him in a great whirlwind. Snow white hair tufted out from under his hat. His chin stuck out long and curved at the bottom, like a hook. His eyeballs were completely white.

May felt dizzy.

And then, as May's legs began to sway, the Bogey smiled at her, revealing rows of pointy teeth. He lifted his odd, knobby fingers to the side of his head and tipped his hat. He would be upon them in seconds.

Arista held up the token, found the slot with one hand, and slid it in.

Zap!

The clock in Arista's study struck ten. May stood watching it as two tiny doors on the bottom slid open, and ten tiny skeletons slid out to dance, circling ten times before sliding back in.

She walked back into the kitchen.

Once they had arrived outside the house after teleporting, Arista had ushered them inside, saying the dogs would be coming to check all the houses in the region, and that they would have to move quickly. Now, just minutes later, Pumpkin stood beside the front door, holding a knapsack. They had each packed packs full of the supplies Arista had insisted on: a bottomless water bottle; a whole slew of soul cakes and skeleton crackers; his last two teleport tokens; a city-finder compass that had three points on it: Right Way, Wrong Way, Scenic Way; and a starlight, which looked like a flashlight and was powered by cosmic dust.

At first May had been too paralyzed with fear to focus on his instructions. The horrible vision of the Bogey was burned onto her brain. She still had to concentrate to keep herself from swaying on her feet.

"What about ghouls and goblins and stuff?" she had finally asked.

Arista shrugged. "If ghouls see you, they'll eat your guts." This had sent Pumpkin into a shivering fit. Now he stood in the doorway, his fingernails jammed between his teeth.

"Arista, the Bogey . . ." May had wanted to say that she couldn't bear to go outside, when she knew *he* was out there somewhere too.

"Will find you here if you don't get moving," Arista completed her sentence for her. "Head north. That'll take you to the sea. You won't see anyone. Hardly anyone ever goes up close to it. But keep an eye out anyway. I hear there are spies in even the remotest areas, though I think that's probably just a rumor started by Bo Cleevil."

"I'll see you when you get back," Arista said, turning to Pumpkin.

"How long do you think it will take us to get to Nine Knaves Grotto?" May asked, still dazed.

Arista shrugged. "I don't know much of the world outside Belle Morte. A week or more, probably."

They walked outside.

"North is that way." Arista pointed. He patted May on the head. "You two be careful." His antennae twitched thoughtfully. "The Bogey will still be in town looking for you. Don't go anywhere near Belle Morte. Write me from wherever you end up, May. Good luck." He hugged her tightly. "I hope you find your way back to your mother and your cat." He peered in the direction of town once, then he turned and hurried inside.

May and Pumpkin looked at each other, May trying to buck up her courage. She hefted her pack up higher onto her back, then looked in the direction they'd come from. Even Arista's little hive house seemed familiar and comforting compared to the path ahead. But then, they couldn't stay. She took a deep breath. "Well, we'll never get anywhere if we don't move forward."

They made their way along the sand, a shy, skinny, black-haired girl and a tall, gangly ghost with a pumpkin-shaped head, leaving one pair of footprints behind them.

CHAPTER FIFTEEN

By the Sea

I'm starving."

May slowed to a stop and let her sack slide down from her shoulder onto the sand. Without a sun above them to show the day passing, she couldn't tell how long they'd been walking, but it seemed like it must have been three hours or more.

"How long do you think we've been at it?"

"I don't know, but I'm exhausted." For the past several minutes Pumpkin had been lagging behind, moving as if every inch pained him. Now he plopped down into a sitting hover above the sand.

May sighed. Pumpkin didn't know much of anything. She wondered if it wouldn't have been better to leave him back at Belle Morte. Then she felt guilty for the thought.

She pulled out her water bottle and swished it around in front of her. She'd drunk out of it many times already, but the level of water hadn't gone down even an inch, just as Arista had promised. She still couldn't quite believe it. She took several huge gulps, then wiped the cool bottle across her sweaty forehead.

"Hey, do you see that?" Pumpkin asked, pointing forward.

There was a black line on the horizon. "Do you think that's it?"

"I don't know."

They both walked another few minutes, and after a few more, they arrived at the sea.

The body of water that stretched itself out before May and Pumpkin wasn't so much an ocean as it was a giant oil slick lying lazily across the horizon. It looked like something that might have dripped out of a car, except that it was endless and vast, so big that they couldn't see any end of it, and it filled May with a sick kind of dread. Up to this point everything she had seen since the portal had had a slight glow to it. The sea was the opposite of that—it was a complete *absence* of glow.

"I guess I didn't know how black, black could get," May muttered softly.

"Mmm-hmmm," Pumpkin agreed.

May wanted to say that the water was also, somehow, enticing. It took effort to tear her eyes from it and look around to figure out where they were. She looked left, then right. To the right was more desert. To the left, cliff met with beach, creating a narrow strip of sand beside the water. Like the sea, the strip seemed to go forward endlessly. It looked desolate and lonely.

She gazed out at the sea, which lapped at the sand lazily with oily little sighs. It was actually hard not to look at.

She must have been staring for a while, because when she tore her eyes away, Pumpkin had laid out a feast in front of her— honey, pomegranates, three tiny cakes decorated with tiny coffins. He'd arranged it all in the shape of a smiley face, and was now lying down a few feet away, resting, his body hovering an inch above the sand.

"Oh, thank you, Pumpkin."

Snort. Pumpkin was already asleep and snoring.

May gobbled up all of the food that had been put out for her, almost guiltily, since Pumpkin couldn't have any. When she was finished, she brushed the crumbs off her bathing suit and stood up, rejuvenated. The water pulled her eyeballs back in its direction. It looked so cool and dark. Maybe she would just dip a toe into the water.

Kicking off her shoes, she padded across the sand. She was just a few feet from the water's edge when she came to a stop. The water glistened and winked at her. It almost seemed as if, just to accommodate her, each gentle wave was reaching toward her softly.

"Umph!"

She felt herself being yanked from behind, and then she was on the ground, a tangle of legs and arms that sorted themselves into Pumpkin's and hers.

"Oh, dear," Pumpkin breathed, dragging her backward like a crab.

"Pumpkin, what's the—"

They both climbed to their feet, breathing hard and looking at each other. May's body buzzed with the tiny electric shocks where Pumpkin had touched her.

Finally, when he'd caught his breath, Pumpkin sighed. "Oh, dear, I should have told you." He frowned and looked down at his feet. "How could I forget? Stupid."

"Forget what?" May demanded.

Pumpkin's mouth settled into a straight, determined line. "You must never, ever touch a drop of the Dead Sea."

May glanced out at the water, then back. "Why not?"

"It'll take you."

May's gut sank. "You mean, there's a water demon?"

Pumpkin shook his head, his large, droopy eyes earnest and solemn. "Oh, no. Much more powerful than that. Anyone who touches a drop of the Dead Sea will be immediately transported to South Place. Way down under the water."

"South Place?" It sounded like some kind of pretty beach. Like in Florida. But she remembered that Arista had said it was where the Dark Spirits came from.

"South Place is a terrible realm. Very bad. The worst." Pumpkin shivered.

"Whoa," May breathed, glancing out toward the water.

"Actually," Pumpkin began sheepishly, tugging at May's finger to get her attention again. "You shouldn't even look at it." A blush crept up his cheeks. "Arista told me to tell you."

May frowned. It made sense now. How enticing the water had looked. How she had felt drawn to it.

May walked over to the spot where her sack lay, and she began packing up.

"I'm sorry, May."

"That's all right."

Pumpkin pressed a palm up against his lips and spoke through the cracks between the fingers. "Are you mad at me for forgetting?"

"No."

"Are you sure?"

May sighed. "Yes."

"Can I have a hug?"

May had never hugged anyone but her cat and her mother. She didn't know what to say. "Um, I guess so."

Pumpkin threw his arms around her and hugged her tight. She accepted it stiffly, trying not to flinch at his strange, cold touch. As soon as he let go, she hefted her pack and smoothed out her bangs with her index fingers, moving them apart.

Pumpkin, who didn't have much in the way of bangs, brushed at his tuft.

When they started walking down the beach again, they stayed close to the cliffs as the Undertaker had advised.

"Hey, look," May said, pointing to a gaping black hole at the base of the cliff up ahead. "The Undertaker told me about those. They're the Catacombs. What do you know about them?"

Pumpkin shook his head. "It looks like a good place to have a sleepover. And tell Live One stories."

"Live One stories?"

"You know, when you sit around with your friends and tell stories about Live Ones coming to the realm and exorcising you. Oh"—Pumpkin blushed—"I mean . . . never mind."

May didn't reply.

"It's just, I think, most Live Ones are scary. But not you."

"I think most ghosts are scary."

Pumpkin shrugged. "Well, anyway, I never really did that. Sitting around telling Live One stories. But I always wanted to."

"Why didn't you?"

"I don't really have any friends besides Arista." Pumpkin sounded like he wanted to sound cheerful. "And he says Live One stories are for ghosts that don't know ectoplasm from their elbow." Pumpkin hunched his shoulders slightly. "Sometimes he says I don't know my ectoplasm from my elbow."

"I'm sure that's not true," May said, after a moment, shyly.

"I suppose you don't have any friends either," Pumpkin said airily.

May shut her lips tight.

A few hours later May made sure they settled far from any cave entrances but still under the cliffs, using their sacks as pillows. They were lying on their backs, May with a full belly and heavy, drooping eyelids. It had been a full day of walking, and her muscles ached. But she kept looking around, scared to go to sleep in case someone happened upon them in the night. She shifted a little closer to Pumpkin.

"I miss my grave," he said wistfully. "I can't sleep when I'm away from it."

May rolled onto her side. "You sleep in one?"

Pumpkin nodded. May was silent, trying to imagine that. "All spirits get one," Pumpkin offered. "Even if you haven't lived. Of course, everybody needs one to get to Earth for haunting."

"What do you mean?"

"That's how I always get to your house. The graves are doors to the spirit pathways. You have your portals, for the spirits of the newly deceased to get to the Ever After. That's what you came through. They only go one way. But each spirit gets a grave in the afterworld, to go back and forth."

May shot up. "But couldn't I just go through one of those pathways to get home?"

Pumpkin was shaking his head.

"But—"

"The grave paths are very complicated. Each spirit can only find his way through his own. If you tried someone else's, you'd never find your way out. You'd be lost forever. A bunch of spirits have tried it. That's why we have Lost Souls Day. To remind us of the golden rule of haunting."

"What's that?"

"Hopping grave-ys is for babies."

"Oh." May tried to absorb this, thinking that maybe the spirits in charge could have done better. She rolled herself up into a ball on her side. Pumpkin did the same. Then she flopped over onto her back and watched the stars.

"Pumpkin?"

Out of the corner of her eye, she saw Pumpkin nod.

"How long have you been my . . . house spirit?"

"Mmmm, don't remember. I moved in when the first house was built there—it was a tepee, actually."

May's mouth dropped open. "That must have been years ago!"

"I don't know. But it was very cramped. Smelled like . . . hmm . . ."—he tapped his lips, thinking—"venison." May pictured Pumpkin cramped into a tent and stifled a chuckle.

"What about our house? Where did you stay?"

"All over. Mostly the attic, but I spent a lot of time in the kitchen. I liked watching you and your mom eat and talk. But sometimes it made me too sad."

May swallowed. "Why?"

Pumpkin shrugged. "Just a feeling. I don't know. You make each other sad sometimes." May picked at her fingernails, her throat tight.

Pumpkin cleared his throat. "And then . . ."

"And then?"

"I spent a lot of time with you. In your room."

Now it was May's turn to blush. She thought of all the times she'd changed in her room. And all the times she'd picked her nose.

"I loved watching you do your little projects—your drawings and your inventions and all the beautiful pictures you hung up on your walls. You kept the sight for a long while." Pumpkin smiled, looking at May but past her. "We were such friends when you had it. You used to lie in your crib, waving at me.

"But then when you got it again, you looked so scared. And that made me scared. You don't get the sight back unless something serious happens. You have to be touched by a powerful spirit. I really didn't know what to make of it."

"You followed me to the lake that night."

Pumpkin was quiet for a long time. "I saw you going into the woods. And I knew the portal was back there. I wanted to make sure you were okay." Pumpkin frowned. "I'm sorry I didn't get there sooner. Then you wouldn't be here at all."

"Well," May hesitated. "Thank you. I'm sorry I didn't thank you for saving me."

Pumpkin was silent for a few moments. "Welcome." They both shifted awkwardly.

"Pumpkin, Arista said you ghosts come to haunt at midnight. But all the stuff you're saying means you were there before then."

Pumpkin shrugged.

"Aren't you supposed to be at my house now?" May asked.

Pumpkin's gash of a mouth straightened into its crooked line. "Yes."

"And you're breaking the rules, for me?"

Pumpkin didn't answer. He blushed.

"Are you gonna get in trouble?"

"A spirit who doesn't show up for work can get fired."

"What does that mean? They don't pay you?"

"They can revoke your Earth privileges."

"You mean you'd never be able to come back to Briery Swamp?"

"I don't know."

May nestled into her sack. Pumpkin did the same. And soon he let out a snore. May, on the other hand, was far from sleep.

She was thinking of all the times she'd holed up in her room, making her art, coming up with her strange ideas, dreaming of faraway places in pictures. All that time she'd thought she'd been alone. She looked over at Pumpkin. He was lying on his back, his skinny arms flung out to the side, long and gangly. And delicate.

Then she closed her eyes. She tried to see her big white farmhouse back in Briery Swamp. Maybe if she concentrated hard enough, she could really see it across all the miles, using mental telepathy. Where was her mom? What was she doing now? She concentrated, but only the backs of her eyelids stared back at her. No farmhouse, no Mom, no Somber Kitty.

She could imagine though. Her mom was probably hunched over the kitchen table with worry, waiting by the phone. Or talking to the police. Somber Kitty was probably snoozing. Maybe he was glad after how she'd treated him. Glad not to get dressed up like a warrior cat anymore or dragged into school for dance shows. Glad not to be underappreciated anymore.

May wished more than anything that she could show them both how much she loved them. She felt very sorry. Her whole heart was sorry for everything she had ever done to worry them. She closed her eyes and tried to send her love all the way to Earth. She didn't know if it could travel that far.

CHAPTER SIXTEEN

Dark Spirits Afoot

always wanted to go to the beach," May said. She and Pumpkin had been walking in silence for two days, only talking when it was time to stop and eat, and even then, only exchanging a few words.

May scanned the sky as they walked, then looked down the beach behind her to make sure there was no one in sight. "I like the woods a lot better."

Pumpkin nodded agreeably.

"Once I get home, I'm never going to the beach again."

Pumpkin nodded again.

May sighed. She'd never wanted so much to talk to someone. In school she'd always kept her mouth closed as much as possible. But Pumpkin was losing his scariness. In fact he was starting to seem less scary than some of her classmates.

"So how do you like being Arista's house servant?"

Pumpkin shrugged. "It's okay."

"You don't like it?"

Pumpkin shrugged. May didn't understand how sometimes he could be so chatty, and then make it so impossible to pull out two words.

They walked in silence some more, May searching her brain for another subject. "Well, what would you do if you could do anything?"

Pumpkin looked at her, surprised. "What do you mean?"

"Well, just imagine you could do anything you wanted to do. What would it be?"

Pumpkin stuck a finger in his mouth, thinking. "Have you ever heard of William Shakespeare?"

May nodded eagerly. "Sure."

"Well, he runs a song and dance revue, out in the Nothing Platte—it's very famous."

"Really?"

"I want to work there. As a singer."

"Wow, really?" May knew she must have looked shocked, because Pumpkin turned crimson.

"I . . . I'm sorry, I just had no idea you could sing. And you seem kind of . . . timid."

"I don't feel timid when I sing."

May smiled. She knew what he meant. She wasn't timid when she was running through the forest being an Amazon.

"Can I hear some?"

"What? Oh, nooo . . ."

"Oh, please? Let me hear you sing."

Pumpkin was shaking his head, but in that way that people do when they really want you to talk them into something.

"Please!" May was practically hopping up and down. "Just not too loud, okay?" she added, peering over her shoulder again.

Pumpkin stopped in his tracks. "Okay." He cleared his throat. "Okay," he said again, getting up his nerve. "I like to imagine that there's a whole bunch of specters who've been in horrible accidents in the audience. And they're missing arms and legs and things and really needing to be cheered up, right?"

May nodded. "Okay."

"I get up on stage, make a few jokes, and then . . ." He thrust a hand out into the air and opened his mouth.

"Iiiii ain't got noboddddddy. . . ."

May stood watching in shock. Pumpkin had the clearest, most fantastic voice she had ever heard.

Pumpkin was wiggling his hips and looking like a different ghost—poised and confident.

"Won't some sweet mama come and take a chance with me, 'cause I ain't so bad."

At the last word he shut his lips abruptly, blinked a few times, then blushed. May burst into applause.

"You were born to be in that Shakespeare revue," she gushed in wonder.

"Nah. I'm a house spirit. That's all I'll ever be."

"That's crazy," May said. "You're selling yourself short."

Pumpkin giggled modestly. "Oh, go on."

After that, a warm glow seemed to have been cast on the walk. Pumpkin moved with a spring in his hover, and May with a spring in her step.

❧ ❧ ❧

Two more days went by, with nothing but endless beach. On the third day May and Pumpkin began to make out something up ahead. It took another ten minutes to figure out that it was a figure. It moved back and forth along the beach, to the edge of the water and back toward the cliffs.

"Uh-oh," Pumpkin said.

"What is that?" May asked.

The way the figure moved made May cross her arms tightly with worry. It didn't float like the other spirits she'd seen—drifty and slow. It jerked and leaped like a flame.

"I don't know."

May looked at Pumpkin, whose face was drawn.

"Who would be out here on this beach?"

He shook his head.

"We should probably walk closer to the cliffs." They had drifted on a soft angle away from them, and now they drifted back, slowing as they continued down the beach. For a while they lost sight of the figure behind a rocky outcropping, and when they saw it again they were much nearer to it than they'd expected.

"Ohhh," Pumpkin said in a low voice, clinging to May's arm with a zap, but a small zap. "Oooh, get down." He pulled her to the sand, holding her in a zappy death grip.

The creature up ahead was horribly ugly. He was red and slimy with black, droopy lips and a long, black spear in one hand. His arms hung at his sides and flopped as he moved. He was far enough away that he couldn't see them unless he looked hard, but close enough that May could see the glinting sharpness of his long, black teeth, curling out of his mouth.

"W-What is it?" she whispered, eyes agape. Pumpkin's body trembling against hers made her own teeth chatter.

"Ghoul."

May slammed her mouth—and her chattering teeth—shut.

The creature loped around the beach in circles, looking up at the stars, then out at the water.

"Ohhh. Very little light from the stars tonight," Pumpkin whispered, his voice shaky.

"What does that have to do with anything?" May hissed, thinking they had more to worry about than the weather.

"It's better for them. Ghouls love the dark."

"Oh." May shrunk closer to Pumpkin.

While they watched, the creature thrust a thumb in his nose and began to pick it, pulling his finger out and examining it.

"Uck," May whispered.

"We should turn around," Pumpkin whispered.

May had to admit, the thought had just crossed her mind. "You can if you want."

Pumpkin shook his head.

"I don't want to leave you. W-We should maybe take one of the caves," he said, pointing to an opening in the rock just ahead. "We can try to go around him."

May followed his eyes. The caves, each one of them that she'd looked into, gaped with pitch-black darkness. "Um, I think we'd better just wait here until he goes away," May said. She didn't want to tell Pumpkin what the Undertaker had said about the caves and turn him into a blubbering mess. What if they had to go in? "If he comes this way, we'll just duck into the tunnel until he's gone."

"But I don't want to lose my guts," Pumpkin said, moaning.

May stared at him, then at the caves again, indecisive. Finally she said, "I promise I won't let you lose your guts."

They settled down in the sand to wait, both sitting cross-legged with their backs against the rock of the cliffs.

The ghoul continued to do his weird little dance around the sand. May and Pumpkin agreed to take turns keeping watch to see if he left or came in their direction. But May, whose turn it was to rest first, had a hard time falling asleep, knowing the ghoul was so close. She kept wondering what it would feel like to have her guts eaten.

Pumpkin woke her some time in the middle of the night, and conked out as soon as she'd taken over watch, snoring loudly. She tried to hold his nose to make him stop, which turned her fingers to ice. She didn't know if the ghoul might have extra-sensitive hearing.

She was just in the middle of trying to roll Pumpkin onto his side when the ghoul seemed to change his routine. He now stood at the very edge of the sea, peering out into the water.

May sank back, alert, and strained her eyes toward the water, but there was only darkness. And then a shadow began to pull away from the black mass of the sea. And then another, and another.

"Boats," May whispered.

A group of three long rowboats was inching slowly across the water toward the shore. The ghoul on the sand seemed to get more excited the closer they got. He snarled and jumped up and down.

Shadows moved within the boats. May shook Pumpkin by the shoulders. "Pumpkin, wake up," May squeaked.

As the tips of the boats reached shore, the shadows began to scurry out, revealing themselves to be ghouls just like the first.

One after the other, they scrabbled out of the boats onto the sand, until there were at least a hundred of them snarling and jabbering at one another. "Bblgggllllbbl."

"Hogubbleeblugghhhh."

May and Pumpkin cowered in their spot, staying extra still.

"What do you think they're talking about?"

"It can't be anything good," Pumpkin said, pulling his knees up in front of his face so that only his eyes showed, and his voice came out muffled. "They aren't supposed to be up here. Oh no, not good at all."

"You think they're up to something?" May asked.

Pumpkin hugged his knees tight. "I just hope they go away."

But the ghouls didn't show any sign of going away. In fact, over the next few hours they built a huge fire and pulled out cases of bottles from the bottoms of their boats, throwing them open and passing the bottles around to drink from. They began to get wilder and wilder, snarling louder, dancing around the leaping blue fires they'd built.

Some of the ghouls stumbled to the outside of the circle and passed out.

May noticed one in particular, sneaking toward the crate of drinks and hoisting it up, then scurrying a little farther down the beach. Another ghoul noticed the first, and as the thief sank down on the sand with his stolen goods, the other let out an ear-piercing shriek. Suddenly all the creatures dropped what they were doing and rushed down the beach, surrounding the thief. From the center of it all came a loud scream. And then all went quiet, and the ghouls straggled back to their fire. The thief had disappeared.

"What happened?" May whispered. "Where'd he go?"

Pumpkin whimpered. "Maybe they ate him."

They looked at each other and moved a little closer together.

That night they moved back to the very mouth of the cave behind them, and Pumpkin kept watch while May's eyelids drooped until she was asleep. In the morning the ghouls were all still there. They had laid out towels all over the beach and lounged on their stomachs and backs, some reading books, some sipping on drinks.

"They're star bathing," Pumpkin explained. "I've heard ghouls are very into their complexions. Goblins too."

May and Pumpkin stayed in their spot at the side of the cliff, May drawing holes in the sand with her fingers. All day the ghouls stayed put. And that night around midnight, another host of boats arrived.

"It's like they're getting ready for something," Pumpkin said.

That night the ghouls erupted into the same loud revelry that they had the night before. It seemed to May that Pumpkin was right. And that it was more and more dangerous to stay.

Around dawn the next day, May awoke to a scratching sound, and something hit her on the forehead. "Ouch." She sat up, staring upward. There was Pumpkin holding onto a tiny ledge of the cliff, reaching above himself.

"Got it," he said, breaking a shiny piece of rock off the wall. He landed, grinning at May and holding up the rock. "Silverstone," he said proudly. As he did, there was a loud crumbling noise above, and they both looked up.

"Ah!" May lunged for Pumpkin and pushed him out of the way, just as a pile of rocks slid down from above and landed in the spot where they'd been standing.

"Uh-oh." Pumpkin said. They both turned to look in the direction of the ghouls. Several were standing up, peering in their direction. And then a few started to walk toward them, sniffing the air.

"Pumpkin!" May whispered. Pumpkin looked at her very sadly. "Sorry."

She looked into the mouth of the cave, then back to the beach. The ghouls were on their way.

Somber Kitty curled up in a tiny nook in the rock and peered out at the strange landscape of the southwest Ever After. He had never lost his bearings before, but he had lost them now, and it was very distressing. Confusion and embarrassment were quickly turning his accustomed melancholy into true sorrow and misery. He was even too sad to meow.

For seven days Somber Kitty had wandered along the banks of the Styx Streamway with only a lady's pointed finger to guide him. He hadn't encountered another soul, living or dead. And though the smell of danger had drifted far behind him, the uncertainty was almost as bad—not to mention the hunger. He hadn't eaten in a week.

Truth be told, Somber Kitty was losing hope.

Curled in his spot in the cave, he was just drifting off into another hunger-induced sleep, when he saw something drifting toward him across the landscape. It reminded him of the sun, or at the very least, a lightbulb. If he had known more astronomy, it would have reminded him of a comet.

Somber Kitty was too mesmerized to hide.

The light entered the cave and drifted down beside him. It laid what felt like warm hands on him and stroked his back, scratched behind his ears and his favorite spot under his chin. The warm touch felt like love itself. And Somber Kitty knew something about love.

The petting only lasted a moment. The light gave him one final squeeze and drifted away.

Somber Kitty stood on his tired legs and pressed on.

CHAPTER SEVENTEEN

Into the Catacombs

May pulled her starlight out of her pocket and held it up to illuminate the walls of the tunnel they had entered.

"Ahh!" Pumpkin cried, and leaped as the walls of the Catacombs came into focus. They were lined with thousands of eyes, staring at them. May stumbled back a few feet, the light glinting along the walls. And then . . .

"Pumpkin?"

He had already run halfway back toward the opening of the cave.

"It's just skulls. Look."

May made a wide arc with her hand, showing that the thousands of eyes belonged to skulls that lined the walls like bricks.

"Whoa," May breathed. Pumpkin started to inch back toward her.

They were in a tunnel that led into shadows up ahead, the ceiling just barely arching above Pumpkin's hair, so that he stooped slightly.

"These tunnels are very ancient," Pumpkin pointed out. "Some of these skulls are thousands of years old."

May was impressed. Maybe she had underestimated Pumpkin. "How can you tell?"

"Look."

He pointed to a skull down at the level of his thigh. Somebody had carved into it with a tiny, sharp instrument: NEBUCHADNEZZAR WAS HERE. APRIL 4, 103.

Pumpkin started skipping along ahead.

"Pumpkin, be careful."

He looked perplexed.

"You should let me lead. I have the starlight."

They trudged forward, May lighting the way with her light, following the winding of the tunnel. A few minutes later they reached a spot where it forked off into two branches. She pulled out her compass. "Nine Knaves Grotto is between here and the city. So if we're headed toward the city, we're headed toward the grotto." May held up the compass toward the tunnel on the left. The needle tipped very definitely to Wrong Way.

"What about this one?" she asked, holding it up in the direction of the other tunnel. The needle tipped to Scenic Way.

"Well." May sighed. She remembered her mom's scenic routes, when they'd drive out into the counties that neighbored Briery Swamp to look for antiques, staying off the highways. *What I wouldn't give for one of those boring trips now,* she thought. Somber Kitty had always tried to sneak into the car in some way—jumping into Mrs. Bird's huge purse or leaping onto the roof of the car. Why hadn't May just let him come?

She choked back the lump in her throat. May didn't really want the scenic route now, but that seemed to be the only choice.

For hours they followed the twists and turns of the caves, May listening for the sound of anything that might be sharing the Catacombs with them. It was much cooler in here, and May shivered. "It's weird being in here without the sky for so long," she said to Pumpkin, who drifted along tentatively a few feet behind her. Every time she waited for him to catch up and walk beside her, he fell back, pretending his shoe was untied or acting like he'd seen something interesting on the ground, until May was again safely in the lead.

May had been hoping the caves would lead them back out into the open before it was time to sleep. She worried that her compass might be wrong, and that they would end up going farther and farther into the heart of the cliffs and never come out again.

The route they were taking did seem to run parallel to the Dead Sea, though there was no telling for sure. Finally they were too tired to go any farther without at least a little sleep. She and Pumpkin lay right down in the middle of the tunnel. There was nowhere else to go. "I hope we get out of here tomorrow," she said.

"Me too. This place gives me the creeps."

In the glow of May's starlight, Pumpkin and May looked at each other.

"I'm glad I'm not alone in here."

Pumpkin nodded. "Me too."

May crossed her arms, squeezing her elbows. "I wish I had a blanket."

She tried to snuggle closer to Pumpkin, but his body was colder than the tunnel was. At least the zapping had faded. May guessed she had gotten used to it.

"I'm sorry," he said. "Ghosts are just cold."

"That's okay."

May snuggled close to him anyway.

"Pumpkin?"

"Mmhmm?"

"Thanks for coming with me."

She smiled at him, and he smiled a jagged smile back. It looked more like a grimace. Then she blew out her starlight.

"May?"

May was shaken awake by the shoulders. When she opened her eyes, she saw Pumpkin leaning over her, frowning. He held the starlight in one hand.

"What is it?"

"Look."

Pumpkin pointed to a spot beside May's hip.

By the dim glow of the light she saw a big black lump in the sand right beside her. May scrambled back a few paces, walking like a crab.

"That wasn't there last night," she said nervously, suddenly wide awake.

Pumpkin nodded.

She snapped her head up and down the tunnel, as if she

might see who had left it there. But the tunnel was black beyond a few feet.

"What is it?"

Pumpkin kept silent, inserting one finger into his mouth.

"How do you think it got here?"

Again, nothing . . . except the rattle of Pumpkin's teeth.

They knelt on the sand, staring at it, as if it might leap up and bite them.

May reached toward the object slowly. But nothing. Her fingers landed on it gently. It was made of fabric, the softest, silkiest fabric May had ever touched.

"I think . . ." May lifted it gently, then began to unfold it. "Pumpkin, it's a blanket."

They both gave each other a meaningful look, their eyes wide. Then May peered up and down the tunnel. "Do you think someone heard us?" she whispered. "Last night?"

It was too much of a coincidence. May's stomach felt heavy.

She pulled the blanket onto her lap and unfolded it all the way.

Glowing green strands of embroidery formed themselves along the top edge, where the blanket came to a silky black border. She ran her fingers along the stitches as they appeared, curving around themselves in cursive letters.

For May. Remember to stay warm.

May gasped, then peered up and down the cave again.

Whoever it was, they were gone.

"What does it say?" Pumpkin asked, staring at the words.

"Here." May held it out toward him. Pumpkin held up his hands in a stop motion.

"Reading is a lot of work. . . ." He sighed loudly for emphasis.

May sighed back and read the words to him. Then they sat staring at the blanket, thinking.

"Who do you think left this?"

Pumpkin shrugged, then his eyes lit up. "Maybe you have a secret admirer," he ventured.

May rolled her eyes. "I don't think so. Maybe it's from Arista . . ." She looked at Pumpkin hopefully, but he was shaking his head so hard that the tuft of hair on top of his skull swayed.

"Arista wouldn't leave his bees," he said. "And he doesn't like surprises."

"No, I suppose it wouldn't be him." Arista didn't seem like the type who would follow them into a tunnel and leave mysterious blankets on the ground for them to find either.

May looked down at the blanket. She reached a hand toward it and undid the last fold. Then she gave into the impulse to pull it around her shoulders.

The world around her went from dark to bright. May blinked, holding one hand up in front of her eyes. And then . . .

"Oh, my gosh."

May had to blink several more times. "Oh, my gosh."

She was in her bedroom back home, sitting on her bed and wrapped in the blanket. There were her pictures of Egypt and Samoa. There was her desk and her bookshelf. Above, her wind chimes tinkled. She reached out and touched them. They were real.

May looked around for Pumpkin, but he was nowhere to be seen. Then she sat forward to peer out her window. There was the view of the front yard and the woods beyond. "Mom?!" she yelled. "Kitty!"

She hopped up, ran to her bedroom door, threw it open, and froze. There was nothing coming from the other side but orange light.

"May?" A voice called. May didn't answer. She didn't want to.

And then the world around her went dark again, and she was facing Pumpkin, who held the blanket in his arms. "What happened?" he asked. "Are you okay?"

"Yeah," May said, trying to shake the image of her house.

"You looked like you fell asleep."

May took the blanket from his hands. "I was home!"

May pulled the blanket around her shoulders again, and once again she was in her bedroom. She reached for her bedroom window and opened it, but when she did, the familiar view disappeared, becoming the orange light again. She pulled the blanket off again, and she was in the cave.

That's when she noticed a little white tag hanging off the bottom of the blanket. In awe May read it out loud: "This comfort blanket was handcrafted by the Spirits of North Farm."

"Oooh," Pumpkin said. "The Spirits of North Farm. Lucky."

May held the blanket out at arm's length. "North Farm," she repeated, unsure as to whether it meant she was lucky or not. In fact it made her feel guilty. Caught.

"I wonder why they would send you a blanket."

May ran her fingers along the words again: *Remember to keep warm.* She wondered whether she could trust Pumpkin with her secret. "There's someone who sent me a letter in Briery Swamp. I guess it could be from her."

Pumpkin looked hurt. "I wonder why she didn't send me one."

May cleared her throat. "The Undertaker said she might have

taken an interest in me. That maybe I have someone on my side."
May didn't say that the Lady had also asked for her help. She was
too ashamed. She hunched her shoulders as if the Lady were in
the cave with her, watching her, disappointed. The scary part was
this blanket made it seem possible.

Pumpkin considered. "I hope she's on my side too. I always
wanted my own blanket." He looked at May pitifully.

It was such a very Pumpkin look that May couldn't help but
smile.

A few minutes later they were on the move again. May reached
into her knapsack every once in a while to sink her fingers into
the soft velvet of her blanket, reassuring herself it was still there.
She had tucked her letter and her picture in alongside it, and she
ran her hands over those too. It all made her feel closer to many
things that were far away, and that made her smile.

Up ahead, Pumpkin seemed to be in good spirits. He was
singing some kind of cheerful tune. *"When we met, after you
crashed in that jet, I thought you were the one for meeee. You floated my
way, all filmy and gray, and I just had to say gee."*

May wondered about it being a love song. Did spirits fall in
love? She didn't see why not. But Arista had said spirits didn't
grow or change. Did that mean they couldn't? She was in such
a good mood, she didn't ask Pumpkin to keep his voice down,
forgetting that someone or something might be in the caves,
listening.

"You say banshee, I say bogey, let's call the whole thing off . . ."

May was reaching around to touch her blanket again when a
sound made her pause. It was faint at first, and then louder, *click*

clack click clack. The skulls on the walls all around them were shaking and rattling. May leaned toward Pumpkin. "We . . ."

Ha ha ha ha ha.

The laugh echoed through the tunnel. It was high and delighted, like a child's. Pumpkin's knees began to knock together. "What's that?" he whispered.

"I don't—"

Suddenly May could see her shadow on the ground in front of her, growing larger and larger. She turned around just in time to see a white flash zooming down the tunnel before it hurtled past them, blowing their hair back and careening off the walls before disappearing into the darkness ahead.

May and Pumpkin both flattened themselves against the wall, breathing hard and peering up and down the tunnel. They stayed that way for several minutes. Nothing stirred. The skulls had all gone quiet.

"I think we'd better get out of the caves as soon as possible," May said.

Pumpkin didn't sing any more after that.

CHAPTER EIGHTEEN

A Deadly Mistake

May watched more anxiously now for tiny caves that might take them out to the beach again. She was starting to think that coming into the caves had been a deadly mistake.

Pumpkin took to whistling softly to pass the time and settle his nerves, and May kept having to remind him to stop. On the fifth or sixth time that he forgot and started whistling again, May came to an abrupt halt. She turned on Pumpkin with a stern gaze and, ignoring the tiny cold shocks that she was getting used to, she reached out with her free hand and physically closed his lips together. They felt like dried worms. May grimaced.

"Pumpkin," she said, "I really need you to be quiet."

Pumpkin stared at her, looking comical with his long eyes searching hers and her hand still on his mouth, his lips puffing through them like fish lips. "Muuvvt?" he slurred.

May scowled at him.

Puffffff.

With a sound like someone blowing out birthday candles, Pumpkin's face disappeared in blackness.

"The light!" May whispered, letting go of Pumpkin's lips. "It went out."

"Maybe I have something in my bag," Pumpkin offered. "Let's see," he whispered. "Food, water bottle, lucky silverstone . . ."

Ha ha ha.

May froze. A high, tinkly laugh had come from behind her.

Pumpkin's teeth began to chatter. "What was—"

Hee hee hee.

This time the laugh came from in front of them.

Haa haaa heee hee haaa.

Laughing voices overlapped one another, climbing on top of one another and seeming to come from all different directions. The skulls on the walls began to shake.

May spun around in a circle.

"Maaaay," Pumpkin moaned. He sounded near tears. "What . . ."

HA!

The laugh was just beside her ear. May spun away.

"Run!"

Dropping her pack with a crash, May started sprinting, and slammed right into a wall. A batch of skulls tumbled down, hitting her heavily on the shoulders and arms and legs.

May backed up and started running again. She could hear Pumpkin wheezing and groaning right behind her.

"Look for a tunnel out!" she cried. But her voice got lost. Hundreds of voices rang through the caves, laughing harder and harder—joyfully, delightedly.

May scraped against each wall as she ran. She didn't even know what direction they were going in now—they could be going back the way they'd come, which meant it would take hours to get outside again. May felt her legs start to give way. Her lungs pounded and squeezed against her ribs like an overinflated balloon. She couldn't run much more.

And then she saw it. It was up ahead, so faint it could have been imaginary, the tiniest slip of dim dusky light. As she got closer, it became more defined: the jagged rock edges that marked the entrance, the gentle rise of the sand outside.

Ha!

She tore through the archway into the light, Pumpkin slamming into her from behind as she skidded to a halt. They emerged onto a tiny patch of beach, no bigger than a few feet across. And there, right at the tip of May's toes, was the oily, greedy water of the Dead Sea.

Before she could back up, the water oozed forward, its tips stretching out and turning into long fingers of water that reached toward her. May sucked in her breath to scream, but a weight around her chest pushed it out of her in a whoosh. Suddenly she was being dragged back inside the caves, her feet making two long lines in the sand.

She only had a second to catch Pumpkin's black, terrified eyes before she was pulled into the darkness.

CHAPTER NINETEEN

The Cave Dwellers

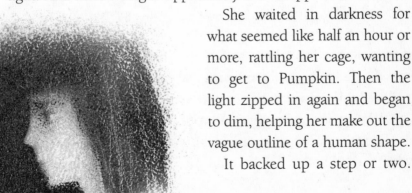

Deeper and deeper into the Catacombs, May was dragged, through low tunnels and tiny crevices no wider than her shoulders. She struggled and kicked, but her feet couldn't find purchase in the sandy floor of the caves, and the light coming from behind her was blinding, making spots swim in front of her eyes.

Suddenly the space around her seemed to expand, and with an unceremonious thud she was tossed into a big cage that swung from the ceiling, right near a wall. She immediately threw her hands up before her face, shielding her eyes against the blinding light. And then the light zipped away and disappeared.

She waited in darkness for what seemed like half an hour or more, rattling her cage, wanting to get to Pumpkin. Then the light zipped in again and began to dim, helping her make out the vague outline of a human shape.

It backed up a step or two.

When the light settled at a faint glow, May couldn't believe what she saw. Staring back at her was a boy, no more than twelve or thirteen, with sandy hair and wide blue eyes rimmed with long eyelashes. He had pale, fair skin, slightly rosy at the cheeks. He was tall and thin, wearing a white button-down shirt under a blue jacket, and a blue-and-tan-striped tie. He stared at her, looking almost as surprised as she herself must have looked.

"I didn't know you were pretty."

The boy seemed to think better of what he'd said, because he blushed scarlet, then he zipped across the room, a flash of white light, disappearing. The hall went dark. May felt something in her back.

"Ahh!"

She swatted between her shoulders, reached down and grabbed whatever it was, and flung it across the room. The glow appeared again. And there, scurrying away along one wall, was a ghostly tarantula.

Ha ha ha!

There was a white zip of light across the room, and the boy was standing in front of her again, holding his hand over his mouth and chuckling. "It's fake, you know! I really got you!"

"I don't think it's very funny," May said boldly. The boy immediately stopped laughing and pulled his hand away from his mouth. He looked suddenly scared and worried.

"Really? I'm sorry."

"W-What are you going to do with me?"

"*Do* with you?" the boy asked, his eyes wide, like doe eyes. "Do with you?" He scratched his chin and began to pace, illuminating the walls as he walked. "I guess the others want to see you. You're certainly a strange type of spirit."

May opened her mouth to say that she wasn't a spirit, but then stopped herself.

She leaned against the back of her cage. "What do you want?" she whispered, trying to keep the trembling out of her voice.

The boy blinked his doe eyes at her languidly, confused. "Want? Oh, I don't want anything. I've got everything I need right here."

With that the boy zipped around the room again in a white flash, bouncing off the walls and ending up across the hall.

"Then why were you chasing us?" May squeaked.

The boy squinted at her, seeming to try to make the question out. "Why? Oh, I don't know." He began to laugh. "You should have seen your face when I blew out your light." He broke into a delighted giggle. May clenched her mouth shut as he walked closer to the cage and stuck his fingers around the bars. Suddenly his eyes were serious again.

"Hey, do you think you might want to be friends?"

"Friends?" May whispered.

"Yeah." The boy smiled tentatively. "Here, shake on it. . . ." He stuck his whole hand into the cage. May couldn't hold back—she slapped it away.

"I'm not your friend! Pumpkin . . ." May's pulse throbbed. She had to get out of here. She had to find Pumpkin.

The boy had gone completely silent, and his glow had all but died. "I didn't mean to upset you." To May's shock, his eyes grew wide and sad. "I thought we were having fun. I'm sorry."

May sat there in her cage, flabbergasted.

"Oh, I didn't mean it!" the boy said with a moan. In a flash he zipped out of the room, leaving May in complete darkness.

"Wait! Come back! Come back!"

Her voice echoed back to her.

"Please!"

Nothing.

May rattled the doors of her cage as hard as she could, but it didn't budge. Then she got quiet again and waited for several more minutes, straining her ears for anything. There wasn't a sound to indicate that anything lived in the Catacombs at all.

May stood up and grabbed on to the door of her cage. "Heyyyyyy! Hey! Please come back!"

She quieted for a moment. Then she had another idea. "I forgive you! Please come back! I forgive you!"

Zip! A flash of light pinged against the walls, one, two, three times, and then there he was, standing in front of her again.

"That's kind of you," he said.

May nibbled her finger. She had to keep the boy by her and convince him to let her out—that much was clear.

"Wh-What's your name?" May asked.

"Lucius."

"Lucius?" May repeated. She'd never heard a name like it. "That's really pretty." She flashed what she hoped was a winning smile.

Lucius smiled back, clearly flattered. "It means 'light.' Appropriate, isn't it?" He held up his brightly glowing arms to underline the point. "What's yours?" he asked.

"I'm May Bird."

"May Bird," he repeated. "That's nice too. I suppose you want out of there then?"

May nodded furiously. She boldly stuck out her hand, and Lucius shook it. Though he was full of warm light, his fingers were ice cold.

"Sorry. I've been stuck in the cage tons of times, playing jail-break. But it drives the other boys crazy 'cause I don't mind it. Everybody else gets sick of it—I forget that sometimes." He floated up to May's cage, pulled a giant key out of the pocket of his baggy, khaki-colored pants, and unlocked the door.

"Thanks." She stared at him, her pulse racing now, like horses at the Kentucky Derby. "Pumpkin . . . did you see what happened to him?"

Lucius seemed to be searching his mind. "You mean the big-headed fellow?"

May nodded eagerly. "Yes, the big-headed fellow. I was won-dering, could you, please, please, just see if he's all right? I'm wor-ried the sea might have taken him."

Lucius seemed to consider this, eyeing her thoughtfully. "Why don't we go check together?"

"Really?" May tried not to show how relieved she was. Something told her not to give Lucius a reason to change his mood. "Can you take me back to where we left him?" she asked gently.

Lucius nodded proudly. "Yes, I could take you with my eyes closed."

"Please, let's just go with your eyes open."

The beach was deserted. May stayed well within the safety of the arch of the cave, but even from there she could tell that Pumpkin was nowhere on the small slip of sand. "No," she whispered softly.

"I think the waves must have got him," Lucius said gravely.

"Yes, remember that one that was right up behind him? Yes, now that I think of it, that's probably what happened."

May's eyes started to blur with tears. She swiped at them secretively.

"I'm sorry about it," he said. "He looked like a perfectly nice fellow."

"You're *sorry*?" May cried, unable to hold it in. "Pumpkin!" She threw her hands up over her face, but then felt another pair of hands on hers, pulling them apart. Lucius had his face right up next to hers, and he was grinning.

"Just kidding. Gosh, you're easy. Come with me."

Back through the caves they went, twisting and looping until they heard a giggle up ahead.

"Ohhh. Ohhhhhhhh."

May's heart caught in her throat. "Pumpkin!"

She ran ahead, bursting into a small round room with a neatly made bed, a Holo-Vision set, and shelves full of model airplanes and old cars. Pumpkin lay splayed on his stomach on the bed, reading a magazine. "Pumpkin!"

May ran to the bed and wrapped her arms around Pumpkin's neck. He rolled his eyes at her, pulled away, and said, "Where have you been?"

"Where have *I* been?" she asked, disbelieving. "What are you doing here?"

Pumpkin shrugged. "Lucius rescued me from the wave, and I've just been here reading these magazines." He waved one titled *Ms. Zombie.* Next to him sat the knapsack May had dropped in the caves.

She looked at Lucius, who continued grinning. "Pumpkin and

I have been getting to know each other. I went and got your bag for you."

"But—"

"Do you like my room?"

May looked around. The room was very old-fashioned. She felt herself getting shy now. "Yes, it's nice."

"You two will stay and play with me for a while, won't you?" He looked from one to the other. "Nobody ever comes to visit."

May looked at Pumpkin, who nodded at her eagerly, knocking his legs against the bed. Personally she didn't think she liked the way Lucius played.

"Um, we can't stay."

Lucius frowned. "Oh?"

"Lucius," May said gently. "I'm in danger. I'm trying to get to a place called Nine Knaves Grotto, to find a certain specter, and I have to get there without being seen."

Lucius frowned, concerned. "You're hiding?"

"Yes, I'm hiding, but I can't hide forever. I need to get out of here." Her voice came out even and calm, but inside she feared that she would say the wrong thing, and Lucius would zip away.

Lucius nodded sympathetically, however, suddenly seeming wiser and sadder than the mischievous boy he'd been a few moments before. He looked over both shoulders, then leaned toward her, meeting her brown eyes with his blue. "I'm hiding too."

"What are you hiding from?" May asked, blushing at being so close to him.

Lucius's eyes widened, and he backed up against the wall behind him, his light dimming. He sank down against the wall, putting his hands up in front of his eyes. "No, please!"

"Lucius?" May hurried and knelt down beside him. "Lucius?"

He kept his eyes buried in his hands for several seconds. But then suddenly, he looked up at her. His blue eyes were as clear and untroubled as a calm Caribbean Sea.

"Where did you say you needed to go?"

May hesitated, confused. "Nine Knaves Grotto."

A huge, delighted grin spread itself across Lucius's face, the fear completely disappearing. "Oh, that's easy. I'll take you there."

With that, he leaped up, his glow becoming so bright that both May and Pumpkin had to shield their eyes again.

"Oh, sorry," he said, dimming to a comfortable level.

He led them through several tunnels that seemed to go deeper into the Catacombs. Every few minutes a sound would be heard from down one of the caverns—muffled whispers, laughter.

"Don't worry," Lucius threw over his shoulder cheerily, "they'll leave you alone as long as you're with me. They all know you're here, of course. We know everything that happens in the caves."

Pumpkin and May shared a worried glance. "Excuse me, Lucius, but . . . who are they?"

"The other boys," Lucius said, turning right and disappearing from sight for a moment, until May and Pumpkin turned after him. "They're all hiding like I am. I hope you'll forgive me for the pranks," he said honestly, glancing back at May. He seemed to be a different boy once again—this one sincere, honest, handsome. "We get so bored, you know. It's lonely in the caves, even with the others."

"You never leave?" May asked, amazed.

"Oh, no," Lucius said. "Too dangerous out there." He looked at her sadly. "I do miss the outside, though. I haven't seen much of the Ever After. I found this place on my way south after I died, and stayed. I haven't been out since."

"But why is the outside so dangerous for *you*?"

Lucius looked at her as if she'd asked the most obvious question in the world. "Well, he might get me."

Again Pumpkin and May exchanged a glance.

"Who?"

Lucius looked all around, then continued to drift on ahead of them. He seemed to have forgotten the question, or ignored it on purpose. "We're almost there."

He floated several feet ahead, where the ground began to rise. Soon they were climbing, not steeply, but steadily.

May watched his back sympathetically, thinking how horrible a life in the caves must be. May didn't know what the rest of this world was like, but she couldn't imagine being happy without seeing the sky, without a mom or a cat, just a bunch of boys playing games.

Lucius zipped farther ahead, disappearing around a bend. He let them catch up to him a few minutes later.

"How old are you?" he asked.

"Ten," May answered. "Why?"

"Oh. I'm thirteen. At least, that's the age I was when I died." Lucius looked at her thoughtfully. "Are there other girls like you out there? Ones a bit older?" he asked, then bit his lip and blushed. May blushed back.

"I don't know," she answered. "I'm sort of new."

"Oh, right." Lucius nodded.

He hurried on ahead of them again, glowing their way through the darkness.

As soon as he was a safe distance away, Pumpkin leaned toward May and whispered in a dramatic, solemn way, "I think I understand. About Lucius."

"What do you mean?"

"Luminous boys," Pumpkin whispered. "Have you heard of them?" He widened his eyes at her for effect.

May shook her head. Of course she hadn't. The path had gotten steeper, and they were no longer on sand but on something harder. May turned to catch Pumpkin as he tripped over an outcropping of rock in their path, then continued.

"Oh, yes, that's got to be it. It makes sense. Hiding in the caves. Arista used to talk about them. . . . They spend Eternity living in fear. Very sad, really. Can you imagine?" Pumpkin shook his head. "Tsk, tsk, tsk."

May yanked at his ragged sleeve.

"Pumpkin? What is it you were going to tell me? About Lucius?"

Pumpkin drew the moment out as long as he could, smoothing his tuft of hair and thrusting his chin in the air knowledgeably. "Oh. Luminous boys are a very particular kind of specter. They all flock together and stay in very tight spaces, hiding because of what happened to them when they were alive." He stuck a pinky in between his lips, looking stricken.

"Well," May whispered impatiently, "what happened to them?"

Pumpkin frowned, his oval eyes huge. "Luminous boys are boys who were taken by the Bogey in their sleep. Sucked into the Ever After through their nightmares."

Just then Lucius zipped back to check on them, giving May a dazzling, sweet smile. May rubbed at the goose bumps along her arms as he squinted at her. "Say, you're not like any spirits I've met," Lucius said. "You move differently, and—"

May gulped, then forced a smile back on her face and interrupted him. "I'm new," she repeated. "Oh, look there." She pointed up ahead.

The light down the tunnel had begun to change. It was much more dim and gray than Lucius's light.

"Oh, yes," Lucius said, leading them farther and finally pointing one arm toward a round opening up ahead. "That's the way to the grotto."

CHAPTER TWENTY

Nine Knaves Grotto

A circle of sky gaped before them, full of zipping stars. May hurried past Pumpkin and burst into the open air. "Whew!"

They were about halfway up one of the cliffs. Below and to the right was the Dead Sea. May breathed in the open air gratefully. When Pumpkin caught up, he did the same.

"It's down there," Lucius said, still pointing.

May scanned all along the shore, which wasn't a shore anymore but a collection of cliffs butting up against the water's edge.

"I don't see anything but water."

"If you stare long enough, you will. It's there," he pointed, "in that little curve in the rocks. It's hidden."

May stared down hard at the curve he'd indicated. She stared for several seconds, so long that her eyes started to lose focus.

And that's when she saw it.

At the base of that curve, nestled in under the shadow of the rocks, was a tiny walled town built on a network of planks and bridges. It looked like the layers of a cake, with small square houses sitting almost on top of one another, reaching from the walkways and canals toward the cliffs. Its seaside side clung to the water, looking as if it might lean forward to peer into the waves and fall in. The wall itself was surrounded by a boardwalk and interrupted only by a tall, open gate. But it all blended so well with the shapes of its surroundings that when May looked away, then looked back, it took her a second to pick it out again.

"Gosh, it's practically invisible!"

"That's the way they like it," Lucius said. "Few spirits even know it's here. Knaves are like that. They're a secretive bunch."

May nodded. They must be, to live in such a dangerous spot— just inches above the deadly water of the Dead Sea.

"I'm sad to see you go," Lucius said gravely, interrupting her train of thought. His long handsome eyelashes fluttered at May.

"You're not coming any farther?" She searched the cliff edge. "But how will we get down?"

"There," Lucius said matter-of-factly, pointing to a tiny indent in the rock, which May now could see was a path.

She walked over to its edge. It was just enough room for one person to stand on, if she hugged her stomach against the rock. "Really? This is the only way?"

Lucius nodded. He stuck out his hand, and May took it, reluctantly. "There's a girl. It was nice to meet you. Good luck, May Bird."

He started to turn away. May and Pumpkin looked at each other. *Poor, lonely soul,* May thought. Pumpkin's eyes said he felt sorry for Lucius too.

"Wait." She threw out her hand to touch him, but he turned around first.

May bit her lip. "Won't you come with us? Just to the grotto? Just to get out of the caves for a little while?"

Lucius looked back at the cave, then at her. "Oh, no. I can't. Really. He might see me."

"But . . . you can turn around whenever you want. And it's not very far. . . . If you could just take us to the edge of town . . . Please?" May didn't want to put Lucius in danger. But she also didn't want him to spend the rest of Eternity hiding in a cave.

Lucius looked bashful. "You mean, you'd like for me to come?"

May smiled sincerely. "Very much."

Lucius gazed down at the grotto. "I suppose I can venture down to the water with you. Maybe I'll even take you to the gates," he said proudly.

With Lucius leading the way, May and Pumpkin grinned at each other. Pumpkin insisted on being in the middle as they made their way down the cliff, zigzagging back and forth along the face of the rock. Several times May lost sight of the town below, and thought for a minute that there must be some other path, and that they were going the wrong way. But finally it came

into view again, and a few minutes later they reached a small platform of rock that marked the end of the trail.

A finger of the sea stretched between the platform, where May
and the others stood, and the wall of the grotto. Dotting the black
oily water that separated them from the grotto were many large,
smooth rocks, lined up in staggered rows.

"I guess those are stepping stones?"

"I'm not going out there," Pumpkin said. "No, uh-uh. I'll stay
here and wait for you."

"Oh, it'll be easy." Lucius zipped right up to the side of the
platform, his feet poking just over the edge. Then he floated onto
the first rock. "See?"

May and Pumpkin stared at the seawater. It lapped at the sides
of the stone eagerly. "What if it's . . . boobytrapped, or something?" May asked.

"Oh, don't be scaredies. Come on."

The next stone over was very close to the first. Lucius floated
onto that one quickly, his arms out for balance, then looked over
his shoulder.

"Well, I guess." May stepped onto the first stone, then waited
to step onto the second until Lucius left it for the third.

He skimmed across the stones ahead of her, finally floating tri-
umphantly onto the wooden boardwalk that edged the wall of the
grotto. May followed, taking Lucius' icy hand as he offered it to
help her onto the planks. "That was easy," May said breathlessly,
flushed with pleasure. Lucius beamed.

He let go of her hand and floated ahead along the wall.
Meanwhile, May gestured at Pumpkin, who still hovered on the
opposite side of the water, shaking his head.

"Pumpkin, really, it's fine."

Pumpkin darted a look at the water, then one at May. He groaned. And then he began to scurry across.

By the time he floated off the last stone, Lucius had drifted back to them. His big, worried eyes filled May with alarm.

"What's wrong?"

"Come look."

Pumpkin, May, and Lucius approached the gate. The main walk that ran through the grotto was completely empty. Along each side of it, the square houses that sat one atop the other like layers of cake lay in various stages of disrepair: doors hanging off hinges, windows covered in spider webs, old pieces of furniture lying forlorn and alone on balconies. Overhead, clotheslines holding curious sacks of liquid dangled up and down the walkways, and above their heads, the same sacks hung from the top of the gate. Now that May thought about it, it was strange that it should be standing wide open. And that it had been so easy to get this close.

She took in the scene before her, letting it sink in. There wasn't a soul to be seen anywhere. The town was deserted.

The companions entered the gate cautiously, peering this way and that for any sign of movement. May's feet thudded hollowly along the boardwalk. Through the slats of the walkway she could see the sinister blackness of the seawater, waving back and forth beneath them.

"Ohhh," Pumpkin groaned, drifting slightly behind the other two and peering this way and that fretfully. He looked like he might turn and head for the hills at any moment. "I think I'll wait outside."

"It's fine, Pumpkin. Everyone's gone," Lucius chirped.

But May wasn't so sure that meant everything was fine. "If John the Jibber is gone, we've come a long way for nothing."

They crisscrossed the grotto three times, weaving up and down different bridges and alleys. Among the houses were several other buildings. May read the signs: N. K. G. SCHOOL OF THIEVERY AND PICKPOCKETING with a banner beneath that said ENROLL NOW FOR SPRING!; AL CAPONE'S ACADEMY FOR THE MUSICALLY GIFTED; HAVE A NICE KNIFE, which displayed all sorts of old daggers and swords in its window; THE REPENTANT THIEVES CENTER FOR CHARITY.

Each time they reached the wall that surrounded the town, they turned and tried a different route. Everywhere the walkway was deserted.

May stood and rested her back against the wall, thinking.

What had happened to all the residents of the grotto? Had they fallen into the water? That wasn't likely. Had something even worse happened? Then May thought about the ghouls back in the Catacombs.

Had something come for the residents of the grotto?

May peered at the space in front of her feet. The walk shook just slightly, as if someone nearby was walking on it.

May looked up. The Repentant Thieves Center for Charity stood just opposite her.

May walked up to the door, a tingle beginning at the base of her neck. She peered at a glowing picture of a beautiful child with huge brown eyes blinking at her. "'This poor, wretched orphan needs your help,'" she read from the poster. "Oh, I don't know," she muttered, backing away, ignoring the tingle.

"What's that, May?" Lucius asked earnestly.

"Nothing, I just . . ." May turned back to look at the sign again. "Ghosts can't change . . . ," she muttered to herself. She stepped forward, put her hand on the door handle, and pulled.

Instead of opening onto the inside of a building, the door opened onto another walkway, one that was much cleaner and newer and also filled with little houses. Pumpkin and Lucius had come up behind her, and they all peered in. May led them forward.

"Good job, May," Lucius said, patting her back. After a few sharp corners, they came to an open space.

Here the boardwalk formed an octagon, dotted in the center by a great fountain. In it was a statue of a man in a green hat, green tunic, and tights.

May smiled. "That's Robin Hood." On his back he held a quiver of arrows, and out of the tip of each arrow arched a black stream of seawater.

Just beyond the fountain was a large building with a sign dangling crookedly from the sloped roof. In glowing letters it read HANGMAN'S NOOSE TOWN HALL. They stepped in through the doors and were immediately overpowered by a smell that was both stale and sour.

"Ech!" They all put their hands up to their noses at the same moment.

May took in the scene. Big stone rafters crisscrossed the roof, and from them hung more giant sacks of liquid. A bar ran along one side, with hundreds of gleaming silver chalices hanging from tiny looped hooks above it. There must have been at least a hundred tables scattered across the floor in various states of disarray, with chairs sitting straight up, or lying on their sides, or broken and smashed on the floor.

Graffiti had been carved into the walls. May read some of the phrases:

"Always be prepared to lie."

"Always watch for seawater."

"Keep your friends close and your enemies at knifepoint."

Then a fourth one caught May's eye:

"John the Jibber is a fibber."

May put her finger on the words for the others to look. "At least we know John the Jibber *was* here."

Below it there was a tiny, jagged carving of a tree, with eyes peering through the leaves. May gasped. Then a movement to her right distracted her.

"Pumpkin, what are you doing?"

Pumpkin held a gleaming silver knife in one hand and was carving something into the wall, biting his lip in concentration.

"Pumpkin!" May reached and took the knife from him. "Where'd you get this?" May looked to see that he had written "Pumpkin was he—"

"It was just lying there on the table. Look how shiny it is."

May put the knife back down on the table and scowled at him. Apparently he'd decided the grotto was safe, because he merely grinned back at her, holding his nose. But May had a bad feeling in the pit of her stomach.

Lucius was peering around the room. "I haven't seen anything like civilization in years," he said, his eyes wide. "You don't think *he* might be hiding here, do you?"

May shook her head, ignoring the bad feeling. "Don't worry, Lucius." She turned and squinted at the carving of the tree again, and then peered at the shelves along the nearest wall, which held various stacks of scrolls.

May walked over to them and pulled one out. Carefully she unrolled it.

"Look!" she called back over her shoulder to the other two. She took several papers from the different piles: *The Lower Realm at a Glance: A Criminal's Guide to the Southern Territories; Top 100 Destinations For Looting and Pillaging; What to Expect When You're Expecting to be Executed.*

Lucius remained on the other side of the room, by the door, hovering unsurely and staring around. Pumpkin came and looked with her, still holding his nose.

Beside the shelves of brochures was a huge book. May scooted over to it and read the cover. *Who's Who in Nine Knaves Grotto and Maps to Where They Live.*

May rubbed the cover with her hand. "Look at this."

Finally Pumpkin drifted over. "Oh, nifty." He grabbed the cover and pulled it open.

Suddenly windows started slamming shut.

Then the two double doors.

Lucius, standing by a window, cast about quickly with his eyes. "It's the Bogey!"

With a lightning fast zip, he careened across the tavern toward the last open door, but just as he did, one of the sacks of liquid fell from above and landed on his head, burst open, and splashed him with black water.

His face contorted into one horrified look. And then he vanished.

"Lucius!" May screamed. She leaped toward him, but Lucius had gone. Only a round puddle of seawater lay on the ground where he'd been hovering. "No!" At the same time May felt breathing on her neck. She turned and leaped back to see she was face-to-face with a man hanging from the rafters by his knees, his hands hanging down below him, one of them holding a watergun filled with black liquid.

May tried to run, but he pushed her up against the wall with one frigid hand, holding the water gun to her throat.

He smiled a wicked, sickly grin at her.

"Welcome to the grotto. I hear yer looking fer me."

CHAPTER TWENTY-ONE

John the Jibber

Pumpkin let out a startled scream and shot for the door. The man laughed. "I'd freeze where ye are, or ye'll end up like yer friend."

Pumpkin, hovering and quaking, slowly turned.

"Get back here where I can look at ye."

Pumpkin complied, sidling up behind May.

In a vaporous swirl the man oozed down from the rafters and came to an upright hover an inch off the floor. He was a gruesome sight. Underneath his filthy clothes, which were ripped and covered in mold, his body was gaunt. His hollow cheeks sucked themselves underneath his cheekbones so that he looked like he was trying to make a fish face. Cockroaches crawled out from beneath his collar and into his hair and scraggly beard.

"A Live One! Look at you." The man laughed heartily again and lowered his water gun. He wore a smile, but his eyes glinted like steel. A cockroach ran along his bottom lip. "I haven't seen one of your kind in years. I couldn't believe it when they said you'd come through the gate! What a sight! I'm John." He thrust out his hand. "Ye can call me Mr. Jibber."

May stared at his hand. "Where's Lucius?" she asked, too stunned to speak above a whisper, her eyes glued to the spot where Lucius had vanished.

John eyed her sympathetically. "I'd say he's about a hundred miles south of us right now, dearie."

"No!" May threw her hands up over her mouth. Tears welled along the ridges of her eyes.

She felt a cold pricking on her chin. John the Jibber had tucked an index finger there and was lifting her face to look at him. "Chin up, lass. Don't waste yer time feeling sorry fer what's already past. Nothing you or I can do."

May shrank back, not just from his words, which sounded mean and hard, but from the unbearable smell. Just when she'd gotten used to the smell of the town hall, he'd appeared with a stench three times as bad. He smelled like maggots and slime and mold and old socks and all the bad things May could think of. As she moved backward she bumped into Pumpkin, who was cowering behind her. She felt stuck between them like ham in a sandwich. She turned back to John and swiped at her tears. "Y-You're John the Jibber."

"Don't like the looks of me, eh? Well, I don't blame ye. But it isn't me fault, what happened to yer friend. Everybody knows not to use the west door of the tavern. Except intruders."

May was speechless. John seemed to take this as agreement, because he once again burst into a wide grin.

"Hey, mates," he called back over his shoulder. "C'mon out! We've got ourselves a Live One in the grotto!"

An explosion of voices filled the hall.

"We're not yer mates, John the Jibber," one voice called. It seemed like it was almost just beneath May's feet.

"You wish, Jibber!" said another.

Slowly specters began arriving from all directions—oozing up through the cracks in the floor, pouring in through the front door of the hall. The women were as rough-looking as the men. Many of them were covered in scars and tattoos, several were missing fingers. One was missing a head. As May watched in awe, they watched her in return, crowding around her and Pumpkin, but only staring at *her.* Some grabbed drinks from the bar before they joined the others.

"Can I touch her?" one woman with three teeth and a rope mark around her neck asked, leaning forward and sticking an index finger against May's arm. They all seemed to think this was a good idea and followed suit. May shrunk back, horrified.

"It sure is an honor meeting you," one man said. "Can I have your autograph?"

May just stared at him, her eyes blurred with tears.

He ran and got a quill pen from behind the bar and shoved one of the brochures toward May. "Make it out to 'Guillotined Gwenneth.' That's me girlfriend."

May did so, stiffly, the ink coming out of the quill pen with a green glow.

Immediately everybody in the room crowded around her, waving brochures. Spirits who looked like pirates, spirits wearing black-and-white-striped prison suits, spirits in cowboy hats. Behind her, Pumpkin whimpered.

John hovered backward a few steps and waited. Soon the crowds drifted back to their tables and began talking, laughing, and drinking, but they continued to cast looks her way. John pulled a long bench away from one of the tables, then came and wrapped an arm around May's neck and pulled her forward. "Now have a seat, and you can tell me what brings you to John the Jibber."

May sat down on the bench awkwardly, sniffling. Pumpkin drifted down beside her, nibbling his fingers.

John stared at her for some time. When she said nothing, he finally leaned toward her, conspiratorially.

"So, what brings you?"

May could feel everyone's eyes on her. She swallowed and sniffled. She didn't know what to do. She looked at Pumpkin, who sat gazing at all the faces with his teeth chattering, offering no help at all.

The Jibber whipped a dirty, rotten hanky out of his coat and handed it to her. "Now, enough o' that snifflin'. If you're worried about us sounding the Bogey alarm, don't worry. Those in the grotto don't bow to the Bogey or Bo Cleevil. Yer safe from that here, missy. Evil Cleevil's a pain in our side, and we sure wouldn't help him fer nothing. Made things tough for us, he has. He'd as soon throw all of us knaves in the sea as he would look at us, and we feel the same about him. And we won't even punish your friend here for trying to take yonder knife."

He eyed Pumpkin, then turned back to May. "Now come on, out with it."

Grief stricken, May took the hanky, pinching it gingerly and eyeing it with disgust. "Um"—May swiped at her nose—"the Undertaker said you'd help us."

A roar of laughter burst out behind her. The whole hall went into an uproar.

"Help from the Jibber, that's a good one!" one woman shouted.

"He'll help you, all right. Right into the gallows!" another man added.

When May looked back at John, he was just grinning at her. She nibbled on a nail. "What do they mean?" she asked, wiping her eyes with trembling fingers.

John smiled confidently. "Ah, they're just jealous of me. On account of me being the wiliest knave in the grotto. They like to make fun, but don't pay 'em no mind." He winked, flashing another horrid smile.

"What do ye drink?"

"Umm, drink? I don't know." Her throat *was* very dry. "Do you have orange juice?"

"Well, let's see." John hovered out of his seat and toward the bar. "No orange juice. But we have That's the Spirit spirits, Spirit of Saint Louis spirits, Let the Spirit Move You spirits . . ."

"Will spirits make me drunk?" The whole bar went into hysterics. May blushed.

"I'll have something," Pumpkin piped in, his teeth ceasing to chatter. He met May's stern gaze with an innocent shrug.

"I wasn't offering *ye* any," John replied hoarsely.

"Do you have anything that's not spirits?" May asked, elbowing Pumpkin in the arm.

As John thought for a moment, a stream of black water went zipping through the air past his head. He ducked just in time to miss getting hit in the cheek. Behind May, Pumpkin wheezed and ducked against her back. John held up his water gun, pointing it in the direction the water had come from.

The shooter was a roly-poly man wearing an eye patch and a T-shirt that said I'D RATHER BE IN BELLE MORTE. He was guffawing, holding his belly as he laughed. "Came close that time, Jib. . . ."

Splash.

Something like a bright turquoise egg splattered against his head, sending out a splash of black liquid. His face contorted into an expression of terror, and then he vanished. The whole room went silent, and then broke out into laughter.

"Old Lefty finally got wet!" somebody cried.

"The ghouls got 'im now!"

What lay on the floor where Lefty had sat were the rubbery remnants of a water balloon.

"I think I'm going to faint," Pumpkin gasped beside her.

May wanted to ask if someone had just hit Lefty on purpose with seawater, but just then, John sidled up to them at the table.

"Things are gonna get rowdy in a minute. We better get moving."

"It's yer turn next, Potbelly Petey!" somebody yelled.

As she said these words, the woman with the rope burn from earlier pulled a water gun out from between her ample bosom and fired at the man who'd just spoken. His eyes widened right before the water hit, and then he disappeared.

With that, the hall erupted. Big balloons filled with seawater went flying in all directions, water guns came out from pockets and bosoms. It was a Dead Sea free-for-all.

"This is no place for a kiddie," John the Jibber said, keeping his gun cocked and looking around pertly. "C'mon."

He expertly led them out from underneath the torrent of water balloons flying overhead. One came so close to May's head she felt it whizzing past her ear. It hit a baby-faced man in a cowboy hat and he disappeared.

"Hey, who hit Billy the Kid? Sure that he didn't deserve it!"

As a fresh volley of balloons flew over their heads, May, John, and Pumpkin burst through the doors onto the town octagon. May had a chance to look back one last time to the puddle of water by the west door, and then the doors swung closed. Two men had already come out ahead of them, and one was trying to push the other into the fountain.

"This way," John said, leading them across the octagon and into an alley, May's feet *clomp clomping* as they rushed along. Pumpkin kept a tight grip to the back of her bathing suit.

"Mr. Jibber, why are they doing that to each other?"

"Just for fun, lass. They'll quit soon."

"But isn't going to South Place a terrible thing?"

"Oh, aye! A fate worse than death."

He took a left, then a right, and another left.

"So you need my help," he threw back over his shoulder breezily. "What is it you're aiming to do? Off somebody? Robbery?"

"I need to get in to see *The Book of the Dead*."

John froze in his tracks. He turned to her, crouched down to May's eye level, and wiped a cockroach off his cheek. There was a steely glint in his eye.

"That's a good joke, lass. Who told you to say that to me?"

"I need to get home, back to Briery Swamp, to my mom and my cat. The Undertaker said my only chance is the Book."

John jerked up straight and yanked on his beard a few times, his eyes still locked on May's.

"The Book of the Dead."

John looked at her for a few more minutes. Then the glint disappeared from his eye, and he became businesslike. "It's a big job. Most would say impossible. The Eternal Edifice . . . It's a fearsome place. I don't know anyone who's gone in and come back out again, except meself, that is."

Beside May, Pumpkin trembled.

"You've seen the Book?"

John frowned. "Yes, I've seen the Book. Had it right at me hands, I did."

"What did you go to find out?"

"Why, the only thing worth knowing, really. Where the greatest treasures are hidden. There are a few in the realm. I been looking for the treasure of Queen Sheba for the past hundred years."

"Where did it say it was?"

John smiled grimly. "It didn't. The Book wouldn't open fer me. Blasted stupid book.

"Anyway, the Edifice is guarded. Heavily. Ghouls, goblins, you name it. All working for Bo Cleevil. They took over the Edifice a few years ago and haven't budged since. What makes ye think yer britches are big enough fer it?"

May shrugged. She thought of telling John about her letter, just to prove *somebody* thought her britches were pretty big. But then she thought better of it.

"Well." John looked at May and stroked his beard, then waggled one of his black teeth and pulled it out. "Nobody can ever say John the Jibber was a yellowbelly. Things have been dull round here anyhow. I'll do it."

"Thank you," May breathed.

"Now, how do you propose to pay me?"

May's stomach lurched. "Pay you?"

John chuckled, but this time his laugh was as cold as crushed ice. "You don't think I do this kind of thing for my health? The city is a dangerous place! Probably the most dangerous in the realm, except that I hear Bo Cleevil's building something fearful in the northeast. We'll all be risking our teeth. I don't risk mine for free."

"But . . ." May's lip trembled. "I don't have anything."

"Jewels?"

May shook her head.

"Bilocation tokens? Fast-forward motion potion? Elixirs of any sort? I wouldn't mind being a bit fatter. Or seeing the future."

"I have two teleport tokens."

"*Please.*" John seemed to rack his brain. "Have you by any chance got an extra head? I might be able to sell it to one of the fellows here."

May just stared now, silently. Then it hit her. "Oh! I have some soul cakes, and Pumpkin has a starlight."

John rolled his eyes, then looked Pumpkin up and down. "I'll take your house ghost."

"Ohhh," Pumpkin moaned.

"You can't!" May gasped, horrified.

"Listen, lass, if you want to see the book, you'll have to pay up." John smiled, friendly. "A trip into the city is bad enough. But a trip into the Eternal Edifice, shooo . . ." John ran a hand along his forehead. "I don't know. It would be the biggest trick of my life getting us *all* in there and getting us out again."

"Maybe I could pay you once I get back home to Briery Swamp. . . ."

"Ha! So long, lassie." John turned and started walking away.

"Wait!"

John kept walking. May felt a cold arm around her shoulders and turned to look at Pumpkin. "Well, I guess that means it's back to Belle Morte," he said, trying to sound breezy.

May slumped against Pumpkin's arm. They had already lost Lucius. This fact was so terrible she almost couldn't believe it. Maybe Pumpkin was right.

She tried to picture never seeing home or Somber Kitty again. Up ahead of them, John vanished around a corner.

May pulled her sack off her back. "Wait! I have something else!"

A moment passed, and then John's head appeared around the corner. May dug into her bag and pulled out her comfort blanket.

"I have this." She held her blanket out. "It's from North Farm."

John eyed them both suspiciously, drifting back toward them, then eyed the blanket.

"No, it ain't."

"Look at the label."

John read it. "A comfort blanket." He jabbed at it with his finger. "How'd you get this?"

May swallowed. She hadn't thought he'd ask.

"It's none of your business," Pumpkin said, surprising both of them. John turned a look of irritation on him.

"But it's yours if you take me to see the Book," May said quickly. Pumpkin looked at her, impressed.

John ran his hands along the fabric of the blanket, his eyes gleaming again. "It's rare. I could get a good price for it."

May waited.

"Ye wouldn't be hiding anything important from John the Jibber, would ye, lass? I don't want to get mixed up with no Northern Spirit business." As he said this his eyes belied his greed. They were glued to the blanket.

May swallowed, then shook her head furiously.

"I'll tell you what, lassie. You give me this blanket. And you promise me something. When we get to the Book, if it lets you read it, you look up where the treasure of the queen of Sheeba is for me."

May bit her lip, and she looked at Pumpkin, who shook his head no. May set her jaw.

"I promise," she said, holding out her pinky. John looked at it, not knowing what she meant, so May hooked it through his pinky and gave a quick shake.

John smiled. "We'll go and pack then."

They headed back through the streets, which were now lit every few feet with glowing blue lamps in glass bulbs. The walkways were still mostly empty, except for a few specters weaving drunkenly, some arm in arm.

Soon they came to a skinny doorway on street level. John pulled out a key. "Through here," he said, opening it. They climbed several tiny stone steps that seemed to lead right into a ceiling. But here, John pulled out another key and stuck it into a tiny hole to the right, and pushed the ceiling over to reveal another stairway leading straight up. At the top of this one, there was a landing, with a metal chest resting on it. John opened it and stepped in. Then, as May and Pumpkin watched, he disappeared. May and Pumpkin peered in, and found another stairway leading down. They climbed into the chest and followed.

At the bottom of the stairs, John was waiting for them on a square platform right on top of the water, just inches from the deadly water of the sea. The platform itself was piled with treasures. Jewels, gold, gigantic diamonds, several crowns, and nestled in the middle, a sleeping bag and a pillow.

John grinned with pride. "Nice, eh? The treasure is mostly from Arabia. Ali Baba nicked it from the forty thieves, but I nicked it from him while he was in his kitchen eating baba ghanoush."

"You sleep here?"

"This is my real home. Any knave worth his salt has a house for show and a hidden one where he lives and sleeps. Keeps me from getting sent to South Place in the middle of the night."

"But if everybody murders one another here, how are there still enough people to fill the town?"

"Ah, knaves are a dime a dozen. There're always new ones coming in. Did you see this golden apple?"

John held up the shiny fruit.

"Can I have it?" Pumpkin asked. May and John both turned to see he was wearing a tiara, a veil, and holding out his hand for the apple.

"Gimme that!" John shouted, swiping the tiara and veil from Pumpkin's head and putting it all back in his pile. He dug some more.

"What do you do with all this stuff?" May asked.

John looked confused. "Well, I *have* it."

"Oh."

"Ah, here it is. You won't find many of these in the realm anymore."

It was a long robe with a hood. John swirled it around May's shoulders.

"It looks great on you. See?" May surveyed herself and gasped. Her skin had become transparent.

"Death shroud. It's only a lender, mind you, and don't get it into yer head that you might keep it. There're a few floating around, with almost all the Live Ones being gone and executed by now." May swallowed and John looked at her apologetically. "Sorry. Anyhow, they've been outlawed of course. So it's a real nice collector's item. Who would have thought there'd be a Live One around again to use it," he said with pride.

"Wow," May breathed.

"It'll get you into Ether undetected. 'Course, if anybody looks closely, they'll be able to tell you're alive. You looking so healthy and still using your feet to get around. But most new spirits take a while to learn to float anyway. And most spirits don't pay much attention to much of anything but themselves. The sniffing phantoms are a different story, though. Frightful careful, they are, about who they let into the city, and it's a frightful penalty for trying to trick 'em. We'll get you nice and fragrant before we go in, don't worry."

John indicated the stairs, and they all went back up. When he had closed the treasure chest, they walked outside.

"John—um, Mr. Jibber, what do you know about Evil Bo Cleevil?"

John's face descended into a deep frown. To cover it, he scratched an ear, pinched at it, and pulled a centipede off.

"Back when I was newly deceased, me and my pals down in Nine Knaves Grotto had the run of the realm. We lived high on the hog in the city then, gambling all night, drinking all day, robbing whatever we could, and the pickings were easy. Plenty of trips into the desert, plenty down south to the pretty seaside towns. Stole everything we could get our hands on." John smiled sadly, his three teeth glinting in the light of the fire. "Good times they were. . . .

"We saw a Live One like you from time to time, missy, and I was pals with a couple of 'em. We heard stories of stirrings in the northern parts, stories of spirits going up there and never coming back. We didn't believe 'em.

"But then I saw the Bogey. We were out riding horses—that was before all the animals got gathered up. And me and my mate Cyril—a Live One, by the way—see this little storm moving across the sand. And then we see the dogs. Poor Cyril, he loved dogs, so he started riding toward them. And then they got closer, and I could see, and I think Cyril saw too, that those dogs meant business—and that there was somebody with 'em."

John paused.

"Well, knaves are no fools, and we kicked our horses into high gallop, but it was too late. Poor Cyril tripped up his mare, and the last I saw him he was lying there on the sand, and then the Bogey was upon him, and then . . ."

"And then?" Pumpkin pressed, his eyes huge.

John was staring into the distance, as if he didn't see either of them anymore. "The Bogeyman has these horrible fingers, with little saucers at the end. He put the fingers on Cyril. And then Cyril was sucked up into them, an inch at a time. Sucked . . . into nothingness." He shook his head. "And we'd thought South Place was the worst that could happen to us."

May and Pumpkin were quiet.

"Anyhow, maybe I noticed it more after that, but everything started changing. All the animals started disappearing. We could see how it was going. Spirits were going out on raids and they weren't coming back. The city started crawling with creatures from South Place, though how they got up here is anyone's guess.

"So we built the grotto. And all is well again. A little more dangerous when we go out on raids, don't get to go on them as much, but still, we are protected."

"You're not scared the Bogey may find you here?"

"As long as I'm in the grotto I don't fear the Bogey. Once we leave, I'll fear him greatly, I will. We won't run into him, though, trust me."

"How do you know?"

"Because I plan on keeping my spirit." John's eyes grew dark and glinty, and his jaw stiffened. The look of mirth disappeared from his face. "An' if we did run into him, to keep our spirits . . . Well, lass, it would take a miracle."

Talk had begun to rise in the south of a living cat with high pointy ears and no fur. Most did not believe it.

In Sour Sands 2 miles south of the majestic Weeping River and 3,750 miles west of Nine Knaves Grotto, he was spotted by a tribe of nomads, drinking from a tributary. His eyes immediately began to tear, a side effect of the water that the nomads had long ago gotten used to. When this happened Somber

Kitty's expression changed from a frown of sorrow to one of irritated confusion, before running off.

At the intersection of the Northern Pass Road and South Bend, he was spotted by an enterprising young goblin who was waiting at the crossroads, selling guitar lessons in exchange for Everlasting Soles, his favorite brand of shoe. The goblin, who was never one to let a potential customer—however banished, or unlikely to actually own a pair of shoes—pass him by, spoke to Somber Kitty, assuring him that, indeed, one need not have opposable thumbs to master a musical instrument. Somber Kitty eyed him coolly and darted away.

He had no idea if he was getting closer to May or farther away. Now he looked down the three possible paths that led away from the crossroads, and waited for what his gut might say. But nothing came. Finally, after much deliberation and sniffing and a small sigh, he turned right onto South Bend, toward a strange grouping of triangular buildings in the sand. A new scent drifted to him on the breeze, making his skinny stomach growl.

Moving toward him were a trio of almond-skinned people with long, black, glossy hair and elaborately painted eyelids. They wore white linen sheets and held a heaping bowl of fava beans low to the ground as they called to him softly.

Somber Kitty hadn't seen food, much less eaten any, since he'd arrived in the Ever After. Being a cat and not prone to guess at the cruelties of men, even dead ones, he ran forward. A net appeared from behind one of the figure's backs, and suddenly Somber Kitty was scooped into the air, letting out a long howl.

With exclamations of excitement, the Egyptians said they

would call him Dinè Akbar, which meant "big ears." But Somber Kitty did not speak Egyptian, so he was not insulted. He only spoke cat, and in a soft plaintive voice he spoke it now: "Meow? Mew? Meay?"

And then he was carried away.

CHAPTER TWENTY-TWO

Into the Outskirts

The whole town of Nine Knaves Grotto came out to see the three travelers off.

Guillotined Gwenneth took hold of May's hand and shook it heartily, holding her other hand to her head to keep it in place. "Yer a nice little girl. If you don't perish in the Edifice, which ye surely will, please remember dear old Gwenneth to the good old Earth, will ye?" She patted May's hip affectionately.

"Good luck," someone else shouted from the back of the crowd. "You'll need it with the Jibber leading you!"

May climbed down off the edge of the boardwalk onto the rowboat that was docked there, following John the Jibber, who sat on the middle bench in front of the oars. The back of the rowboat bore a painted message: PROPERTY OF TUNNEL OF HORROR, PIT OF DESPAIR AMUSEMENT PARK.

Pumpkin hovered on the edge of the dock, looking unsure. "What if the boat sinks or we get splashed?"

"We don't have a choice. Come on, Pumpkin," May urged.

"Hurry up or we'll leave ye behind," John added.

May reached out her hand, and Pumpkin took it, making a face at John, then turning to May. "I don't see why he gets to be boss."

John had a pair of rubber gloves in his hands. He blew into one, then the other.

"Why'd you do that?" May asked.

"Heh? What'd ye say? Yer so quiet I can hardly hear ye."

May repeated herself, this time more loudly.

"The gloves are protecting ye from the water that might be on the oars, but tricky knaves are always putting holes in 'em, so tiny ye can't see 'em."

He watched the glove in his hand to see if it would deflate.

"Looks like I got a good pair this time." He paused for a minute. "I don't suppose yer skinny-armed friend would be any good at rowing?"

Pumpkin crossed his arms around his knees, which he pulled up in front of his face, and looked at May. "Will you tell him that I'm an excellent rower, but I just don't feel like it right now?"

May put her thumbs to her temples. It was going to be a long ride.

Once he had the gloves on, after a lot of mumbling about Pumpkin under his breath, John leaned into the oars. Pumpkin and May watched the crowd on the pier of the grotto shrink into the distance. A few seconds later they passed a red buoy bobbing in the water. To May's surprise, two men—as skinny as John the Jibber and as ugly—were standing on it, hugging tight to the buoy and watching them.

"Seen anything interesting, Chippy?" John asked.

"No sir, Mr. Jibber. I say, do you think they'll be coming to get us anytime soon?"

"I wouldn't hold yer breath, mateys. Could be another couple years or so. Just ye mind to sound the alarms if ye see any intruders."

"Yes, sir."

Once they were out of earshot, John rolled his eyes at May. "They were caught trying to murder the mayor. He takes that stuff seriously. So now they're on watch out here. There's nobody willing to do it. Personally I think it's a bit harsh, as the mayor's certainly murdered his share of folks." He held his hand up to the side of his mouth. "Poor fellas. Must be boring as anything."

And then they were alone on the sea, just listening to the lapping of the oars against the water and the waves against the cliffs.

John rowed for several hours until the cliffs seemed to shrink from massive to just huge, then huge to large, until finally they'd settled into rocky, rolling hills alongside the shore.

After hours of snoring, Pumpkin sat up, rubbed the tuft on the top of his head, and spoke. "I wonder what those ghouls are doing now."

"What ghouls are they?" John asked, perking up.

"We saw them, back at the beach," May explained. "That's what forced us into the Catacombs."

"Ghouls outside the Catacombs!" John looked deeply troubled.

May stammered. "I didn't think to tell you earlier, I just . . ."

John looked stricken.

She swallowed. "Do you think . . . they might be looking for the grotto?"

John nodded once, decidedly. "Ah, I'm almost sure of it. Why else would ghouls be in these parts? There's nothing here but sand and sea and the caves. And I said, Cleevil wants us all wiped out. Ay, the trouble my dear friends are in."

"We should go back and warn them!"

John's face was grim and as still as a rock. Then he took a deep breath and sank back into the oars.

"Wait. Don't you think we should turn back?" May asked.

"It's too late, most likely. Ghouls move fast when they want to. But the knaves know how to take care of themselves. Nobody can get in who we don't want in."

"But *we* got in."

John winked at May. "You don't think we let you, dearie? You and that house ghost of yers?"

"How do you know Pumpkin is a house ghost, just by looking?" John nodded.

May looked at Pumpkin, who looked suddenly humble and unsure, and back at John. "How?"

"Look at him. House servants are dimmer than the rest. And anyhow, ghosts just ain't as important as specters."

May looked at Pumpkin, who was looking down at his feet, his shoulders hunched. "He's important."

John laughed. "Right, lass."

"I don't think *you're* so important, cockroach lips," Pumpkin muttered to his feet.

"Why, you . . ." John thrust his oars to either side of him, moving forward—

"But about those ghouls," May interrupted, sliding between the two. "Shouldn't we at least warn—"

John sat back as he interrupted her in return. "Each knave has to look out for himself."

It was the end of the topic, clearly.

After several minutes Pumpkin lay down and began to snore

again. May lay back beside him protectively and watched the sky, occasionally sneaking a look at John the Jibber. They needed him. And he seemed to want the same thing they did. Still, May wondered if it wouldn't be wiser to take their chances on their own.

When they finally docked, she was in such a daze she hadn't even noticed they'd turned toward shore. And then she heard and felt the crunching of sand underneath the boat.

They were sheltered by an overhanging of rock, and it was cool. John stretched, his bony ribs poking out against his ragged shirt. "We should build a fire."

After May ate, the three sat around the fire John had made from stardust kept in a pouch in his coats. They sat with crossed legs, staring at the flames. "Ye know," John said, "it's a quick walk to the top of the hill, and from there you can just see Ether. Do ye want to go?"

"You mean, we're that close to the city?"

"Ay."

"I'd love to!"

May jumped up and brushed herself off and followed John, who led her out from the overhang and up a narrow, rocky path. She thought to herself how amazing it was that she was here, walking at dusk with an old pirate—*her,* May! If only Somber Kitty could have seen her. Maybe he *would* see her, soon. The thought lifted her spirits.

John reached out his hand to help her up the last few steps. May stepped up beside him and followed his gaze.

"There she is. Most beautiful city in this world or the other one, though I admit I haven't seen the other one in quite a while."

They were at the end of a long, dry plain, and there, across it, glowing and spiking above the horizon, was the City of Ether.

"Gosh, it's farther than I hoped," May lamented.

"Not as far as ye'd think." John sighed. "Sometimes I wish I could give up the life." He sighed again. "I'd love to live like normal spirits do. With their nice graves outside the city and their Earth houses to haunt, and going to the Pit of Despair for holidays. But alas, I am what I am."

He turned to May. "Yer lucky. If I were still livin', like ye, ah, the things I'd do. . . . I'd change, I swear, be the person I want to be. I'd give up the knave's life! Get married. If I hadn't died—"

"Um, how *did* you die?" May ventured shyly. She'd been dying to ask.

John studied her, the usual twinkle in his eye gone. "If you want, we can sit awhile and I'll tell ye."

They both sat on the rock overlooking the city.

"Back in England I was running with a band of thieves, doing the usual. Stealing, holding up ships, things like that. I was out working on me own one afternoon, slipping into the local rectory to steal the communion cup, when the law nabbed me. The royal guard heard our gang was around, you see. And they were looking.

"Well, they hadn't been able to find the others, because we had a nice tucked-away spot that we used to hide in. It drove the guards crazy, and they told me if I told them where me mates were they'd let me go."

John shrugged. "I told them all I knew, and they let me go, on condition I wouldn't say a word to me mates. When me mates asked me what had happened, saying they'd heard I was caught, I told them they'd heard wrong. That evening, knowing the royal guard would be coming at nightfall, I left them and went to the pub, had a nice mutton dinner, and didn't think more about it except that I'd have to find me a new gang. Only, I get the news that me mates were too wily for the law. How I got the news was that me mates showed up at the pub, grabbed me, and threw me in a sack. They took me to a cave and put me in a barrel and hung me from the ceiling. I was in there seven days before I finally died."

May sat stunned.

"Terrible, ain't it?"

"Yes," May breathed.

"Can you believe me own mates treated me that way?"

"But . . . you betrayed them."

"That's true. But two wrongs don't make a right," John insisted, crossing his emaciated arms.

"No. I guess not."

John's cracked, dry lips turned downward. "You're taking their side."

"No, I'm not. It's just, don't you feel bad for betraying them?"

"Sure I do, lassie. But I'm a changed man now. All I can do now is be the best knave I can be."

May stared. "But . . . spirits don't change. . . ."

John cleared his throat. "I guess that's what they say." He shrunk from May defensively. "Ain't you ever done a betrayal to one of yer friends?"

May thought, then picked at her fingernails, not meeting his eyes. "I don't really have any friends."

"Well, that's a shame."

"I have a cat."

"A cat's not a person."

"Yeah, but he's my friend." May thought of the night at the lake and crumpled a little inside. She thought of how she had never realized just how much of a friend Somber Kitty had been. He had been her best and *only* friend. "And I guess I did betray him."

"See?" John smiled with satisfaction. "But still, I say a cat ain't really a friend. I hate cats meself. Except in stew. I liked a good cat stew when I was livin'. I used to make up a mean batch for me mates."

May winced, feeling depressed. Even a man with cockroaches crawling out of his mouth had more friends than she did.

"Pumpkin's sort of . . . my friend," she offered hopefully.

John laughed. "Ha! A cat and a house ghost. That's rich. You won't find a house ghost that's worth much in the way of smarts *or* courage. When the chips are down, he'll run the other way, mark me words. And as fer cats—well, ye won't find one in the whole o' the Ever After."

May pondered what John had said about Pumpkin. It *did* seem like the truth. "Why do you think the animals were banished, Mr. Jibber?"

John shrugged. "Who can explain anything Evil Bo Cleevil does? A bunch of ghouls that worked for him rounded up the cats first. The ghouls ain't very bright, and I think they had a hard time telling cats apart from the other animals. I don't know that he didn't just decide to get rid of all the animals altogether, to make it simpler. It was right around the time we started hearing reports of the Bogey. Lord knows why he didn't send the Bogey's dogs to do the job. I reckon they could tear a cat apart in less than a second flat. Curious, that."

May sidled a little closer to John, thinking about the Bogey's dogs. She hugged her arms around herself.

"Look over there," John said, pointing across the sand in another direction. There was just the tiniest hint of movement. "That's the Interrealm Soarway. It goes all the way from the Southwest Portal up around the city, where it intersects a set of train tracks that run all the way to the Far North. Quite a marvel, it is, the train. It stops outside Ether, and that's it. Doesn't stop again till the tip-top of the realm. Though nobody rides it anymore, if they can help it.

"I believe it goes all the way to North Farm, where yer blanket is from." May's throat tightened. "That's one place you wouldn't find me goin', even fer treasure. There's nothing but strange spirits up that way. Powerful types, like what made yer blanket. How'd you say you got that, anyway?"

May's heart sped up. "We just . . . found it." She wished he hadn't said anything about the train. Knowing it even existed filled her with shame.

John nodded, seeming suspicious. "Anyway, no need to worry about the North—Ether is our concern. Ye see"—he pointed— "the city is surrounded by a high wall, with a gate at each corner. Each gate is guarded by a sniffing phantom."

He leaned toward her and looked her in the eye for emphasis as he said this, sending a waft of horrible stench over her face. "Ye know what that is?"

May shook her head. She'd heard it before—even from John— and it didn't sound very scary.

"The thieves used to dress up to get into the city, once Evil Bo Cleevil's spirits started taking over. But Cleevil caught on to that.

So he brought up the sniffing phantoms from the Stench Swamps down in South Place. Highly developed noses. Now you have to get checked for scents before you can get through the gates."

"What kind of scents?"

"Oh, the scent of thievery, for one"—John sniffed his armpit, and then poked her in the side—"and the stench of life. But we'll fix that."

May's mind darted to Lucius. She didn't want to think about it. "And if we're caught?"

"They throw ye in a gadget called an incarnerator. Ye come out a bug or a worm or else a rock, and that gets sent in the mail to yer nearest relative. Me cousin Iago got turned into a twig that I kept in me pocket fer a while, till it got washed out in the laundry." May's face must have shown the worry she felt, because he winked and added, "Don't worry. Ye stick with me, and I'll get ye through."

May wondered what she and Pumpkin would do without him. They'd be lost. Suddenly she felt guilty for doubting him. "Mr. Jibber?"

"Yes, dearie?" He leaned an ear close to her. "Speak up."

"Thank you for taking us."

John grinned, his deep-set eyes getting a little moist. "Why, it's good fer me to be challenged. Eternity gets real stale, I'll tell ye. Sometimes I don't think it'd be half bad to disappear into nothingness after all." His limbs shook for a moment, and then settled.

"What is it?" May asked, touching his arm. She was getting less and less sensitive to the cold zaps of the spirits.

John forced a small, nervous laugh. "Just a goose walking across my grave."

With that, he turned and drifted back down the hill.

Far across the realm, Somber Kitty paced a large, stone-walled room, occasionally gazing toward a large open window, like a caged tiger.

On the first day of his captivity his net had been substituted with a triangular room at the top of the tallest pyramid in the Egyptian settlement. It had a sumptuous carpet, a gorgeous linen scratching post, and gilded catnip balls. There was also a breathtaking view of a city far in the distance. But looking at the vista made Somber Kitty meow darkly.

He placed his paws on the sill of the window, sticking his head out into the dry desert air and looking toward the ground longingly. As he did so a large group of people, who were milling about at the base of the pyramid, fell on their knees and bowed their heads to the sand.

They did this every time Somber Kitty showed his face. At first it had made him curious, but now he barely noticed. He had no way of knowing that the Egyptian spirits had adopted him as a god. And if he had, it wouldn't have made him any less melancholy.

With his paws still on the sill he looked around the room once again for a way to escape, and then turned to the window with a mew. He peered at the people below thoughtfully as if they might be able to answer the one question that really mattered.

"Meay?"

CHAPTER TWENTY-THREE

The City of Ether

May woke to wet drops landing on her face. She blinked her eyes. Large green drops were falling from the sky, and John the Jibber was sitting beside her. He had her knapsack in his hands.

"Er, time to go, lass."

May sat up, her eyes darting to her bag.

"What's happening?"

John laughed. "Just a little ectoplasm shower. Get yer house ghost up and let's go." He handed her the sack as if that's what he'd been meaning to do. May looked at it for a moment, uneasy.

She shook Pumpkin awake. He grunted and sat up, rubbing his eyes and looking around. He grinned pleasantly at May, let out a long, leisurely yawn, then he stuck out his purple tongue to collect a few ectoplasm drops. "Can't I sleep a little longer?"

May groaned and pulled him up. They climbed the hill together behind John.

"Look lively, Pumpkin. There'll be no time fer yer laziness today," John chided.

Pumpkin stuck out his tongue at John's back, but sucked it in again when he saw May frowning at him. As they reached the ridge, and Pumpkin got a view of the city, he thrust his fingers into his mouth and dropped his mischievous mood altogether.

John had knelt down and was digging in the dirt, and now he pulled out a handful of worms and centipedes, then dropped them into May's hair and down into her bathing suit.

"Ah!" May jumped up and down, trying to brush them off.

"Stand still, girl!" John said, grabbing her wrist to stop her from jumping. "Do ye want to make it past the sniffing phantoms or not?"

May considered. Then she let her arms drop to her sides.

"Now, I gathered up some mold this morning, and I've got this stuff on the bottom of my shoe that's been here for about fifty years. . . ." John reached beneath his shoe and pulled out a decayed mass of brown goo. Then he rubbed it over both hands and smeared it on May's arms and legs. May thought she might vomit. She retched a few times and held her nose.

"There, that gets rid of the living scent nicely. Now for me."

John reached into his pocket and pulled out a tiny bottle of clear liquid, then squirted himself several times. May read the label: Crook-Be-Gone.

"Mr. Jibber, shouldn't this wait till we're closer to the city?"

"What do you mean, lass?"

"Well, won't it wear off before we get there?"

"My dear, it'll take us ten minutes to get to the city. Perhaps fifteen."

May blinked at him several times, then looked across the long wide plain separating them from the tiny city in the distance. It had to be hundreds of miles away. "Really?"

"It's right there." John pointed in the same direction she was already looking.

"But it'll take days to get there." She looked at Pumpkin, as if to verify she wasn't crazy.

Pumpkin, though he didn't need to cover up his normal ghost scent, had dug up a handful of worms anyway and was dropping them into his ragged shirt one by one. "The City of Ether's in a wormhole," he said absently, dangling a long slimy worm next to his neck, "*everybody* knows that."

John started walking across the field, with Pumpkin traipsing along behind him with his worms, leaving May with no choice but to follow. She trailed behind, only noticing after several steps that something strange was happening to the view as they walked. The farther John and Pumpkin got from May, the bigger they seemed to get, compared to the city. Or was it that the city was getting smaller? Yes, the more they walked, the less and less the city looked like something huge in the distance and more like something tiny on the ground. May hurried to keep up with them, catching up breathlessly when they came to a halt. All three of them stared down at their feet. There was the city, the size of an anthill. It reached to May's shins and was surrounded by thousands of tiny curved pebbles stuck in the ground. A spiral pattern was furrowed in the dirt encircling the city scene.

"Wow," May said, kneeling down. To her astonishment she could just make out tiny figures drifting up and down the tiny streets. "I can't believe it." She reached out a hand to touch the top of the tallest building, a white structure that towered over the rest of the city, but as she did, a powerful zap traveled up and down her spine, knocking her backward. She landed on the ground with a thud.

"My, yer daft, lass. It's protected, of course. Wouldn't do at all if it weren't," John said.

"Thanks for warning me," May muttered, standing up, embarrassed. John and Pumpkin looked at each other, then at her, and burst into laughter.

"What?" May went to pat her hair, and noticed it was sticking straight up. "Oh, ha ha." A tiny smile snuck onto her lips. She stuck her hands in the dirt and grabbed two fistfuls, rubbing them into her hair.

"Don't ye know about wormholes, dearie?" John asked when she was finished, swiping a jolly tear from his eye.

May shook her head.

"There are lots of them all over the realm, but this is the biggest one. Wormholes make space all distorted. So a giant city can fit into a tiny area."

May stared at it. "But, how do we get in there?"

"Why, right there."

John nodded to his left. Beaten through the dirt a few feet away was a smooth path that seemed to lead forward, away from the city. A sign beside it announced it to be PAIN IN THE FOOT TRAIL.

"Well, come on, then," John said, walking ahead. Pumpkin and May trailed behind him. The train trickled to a stop.

Though the trail had looked like it would go straight, it actually curved hard to the left a few paces in, and curved and curved, making a wide circle around the city.

"What are we doing?" May asked.

"Ay, lass, it's a wonder you ever made it to the grotto in the first place with that feeble mind of yers. We're going to the city, remember?"

May scowled, feeling foolish. "But we're walking in circles."

"We're walking in a *spiral*," John answered, shaking his head in exasperation.

"Yes, a *spiral*," Pumpkin added in a superior tone, also shaking his head.

May fought back a sigh of frustration. She didn't know how that was much different, but she kept her mouth shut. And after a few seconds she realized, where the city had gotten smaller before, it was now bigger, closer. With every few steps it got much larger in front of them, the spikes that surrounded it taking on a more distinct shape.

By the time the path finally came to an end, May had gone speechless. They were at the edge of an enormous, desolate cemetery, filled with tens of thousands of gravestones. Across it gaped the enormous City of Ether.

"Ohhh," Pumpkin moaned. May moaned in her heart too. It looked to be a hundred times the size of New York, which—in the Saint Agatha's brochures—had looked gigantic. It glowed brightly, with an enormous, slate gray rock wall surrounding it and impossible rooftops reaching toward the stars. And these were all dwarfed by the tallest building, the soaring spire of which disappeared into the dusky starry sky, so that the point of it was invisible.

"There"—John pointed a bony, dirt-caked finger toward the place where the spire disappeared into the sky—"is where the Book lies."

Pumpkin let out another groan.

"Oh," May whispered, feeling very small in all sorts of ways. "Up there?" It was so high. Way, way too high. May thanked her lucky stars that John the Jibber was with them. Maybe he would go up to the top and bring the Book down. Without him she would have turned around right then and there and given up.

Beneath the shadow of the city, and outside the wall, a huge shape was moving back and forth, with what looked like arms stretching out and making long scooping motions toward the ground.

"Is that . . ." May brushed her soggy hair aside.

"The south gate sniffing phantom," John finished for her. "Sure is. And this,"—John pointed to the field full of millions of headstones and gaping grave holes—"is where the city ghosts come for haunting."

May's eyes met Pumpkin's.

"Well, we best get moving, you two. We want to miss rush hour, that's certain."

May tightened her death shroud around her and started walking.

They picked their way across the graves, which May realized were what had appeared as pebbles from above. She and Pumpkin zigzagged back and forth behind John the Jibber, careful not to get too close to any of the holes for fear of falling in. John was a faster zigger and zagger, however, and he was soon several feet ahead of them.

"Now, no need to be squeamish, you two. Now's not the time for lollygagging. When the bells on that yonder church ring midnight, the spirits'll come out for work, and if we're out here then, we'll have *our* work cut out for us."

May tried to pick up her pace, stepping faster around the stones and taking longer strides.

"That's it, c'mon." John turned his gaunt, curved back toward them and picked up his pace.

Up ahead May could see a bridge rising from the ground to the top of the gate and a line of spirits straggling its way along it. The sniffing phantom stood beside the bridge like a tall white pillar. He glowed with faint white light and had the face of an old man covered in snow, with droopy wrinkled eyelids over pale gray eyes, each the size of a small house. His nose was his most striking and exceptional feature—it was large and hooked and had enormous flaring nostrils to which he lifted one spirit after another with his massive palms. Each time he did, he made a deafening sniffing sound, and the spirit in his hands was sucked right up into one of his nostrils. He had to blow hard to get it out, using his hands as a hankie to catch the spirit before laying it down on the bridge again and nudging it toward a small archway through which it disappeared. Pumpkin reached for May's hand, his frigid white fingers finding their way into hers.

On the walls of the city huge stone gargoyles perched, looking ready to pounce and wearing Holo-Pix cameras strapped around their necks. Behind them rose a giant clock tower, announcing the time to be eleven minutes before midnight.

Behind the phantom was a giant green can emblazoned with the word INCARNERATOR and covered tightly with a lid.

May could see, when John turned to look back at her, that a deep wrinkle had creased his brow. "Almost fergot. Don't ferget to hold your breath, lassie. Breath smell is a dead giveaway."

The fear on his face made May's own courage falter. She adjusted her death shroud nervously. "Are you okay, Mr. Jibber?"

"I'm a bit nervous, that's all. Listen, if we get separated for any reason, we're staying at the Final Rest Hotel, room nine thousand nine hundred ninety-nine, got it?"

"We won't get separated, will we?"

John grinned falsely, showing his black rotted teeth. "Nah. Ye got nothing to worry about."

They got to the foot of the bridge, May and Pumpkin's heads falling back on their necks to stare up at the phantom. "Ohhh, my," Pumpkin groaned. May tightened her grip on his hand. "It'll be okay," she whispered.

"Well, hold on to yer booty," John said.

May tugged on Pumpkin's hand, and they followed him up the walk.

The group of spirits in front of them appeared to be a family of three—two parents and a very little girl. The little girl kept turning to goggle at May and make funny faces. May crouched down and made funny faces back.

"Why are you going to the city?" the girl asked. Her eyes were large and gaunt.

"I'm looking for something important. What about you?"

"Mommy says the territories aren't safe anymore. She says at least the High Ghosts in the city will look out for us."

"Oh." May nodded. She wondered who the High Ghosts were.

The family inched ahead, the mother tugging her daughter along by the hand. Her small feet floated out behind her as she was dragged, then she came to rest again above the walkway, the tatters of her ragged dress settling around her.

May held Pumpkin's hand tighter, watching the spirits being

lifted and sucked one by one into the phantom's nose, then dropped by the small archway up top. Each floated through the arch and disappeared, seeming to fall out of sight. Some gave a little squeal as they went.

The giant white hand descended right in front of May, pinching the mother between one giant thumb and one giant forefinger, and lifting her way up out of sight. It was all May could do to keep from stumbling backward. The mother came back down and waited there for the rest of her family. The same happened to the father. While she waited, her big blue eyes huge, the little girl locked her gaze on May. Then her eyes seemed to widen in recognition. "You're not dead," she whispered.

A shock ran its way up and down May's spine. "Yes, I am," she lied.

But the girl was reaching into the top of her dress and in another moment, the gleaming Bogey whistle appeared.

"No, you're not." The girl narrowed her eyes and lifted the whistle to her tiny pink lips just as large fingers descended and lifted her up. The whistle was knocked out of her hands, and the girl disappeared into the air. When she came back down, she gaped at May in horror, then ran toward her mother while the enormous hand closed around May's body and lifted her up.

May felt the roller-coaster feeling of her stomach dropping as she sped through the air, up, up, and up. She was being lifted so fast that the force blew her black hair around her face and some of the cockroaches flew out. As soon as she caught her breath, she sucked it in and held it, her cheeks puffing out like balloons. She had the stabbing, prickly feeling she had gotten in third grade, when she'd cheated on a math test. It was the throbbing, gut-pounding feeling that she was a big fake about to be caught.

The giant fingers rolled her into the palm of his phantom hand and, May sat up, face-to-face with a gaping nostril that was twice as wide as May was tall. There was a great roaring sniff, and May went flying upward, her body catching deep in the nostril, like a plug. Everything around her had gone black, and May wriggled, nearly retching when she realized that she was rubbing against a layer of slime, her lungs ready to burst.

Sniff sniff sniff. With every sniff May was pulled upward, deeper into the nose, her bare arms rubbing against the slime. She couldn't hold her breath anymore. The phantom began to blow. . . .

Puff. May's breath went rushing out of her. As quickly as it had happened, she sucked more air in and closed her mouth again. But it was too late. There was another loud sniff, and she was sucked back in.

Sniff.

She could feel the phantom's head tilting slightly. *Sniff sniff sniff sniff sniff.*

Please please please.

Ding.

For a moment everything around May vibrated, and then she was shot out of the phantom's nose in a big huff.

Ding.

To her left the clock tower was striking twelve, and she peered over the phantom's giant thumb to see that the gate had cracked open and that crowds of spirits, thousands, had begun pouring out into the cemetery.

The phantom gave May another, gentler, sniff, then began to

lower her. Again May's stomach dropped as she sailed through the air, before arriving back down at the top of the wall and landing gently on the walkway. She put her hand over her chest. Her heart was thumping against her ribs heavily. She peered around for the little girl with the whistle and met her sunken blue eyes as she was being dragged away by her mother. "That's nonsense, honey," May could hear the woman saying as they disappeared through the archway. "There are no Live Ones in the Ever After." The girl extended her pointer finger one last time toward May, and then a twin pair of squeals, and they were gone.

Pumpkin was the next to disappear. He came back quickly, smiling with pride. "I don't know what you two were worried about," he said, brushing his hands together as if he had actually accomplished something. And then John the Jibber went up.

May squeezed up against Pumpkin nervously and watched the sky. Far above them the phantom pulled John close to his face, sucked him into his nose, then quickly puffed him out. A hiss of white breath came out of his mouth.

"No, sir." John's voice echoed down to the bridge, sharp and edgy as a knife. "Knave?" Chuckle chuckle. "I've been told I smell like knave before, but no, sir. Never nicked a thing in this life or the other one."

May tightened her grip on Pumpkin, her whole body going cold. The eyes of several of the spirits on the bridge glued themselves onto the scene above.

"Not even a pack o' gum. A good, honest boy, I've always . . . Sir, I resent that. If you just put me down, I'll forgive your rudeness. Wait, no!" The phantom's hand swung downward, toward the incarnerator. The lid flung open, all on its own, with a creak.

Everywhere spirits peered toward the spot. Murmurs drifted from the crowd.

"Pumpkin!" May whispered, grabbing Pumpkin. "No!"

An agonizing moment passed as the giant hand soared. John's legs swung into view, and then the rest of him, so that he was dangling from the phantom's finger. Hurling himself with gymnastlike grace, he swung from the giant pinky onto the phantom's sleeve, and then began to clamber up his arm, holding tight to the fabric of the cloak. May had to clamp her hands over her mouth to keep from screaming. The crowd of spirits itself was stunned into silence, its surface spiky with pointing fingers.

John scrambled down the phantom's chest, but with one long, gaunt arm the phantom swiped at him, and he went flying into the air. He landed on the sand below the walkway.

"Oh," Pumpkin moaned. He looked at May. "Do something!"

May was rooted to her spot helplessly, her mind racing. *Do what?* What in the world could she do?

Several hundred spirits backed into a wide circle around John, who looked back at May once in a horror-stricken plea for help.

May balled the fabric of her death shroud in both hands. She dropped to her knees and tore open her knapsack, rifling through it for something, *anything* that might help. Maybe if she threw John a teleport token, or used the comfort blanket to . . .

Then she stopped. The photo of May the Amazon stared back at her.

May glanced up. John had turned and run into the crowd. But for all his many steps, the phantom took just one and plucked him out easily. Again the giant hand swung him toward the incarnerator.

May looked back down at the photo and set her jaw. She *was* that girl. With renewed courage May clasped the hem of her death shroud as she rose from her knees. "Wait!" she yelled at the top of her lungs. In one flash movement, she whipped off her shroud and waved it violently above her head, then shoved it into Pumpkin's arms. "Over here!"

Silence fell over those nearest her, and all eyes, even those of the phantom, turned to May. For a moment, everyone froze.

Then the spirits on the bridge went into chaos, plunging off the sides, rushing away from her, screaming. Within seconds most of them had their Bogey whistles to their lips. The phantom stumbled backward. As he did, he dropped John—right into the incarnerator.

May screamed. Pumpkin screamed. But John's scream was the most earth-shattering shriek May had ever heard.

The Jibber went hurtling into the can, at the same moment the phantom's hand took a giant defensive swipe at May and Pumpkin. Seeing it just in time, May grabbed her knapsack with one hand and the back of Pumpkin's shirt with the other and yanked him through the archway.

Still screaming they flew forward, landing on a silver slide that swept them downward, hurtling them into a pile on the ground inside the city gates. They quickly pulled each other up, clutching each other's arms like survivors of a shipwreck.

At a glance they saw they were on a wide boulevard that shot like an arrow between the enormous buildings of Ether. Alleys stretched this way and that off the boulevard. And all around them stood a horde of stunned spirits, frozen in their activities of moments ago—pushing baby carriages, driving carriages, selling soul cakes from gleaming carts. The spirits watched the two intruders for a moment. A man in brown knickerbockers pointed and screamed. And then they all scattered like marbles.

Above it all an ear-piercing siren began to wail, and May looked up, gazing at the impossible heights of the spiky gray buildings. A deafening crack behind her brought her attention to the city wall. "Oooooh," Pumpkin wailed. The stone gargoyles overhead had begun to move, layers of rock shattering and sliding off them, claws stretching and wings flapping slowly into motion.

"Oh, my . . ." Both May's and Pumpkin's heads lolled back on their necks senselessly.

"Do you hear that?" Pumpkin cried.

"Of course I hear . . . ," May snapped, but Pumpkin was already shaking his head. Their eyes met. The world around them seemed to go still.

"Not that," he said, tucking a finger between his lips, waiting for another sound, and then pulled the finger out and pointed. "That."

May strained her ears. Above the siren, above the crumbling of rock behind them, there was the sound of dogs.

May grabbed her shroud from Pumpkin's hands and fastened it around her neck. And then they ran. May's legs kicked behind her, throwing up gray dust and debris. Pumpkin floated at her back, covering his head with his skinny arms and hunching his shoulders.

"In there!" May shouted, pointing to an alley just to their left. A giant swish brushed past her ear, and a pair of talons sliced the air next to her extended hand. She screamed and looked up to see the gaping jaws of the gargoyle poised above her head.

Scraaaawwwwwwwkkkkk!

They entered the alley at a bursting pace, and the gargoyle vanished. May turned to see he had crashed into the entrance, too large to fit through it.

Now they were in a tangle of alleys, all cutting right and left and looping in on one another. May, with Pumpkin behind, crisscrossed at a sprint, trying to dodge two, then three gargoyles that soared above, unable to squeeze into the alley behind them, but right on their trail. Sharp talons swooped within inches of them, several times, forcing them to duck or roll across the ground, then get up and keep moving.

They were just turning another sharp corner when suddenly the area before them opened up into a wide space, and the next thing she knew, May was tumbling forward, landing underwater with a splash. She spluttered to the surface, finding herself in a canal full of green liquid. The smell of it hit May hard, taking her breath away before she looked up to see Pumpkin several feet in front of her on dry land, getting farther and farther away. She was being carried quickly away from him by the stream.

"Pumpkin!" she called. Pumpkin, his arms and legs flailing, was running after her along the side of the canal, reaching out his skinny arms toward her and calling "Wait!" She tried to paddle back but the current was too strong. She turned to looked behind her and groaned when she saw there was a tunnel up ahead. When May looked back at Pumpkin, she had time to see a gargoyle—its talons cracking loudly, its giant teeth bared—swoop in just above his head, before she disappeared into blackness.

Far beyond the walls of Ether, at a settlement that was merely a gaggle of tiny triangles in the distance to anyone looking, Somber Kitty lay on his back, swatting irritably at a ball of silk thread that had been hung from the ceiling. He had already rubbed his nose and cheeks against the jewels that had been piled all over the floor for him to play with that morning. Miserably he had batted around a gold and diamond staff, watching it roll across the floor. Occasionally he had laid down in the sun that poured onto the chamber floor, his bald body stretching as long and drawn out as a sigh.

Whenever Somber Kitty looked away from his string toward the direction of the window, the sight of the tiny city on the horizon filled him with a strange sense of dread. The dread was lying heavily on his heart, when he heard the door to his chamber slide open, and he hopped up, his body spinning in the air and landing on all fours.

The woman standing in the doorway was the one who brought his milk tray every afternoon. She padded in, knelt on the floor in front of him, and bowed. Then she poured the milk into the gilded bowl by his bed.

As she repeated this ritual now, Somber Kitty scanned the area behind her, his tail going straight as a lightning rod. Usually when the woman walked into the chamber, she closed the door behind her.

The open doorway seemed to wink at Somber Kitty. And Somber Kitty's ears twitched in reply.

His slitty green eyes moved to the woman, still leaning over the bowl and dribbling honey into the milk. Then the eyes moved to the door. Back and forth.

Somber Kitty's body coiled up like a bedspring. He knew if he hesitated, the moment would be lost. In one glorious movement, he flew across the room, not landing until he was already through the doorway.

Behind him he heard the woman yell something, but he was already moving, dashing down the dark hallway, his claws sliding along stone so that he bumped into every wall he met. Finally he came to a place where he could turn either right or left. Again, without a moment's hesitation, he turned left and ran full speed, somehow coming to a perfect, graceful halt right at a huge square opening. He teetered at the edge of the open air, glancing along the wall that angled out beneath him. He surveyed the scene on the ground below. Impossibly far below. He looked behind him, seeing the group of guards running toward him.

Then he leaped forward, curled himself into a ball, and rolled.

CHAPTER TWENTY-FOUR

May, Alone

t was several minutes before May emerged into the light again. She had just begun to think this was how her life would end, drowning in a stream of ectoplasm, when the glimmer of dusky light made its way into the darkness, and she finally drifted out into the open air. She caught at a brick poking out of the sidewalk above and latched on to it, dragging herself onto the cobblestones, and finally, pulling her death shroud over herself.

Panting hard, she looked around and saw that she was in a deserted alley lined along one side with solemn, gray, ornately carved buildings. Wherever she'd drifted, it was very quiet and far from the chaos of the boulevard.

The gargoyles were gone. Pumpkin was gone. John the Jibber was gone.

May hung her head between her knees, fighting back the sharp pain in her heart. In the distance she could hear the sound of dogs somewhere in the city.

She was completely alone.

May fell onto her back, watching the zipping stars, which tonight were covered lightly in clouds, and feeling the darkest despair.

"It's all my fault," she squeaked to the sky, thinking of John, and Lucius, and Pumpkin. She closed her eyes, her lids forcing twin tears out of the corners and down her cheeks, and where they hid in her ectoplasm-soaked hair.

Pumpkin, Lucius, and John were gone. And she was still a million miles from her home.

May curled into a tight ball on her side and lay still for a long time. Whenever she'd been sad at home, she had always had Somber Kitty to tuck up in her arms to catch her tears on top of his soft ears. Now she had nobody.

When May finally opened her eyes again, she rolled slowly onto her back and blinked at the sky, squinting at a strange cloud that had settled directly above her. It took a familiar shape—of a tree, with eyes peering down at her.

May scrambled to sit up. But by the time she did and blinked at the sky again, the cloud had been blown into a new shape.

May looked around and adjusted her shroud nervously. Slowly she climbed to her feet and gazed at the sky again. Was the Lady looking out for her? Or frowning down on her?

"I just want everything to be like it was before," she said out loud.

A *scrawwwwwk* sounded in the distance.

May shivered. She should probably hide for a while, just in case. And then, when the city had calmed down and the sound of dogs had died, she could go look for Pumpkin. If there was any hope of finding him at all.

She scanned the street again.

The building straight ahead of her stood wide open. Above the door it read MAUSOLEUM 387A.

Walking very slowly, May peered through the open doorway. The mausoleum was pitch-dark inside, clearly deserted. She shifted from foot to foot, then stared up at the sky, then back at the door. She walked into the mausoleum at a snail's pace, feeling her way along a wall.

Pssssspppppsss.

Voices were whispering in the darkness.

May shrank back against the wall, her heart racing.

Suddenly a blue flame leaped into the darkness, illuminating a tall starlight and a man holding it, surrounded by a circle of other spirits. May shrank farther into a corner and tried to make her breathing as low and quiet as possible.

"You see, that wasn't so bad," the man holding the starlight said, pushing his glasses up onto the bridge of his nose with his free hand. "Now let's try again. Laura, this time you do the honors."

A pretty woman with curly black hair leaned forward and blew out the light.

"Hoooooh." Voices chimed in from all over. "Hooooooooh."

The inside of May's throat began to itch from the dry, stuffy air of the room. She dared to put her hand to her throat to rub it.

The candle leaped back to life, and she froze.

"You see. If you just do your 'Hooooh' chant, it'll really calm you down. Feel the positive energy. Say to your—"

Cough.

May couldn't help it. It was one of those coughs that just popped out.

The spirit with the starlight locked his eyes on her. The others turned to follow his gaze and shifted around in surprise. The woman with the black curly hair frowned—her upper body having come detached from her lower body at the waist—and absently pulled herself back together again.

May waited for a scream, pointing fingers.

The ghost who'd been speaking cleared his throat. "Hi, friend, can we help you?"

"Um, um, yes . . . um, I'm lost. I just stepped in here by mistake. Sorry about that, I'll be . . ." May was tiptoeing toward the door.

"Wait."

Her stomach doing a little flip, May turned.

"You're not really lost, are you?"

"Umm . . ."

"It's nothing to be ashamed of," the man said. "You've come to the right place. Mausoleum 387A. We don't judge one another here. I'm Albert."

"I'm May."

"Well, May, lots of specters are scared of the dark." Albert smiled warmly. "Especially those who died at night. Laura here just got in from a night-boating accident. How did you die, May?"

May's mind raced back to the night of the lake. "Um . . . I drowned."

"It was probably at night, am I right?"

May nodded.

"That'll do it. I myself died in a caving accident in Peru. Don't worry, you'll get over it. We were just doing our darkness chants. Something to help you feel less afraid when you're assigned a house to haunt. Have you gone to get your assignment yet? You can be arrested if you don't, you know."

May shook her head, befuddled.

"Mmmm. Well, anyway, here's the chant." Albert pursed his lips, his eyes on May's. "'Hooooooooohhhhhh.' You try it."

May glanced at the doorway again.

"Okay, here we go. I'm going to blow out the starlight candle. Are you ready?"

Everyone nodded and muttered that they were.

Albert held out the candle for May to blow on. She did, and joined in when everyone started hooohing. They did this several more times.

"Oh, I feel much better, thank you!" May said, backing up quickly.

"Wait."

"No, I really have to go."

"Well, if you must. But be careful out there. The gargoyles have been out. Supposedly there's a Live One on the loose."

May froze.

"Say what you want, but I feel sorry for that poor soul," one woman said, shaking her head and tsk-tsk-tsking.

"Can you imagine running into one? That would be the thrill of my afterlife! I'd have my whistle to my lips faster than you can say 'undead,'" another woman added.

Everyone agreed.

"And I heard there was a knave helping her. And a ghost. My wife was just calling about it." Albert looked around at the other specters apologetically, gesturing to the small skullophone clipped to his belt. "Of all the unlikely—"

"Did the ghost get away?" May leaped forward, startling Albert.

"Oh dear, don't scare me like that. She didn't say. She said the knave was incarcerated." May's stomach flopped sickly. "And oh, wait, the ghost, let's see . . . she did say, I think he escaped. Frightful ugly ghost, by reports. So many ghosts *are*. . . ."

May, her insides lighting up with hope, rushed toward the door, then on second thought, she turned around one last time.

"Hey, do you know where the Final Rest Hotel is?" she gushed. May knew it was unlikely Pumpkin would even remember the name, but if he did, he might find his way there.

Albert tapped his chin. "I think it's on Sewerside. Not a very pretty place. Are you sure you want to go there?"

"Thank you."

May slid outside and looked both ways, up and down the narrow cobblestone street.

May walked through the city like a ghost, mixing with spirits up and down the busy streets, and drifting through the dark alleyways that crisscrossed Ether like a giant web, searching for Pumpkin.

She had decided the hotel would be her last resort. Most likely, if Pumpkin had escaped, he was somewhere in the city, lost.

All around were marble mausoleums, small pointy churches, tall apartment buildings with broken windows and fire-singed doorways, grand hotels with vaulted roofs, and old stone cottages, temples, and shrines. Every time May turned a corner, she expected to see Pumpkin standing down the next street, but the city was vast and crowded, and she finally began to feel discouraged. She wondered if she shouldn't head straight to the Final Rest after all.

She came to a stop in front of Specter's Sweets Suite, which had a variety of skeleton bread and skull cakes in the window, beneath a sign that read FRESH! SACRIFICED TODAY AT VARIOUS WORLD ALTARS!

May's stomach growled. She laid down her bag on the bare sidewalk next to a skullophone booth and rummaged through it. All of her food was covered in green gook, and most of it had disintegrated.

She looked back up at the sign, then into her bag again, pulling out one of her transport tokens. Then she squared her shoulders and walked into the shop. "I want three of those soul cakes," she said loudly, pointing to the second shelf behind the chubby man at the register, who wore a big white baker's hat. "But will you take this for them?" She couldn't remember ever being so bold with a stranger in her life, but the words had come out easily. She blushed and held out the token.

The man surveyed the token and grinned at her. *"Oui."*

May handed over her coin, and the man grabbed a pair of tongs and lifted three soul cakes into a bag.

"Thank you."

"Newly dead, eh?" he asked with a thick French accent.

May nodded. "Yes, sir."

"Don't forget to peek up your houze azzignment," he advised.

May thanked him, then stepped out into the street and bit into her first soul cake ravenously, hardly noticing where her feet were carrying her. When she looked up, she stumbled backward a few steps.

Ahead of her was the Edifice, gleaming white against the gray of the other buildings, several blocks wide, and soaring into the sky. May craned her head back on her neck to take it in, unable to see where the building ended, then slid her eyes back down the sides to stare at the gleaming golden doors, shielding her eyes from the glow. Finally she took in the area around her.

She was standing in a large square packed with thousands of spirits—ghosts and specters milling along in one endless line that curled around itself over and over again, its tail disappearing around a corner and down a wide boulevard. For a moment May shrank back with a shock, sure that the crowd had something to do with her—that they all had gathered because they'd heard there was a Live One in the city.

"It's impressive, isn't it?"

A teenage girl in overalls, missing her left arm, had just floated in front of her.

May focused on her with difficulty, she was so dazed. She nodded.

The girl leaned in close to May and whispered, "Hard to believe Bo Cleevil owns it now, huh? What's the afterworld coming to?"

May followed the girl's eyes up to a set of enormous white steps that led to the doors of the Edifice. Staggered all along the steps, their black teeth dripping and their bodies slick with slime, stood a whole troop of more than fifty ghouls, looking over the crowd suspiciously, scuttering back and forth beside the line that wound its way up the steps and inspecting each ghost by poking and prodding them with the points of their spears.

Two gargoyles lay on their haunches in front of the doors, and two others perched at either corner at the top of the doors, ready to pounce. And in the middle of it all, at the very center of the landing and standing several stories tall, was a marble statue, its arms crossed, its features hidden in the folds of a marble cloak. Only its eyes showed, glowing a deep, burning red from underneath a marble hood.

May felt a shudder run from the tips of her toes to the ends of her hair. She didn't need anyone to tell her who the figure was. She just knew it deep down in the very root of her soul.

"They say a spirit's more likely to fit through the eye of a needle than get into the Edifice unnoticed," the girl continued in her low voice, not noticing that May had turned the ghostly shade of pale that was more suitable to her surroundings. "All sorts of secret stuff in there. Nobody knows what."

May let out the deep breath she suddenly realized she'd been holding. How on Earth had John the Jibber ever made it in? If she'd had even the tiniest hope of getting to the Book on her own since she'd lost him, that now disappeared.

"It's a shame. The city's gotten to be so serious since the Dark Spirits moved in. So many rules. Well, that's the afterlife for you, I guess. Just the way it goes."

The weight of despair that had been with May for the past few hours dragged her down even farther. "I guess," she murmured.

"You may as well get in the line."

May once again tore her eyes from the Edifice. "The line?"

"For haunting assignments, from the High Ghost Court. I could tell you were new." The girl smiled sadly, chomping gum between her teeth. "Every spirit has to go. It's where you get assigned your house to haunt."

"Oh."

May surveyed the crowd.

The girl continued, waggling her left stump sociably. "You can request a house if you want. If another spirit is already there, the High Ghosts will just assign you somewhere else."

May blinked at her. "Who . . . who are the High Ghosts?"

"Gosh, you really just got run over by the potato wagon, didn't you? It was a tractor that did *me* in." The girl blew a bubble with her gum. "They're part of Ghost Court, the highest law in the land. They still get their orders from the North, though the court's in the Edifice. I'm sure it makes Bo Cleevil crazy angry. But he can't do a darn thing about it. Not for now, anyway. I guess he'll figure it out eventually."

The girl nodded over her shoulder. "You better get going. End of the line's that way. If you get there in time, they'll give you a number to mark your place. See?"

Chomping, the girl held up her number, which was scrawled on a glowing tile: 30,090.

"Uh, thanks." Glancing from time to time at the Edifice, May drifted along the crowd, hoping that she might catch a glimpse of a round pumpkin head and a yellow tuft of hair. She happened to see the front of a newspaper held in someone's hands. May could just make out part of one headline: LIVE ONE BREACHES CITY GATES . . .

Suddenly the crowd began to rustle and move about. Everyone gazed at the landing on top of the courthouse stairs. A figure draped in a white cloth, with two holes for eyes, drifted out, ghouls on either side of him.

The ghost spoke loudly, his voice booming. "Hear ye, hear ye. Today's session is closed. Please come back tomorrow, thank you." All over the square a resigned grumble arose, and spirits began to drift and disburse in all directions.

In a matter of minutes, though, the square was empty, and there was no Pumpkin. The only thing that stood between May and the Edifice was empty space, dotted with a couple of stragglers. "Pumpkin, where are you?" she whispered sadly.

Keeping wide of the front stairs and the entrance, May walked with unsure steps to the west wall of the Edifice, stopping inches away. Etched into the marble, in every spare space, were words in different languages. She read the ones that she could.

I wish my mom would feel better.

I wish I had a parrot.

I wish I could fly.

Before her eyes, new words would squeeze their way in with the ones that were already there. May reached out to touch the words, and a bolt of lightning ran through her fingers.

She leaped back, staring at the Edifice. Then she walked back across the square and into the nearest alleyway, dragging aimlessly until she found a sign pointing toward Sewerside.

Sewerside turned out to be every bit as undesirable as the spirits at Mausoleum 387A had promised. May tried to blend in as she walked along, but she had to fight not to gag at the smell. Now that she had arrived, she realized she had no idea how to find the hotel. The whole area was much bigger than she had expected.

Eventually she noticed a skullophone booth standing on a corner. On a hunch, she ducked into it and looked for a phone book. There was one in the slot below the skull. She flipped through the hotels section. Final Rest . . . Final Rest . . . There it was, right between Fade to Black Bed-and-Breakfast and the Float On Inn.

Next to the name of the hotel were two and a half gravestones. May read:

> Located on one of Sewerside's quietest streets, the Final Rest is a popular haunt for outlaws, lost souls, and other spirits looking for a resting place that combines privacy and

discretion. We recommend that families and those not desiring to associate with scalawags look elsewhere for their accommodation needs.

"One-seven-eight Many Moans Way," May read, out loud this time. She looked around her. "Well, that helps," she muttered sarcastically.

"What else do you need?" a nasal voice asked. May looked at the skullophone. Then at the skullophone book. Then at her feet. A woman was sitting under the grating, with plugs in her ears, staring up at May. "It's no Shangri-la, but we like to think we're an efficient city. What more were you looking for?"

"Um, I need to find out where one-seven-eight Many Moans Way is."

The woman rolled her eyes. Her face was blue. "Just look at the map. In the back." She pointed one stump of a finger toward the book.

"Oh." May flipped through to the last few pages. There it was.

May looked at the index, then traced a line to Many Moans Way with her fingers, then looked outside the booth to see what street she was on.

"That's only three blocks away! Thank you."

The woman nodded.

A few minutes later May arrived at two large but decrepit doors, covered in cobwebs, with ghostly spiders dangling from every corner. The building itself was small and squat, and looked like it would be too cramped for a house, much less a hotel. There was no mark on the door but for the street number.

May pulled on one of the handles—gently at first—and then

with all her might. It opened with a loud groan, sending a cloud of dust flying at her face and setting off a jangling bell.

May hurriedly stepped inside and waved her hands in front of her face, coughing.

When the dust cleared, a small man in an ascot stood before her, grinning with a mouthful of crooked teeth. His face was covered in red bumps, a few of which oozed green.

"C'min C'min." He waved May forward. A name tag on his vest read CONNER O'KINNEY.

He ushered May into a dingy marble foyer that sprawled below a giant chandelier covered in webs and spiders. At one end a large marble staircase with an ebony banister that had been mostly rotted away spiraled upward. May could hardly believe she was in the building that had looked so tiny from the outside.

"What can I do you for?"

"I'm looking for a room, sir, room nine thousand nine hundred ninety-nine."

"Ah, you want that one, do you? Not a problem, not a problem."

Conner walked behind a large wooden desk that was missing one leg. May watched him as he flipped through the pages of a book, unable to keep from staring at the scars on his face.

"The fever, it was," he said, making May blush and look at her feet. "No need to be embarrassed, child. Took my whole town. Plenty of nice specters walking around with boils like this. Let's see, nine thousand nine hundred ninety-nine, nine thousand nine hundred ninety-nine. Oh." Conner frowned. "Oh, I'm sorry, that's right, the room's taken."

"By a ghost with a big head?" May begged breathlessly.

"Mm, no, it was a specter in fact. Can I interest you in another room? I have a suite just a few floors below that's quite as popular, and available."

May shifted from foot to foot, crushed. "Well, do you mind if I wait in the lobby awhile? I'm hoping to meet someone."

Conner frowned. "Most spirits coming in here don't relish being looked at. Discretion is one of our selling points."

"Well, can I just get a room on that same hall?" May couldn't quite believe her own pushiness. But she set her chin.

Conner, apparently annoyed now, looked in his book. "Ninety-four forty is available. Just follow the stairs up to the ninth floor. Turn left and it's the four thousandth, seven hundred and twentieth door on the left."

"But, four thousand . . ."

Conner already appeared preoccupied, so May did what he'd said.

She followed the marble staircase, which swept past each floor regally. Again May marveled at how so much space could fit into such a tiny building.

When she reached the ninth floor, she entered into a seemingly endless hallway and started walking. But it only took a few minutes to get to door 9440. She stopped, deciding to walk down to room 9999 and, if she could get her courage up, knock on the door and ask the spirit there if they would mind changing rooms or if they'd keep an eye out for Pumpkin.

The hallway was lined with several full-length portraits. Each was a painting of Conner himself, standing with a spirit who, May assumed, had been a customer. The one she stood in front of now had darkly slanting eyes, tan skin, and a massive beard. TO CONNER, it was inscribed, THANKS FOR THE COMFY BED AND THE FABULOUS SERVICE. XO, ATTILA.

"Excuse me, miss," a voice said, and a hand clapped down on May's shoulder, giving her a little jolt before spinning her around.

A figure stood there, looking no worse for the wear, and grinning. He was wearing a big straw hat, a jangly necklace with a miniature Eternal Edifice dangling from the bottom, and a sack over his shoulder. A length of chain curled out of one side of it with a tag attached that read MY HOUSE GHOST VISITED THE CITY OF ETHER AND ALL I GOT WERE THESE LOUSY SHACKLES.

Before May could throw out her arms to hug him, or even exclaim, Pumpkin wrinkled his nose at her. "You smell horrible," he said.

Standing on the balcony of the ninth floor of the Final Rest Hotel, a guest was treated to a view of the seedier buildings of Sewerside, a slice of the city wall, and in the distance, a gaggle of pyramids far across the desert.

Tonight those triangles were surrounded by giant points of light—fires lit for an all-night vigil being held while the inhabitants of the pyramids looked for Big Ears.

When the alarm had sounded the evening before, just as Somber Kitty's paws had hit the ground after his long tumble from the sky, every inhabitant of New Egypt had fanned out over the desert after him, swinging their nets and beating the small desert bushes in search of the missing cat.

Hours later, long after most had finally floated back to their homes for rest, Somber Kitty crept out from behind the reeds along a wide stream full of green liquid and peered around to make sure the coast was clear. His ears tilted in the direction of the pyramids, listening for any suspicious sounds.

It seemed that he was safe.

Staying alert, he crept up to the edge of the stream, where he discovered several handwoven baskets, apparently made by the Egyptians, sitting on the bank.

Somber Kitty sniffed them, then touched the surface of the stream with one dainty paw, shaking off the liquid with a wrinkle in his nose. It smelled horrible.

He backed up and let his eyes follow the current toward the horizon, where the city he had seen from his chamber rose up, far away and majestic. It still gave him a trembly feeling to look at it, way down in his gut.

Somber Kitty looked at the baskets resting by the river and, after thinking for a moment, nudged one into the stream with his nose. He stood back and watched it float along and out of sight.

He looked back toward the city.

"Meay?" he asked.

A noise arose from behind the bushes.

Somber Kitty didn't think twice. He put his front paws into the next basket and pushed it forward with his back legs, yanking them inside at the moment the basket hit the water.

The basket tottered, but stayed afloat, and only his tail could be seen above the lip of it as it drifted with the current, in the direction of Ether.

CHAPTER TWENTY-FIVE

Beatrice and Fabbio

May stood on the decrepit balcony of room 9440, staring down toward the streets of the city and listening to the noises that drifted up. Everyone moving around below looked tiny, like little toy ghosts. Pumpkin still lay snoring in the room behind her.

The beds—there were two—were moldy and rotten, sagging in the middle and covered in dust, which Pumpkin had found delightful. They had burst into the room, laughing and joyful and hugging each other, talking about their adventures—May relating what she'd seen at the Eternal Edifice, and Pumpkin talking about slipping away from the gargoyles by ducking under a souvenir cart. They'd bounced on the beds awhile and played Old Maid with a deck of cards they'd found in the drawer, and May had let Pumpkin cheat. Then Pumpkin had shown May all the things he'd bought.

He'd presented her with a locket he'd bought in a trendy neighborhood at the edge of Sewerside. It was in the shape of a coffin that broke into two

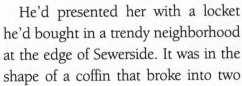

halves—one for each of them to wear. Put together, it read BEST FRIENDS, and words had been engraved on the back: PUMPKIN & MAY, NEVER TO BE DEARLY DEPARTED. Afterward they had listened to the sirens of the city, which had gone off three times in a row.

"Do you think that's for us?" May had asked, peering through the sliding glass door at a distant gaggle of gargoyles circling at the edge of the city.

Pumpkin had yawned and crawled into his bed, shrugging.

May twisted her half of the locket between her fingers, smiling with relief that Pumpkin was okay. But after a few moments her smile faded, and her heart became as heavy as a sack of beans.

Pumpkin had escaped, but just barely. John the Jibber was gone. And there was Lucius, somewhere far below the Dead Sea. She'd caused nothing but disaster to the spirits who had helped her. She couldn't forget what the Undertaker had said, about the danger that surrounded her. She knew as long as he was by her side, Pumpkin was surrounded by it too.

Down on the streets all the spirits seemed to be going somewhere, and May wished she were going somewhere as well. They all had homes. Sighing, she walked back into the room, then dug through her sack for her comfort blanket. She wrapped it over her death shroud.

Suddenly she was lying on her bed in White Moss Manor. There was the tiny hairline crack in the ceiling she used to stare at while daydreaming.

May sat up and peered around at the shelves lined with quartz rocks, picking one up and rolling it around in her hands, her heart aching. Her eyes skipped across the books on her desk and the materializer lying on the floor beside it. She stared at the bedroom door.

"Somber Kitty?" she called loudly, knowing it wouldn't work, but hoping. She waited for several seconds, then slumped back down onto her bed in misery. Finally she tugged the blanket off.

She looked at the embroidered words: *Remember to keep warm*, and she thought she understood them differently than she had at first. Maybe it meant she should remember and that would keep her warm. Only right now, it made her sad.

Pumpkin was still snoring.

May went to her knapsack again and tucked the blanket inside, then swung the pack over her shoulder and looked at Pumpkin, thinking.

She pulled out the blanket again and laid it over him, wondering what kind of place he would wake up to, lying under it. What memories kept Pumpkin warm? "Good-bye, Pumpkin," she whispered softly, gently patting his tuft of yellow hair. Then she tiptoed out of the room, closing the door behind her.

In room 9440 the comfort blanket had already transported Pumpkin's dreams far away, to the same place it had taken May: Briery Swamp. He too was in May's bedroom, sitting on a chair. Only he was waiting for a skinny, dark-haired girl to come upstairs and draw her pictures or read her books.

Still sleeping, he smiled.

Dragging her feet sadly, May walked down to the lobby and plucked a few travel brochures off the shelves by the front desk. She flipped through them, bewildered. *What to do, where to go?*

On a sofa a few feet away, a blue-faced man with a bright red nose and a curlicued mustache, wearing a blue military uniform, and with what looked like an old parachute case strapped to his back, met her eyes as she glanced up. Next to him was a girl who looked to be about May's age. She was possibly the prettiest girl May had ever seen, with long blond hair, and huge blue eyes, and a long white dress with a sash going through the middle.

May surveyed a map of the city, tracing the streets with her fingers, not knowing what she was looking for. When she glanced up a second time, both the girl and the man were watching her intently. They both looked down quickly. May noticed the girl was holding a newspaper.

Uneasy now, May stood up and tucked the brochures into her knapsack, walking toward the door. The man and the girl stood up at the same time and followed her.

Out on the street, May picked up her pace. The two kept up with her. No matter how fast May walked, they drifted effortlessly just behind her. May balled her fists and spun around.

"If you're going to call the Bogey, do it!" she cried. The man and the girl both floated back in surprise.

"Excuse us," the girl said. "We didn't mean to startle you. Can we talk to you for a moment?"

May didn't reply.

"That's a pretty bathing suit," the girl said. "It looks just like stars in the sky. Isn't it nice, Fabbio?"

The man, Fabbio, looked May up and down with an air of dissatisfaction. "Eh. Is all right."

"Don't you find it dusty in the street this time of year?" the girl continued, looking slightly embarrassed. "We do."

May glanced around, confused. Really what she noticed on this street was the smell. "Um, I guess so."

"Mmm." The girl nodded her head politely, seeming to be at a loss for more to say. "Oh," she finally said. "I'm Beatrice; this is Fabbio."

"*Captain* Fabbio Fabbiani," Fabbio added.

"I'm May Bird." May eyed both of them, suspiciously. They seemed to want something. But she couldn't imagine what. Beatrice reminded May of the girls at school—perfect, normal, pretty. But Beatrice was gazing at her with much more friendly interest than any girl at school had ever had.

The three stared at one another for several seconds in awkward silence. A couple of ghosts holding hands drifted by, and Beatrice eyed them before continuing. "Maybe . . . maybe we could talk in private?"

The two strangers drifted into a small, decrepit gazebo, full of spiderwebs, that looked out on a particularly wide canal. May followed, crossing her arms over her chest and expecting very little. But what did she have to lose?

The three sat down. Fabbio shifted his parachute tighter onto his back.

"Ask her," Fabbio finally whispered, elbowing Beatrice and rubbing at the tip of his red nose.

Beatrice gave him a stern look, then elbowed him back. "You ask her."

"You."

"No, you."

Captain Fabbio flung out his hands in a rock-paper-scissors gesture. "Shoot you for it."

Beatrice's chest heaved in a big sigh. "Don't be childish." She looked at May. "We were wondering, are you by any chance here for the Book?"

"Book?"

"The Book of the Dead."

"Um." May tried to think fast, wondering how they could know, and whether she should say yes or no. "Ummmmm."

Beatrice thrust a newspaper into May's hands. "It's all over the news that there's a Live One in the city. I saw you in the lobby, and I saw this article."

The front page of the newspaper was covered in a huge headline:

LIVE ONE BREACHES CITY GATES, PHANTOM FIRED AFTER 150
YEARS OF SERVICE

Below it was a glowing, moving picture of May and Pumpkin running. It looked like it had been taken from the sky. Just the tops of their heads and their running legs and flailing arms were visible, and May's cloak trailed behind her. A tiny line along the bottom read: "Courtesy of Holo-Pix."

"Why do you think this is me?" May said, looking back and forth between them.

"Beatrice is very smart," Captain Fabbio said tightly.

Beatrice laid a hand on Fabbio's wrist gently. "I just saw you and thought, *maybe.* And I . . . we couldn't think of any reason a Live One would come to the city, except if they were looking for the Book."

"Um."

"You see, I'm looking for my mother. And Fab—Captain Fabbio here is looking for his retinue who died in the Alps. And we thought the Book might tell us where to look. It's supposed to have the answers to everything."

May was silent.

"I thought, well, three is better than two. Safety in numbers and all that. And it seems that you're so brave. That photo took my breath away! And coming through the gates like that! And *escaping!*"

"Oh, oh," May stammered, blushing. "Well, the truth is I don't know if I'm going after the Book anymore."

"Please," Beatrice pleaded. "We need someone like you. And I can't spend Eternity without my mother. If I have to, I'll . . ." Beatrice's bottom lip trembled, but she set her jaw and composed herself. "We've already tried to get into the Edifice three times. I'm afraid neither Captain Fabbio nor I are very good with strategy."

"I beg your pardon." Fabbio stiffened and tugged tightly at his mustache.

Beatrice rubbed his arm affectionately. "I'm sorry, Captain." She turned to May. "I read somewhere that Live Ones are nine times out of ten more likely to be able to read the Book. And then, you're so heroic."

"Anyway, we can't afford to stay here anymore. Neither of us has reported for haunting duty. Which is why we had to come stay in Sewerside."

May tugged on her fingernails with her teeth. "I'm sorry. I'm not here for the Book. And if I did go, I'd only be trouble for you, trust me."

Beatrice nodded, her pretty pale lips coming together in a thin line. Tears trembled on her eyelids. "Okay, well, we thought we'd give it a try. Thank you for your time."

May swallowed the guilty lump in her throat and stood up. She liked Beatrice. She liked them both, and she didn't even know them. She couldn't help it.

Fabbio's eyebrows had lowered into an angry V, directed at May. His cheeks flamed. "You should be ashamed at yourself. No helping poor innocent Beatrice. Look at her, she is angel."

May clasped her hands together tightly. "I'm not heroic, you know. You think I'm someone that I'm not. Trust me, I'm really doing you a favor."

Fabbio threw his hands in the air. "Favor? Pah! Someone in this world ask for help, nobody is giving it. How is that favor? And all she wants is to find sweet, beautiful mother. And now she may never find. I am not so sad for me. I am captain in Royal Italian Air Force, I am strong and courageous, I can withstand anything, but Beatrice . . ."

Fabbio turned stiffly, clicking his heels together. "Beatrice, we go."

"Wait . . . ," May said. She kneaded her fingers together, deciding. "You know how dangerous it will be?"

Fabbio and Beatrice nodded. "Most likely, we do not survive. But Beatrice and I think, it is worth the risk."

"You're going to go anyway?"

Beatrice nodded.

"Well . . . I guess . . . I don't really have anything here. I . . ." May faltered.

She closed her mouth into a thin, firm line. And nodded her chin, just slightly.

Watching Beatrice's face light up was like watching the sun rise. She threw her arms around May and kissed her cheek, making May blush.

And without May saying the final word, it was decided.

☙ ☙ ☙

Minutes later the three of them were a cozy trio drifting down the sidewalk. As they talked about what things the Book might tell them, May marveled at how kind and beautiful Beatrice was, and how quickly her shyness was fading. Beatrice had linked her arm through May's as if they'd been friends forever. Of course, she had never seen May fly off a car while tied to balloons.

"I haven't felt this hopeful since before I died," Beatrice said.

May, catching the spirit, got up the courage to ask, "How did you die?"

"Typhoid." Beatrice's big blue eyes became doleful. "My mother died before me. When I got here, I couldn't find her. I've been looking ever since."

May looked at the ground.

Beatrice tried to smile. "Poor Fabbio and I met at the Spectroplex. He is in the same situation I'm in, in a way."

"My men and I, we die of frostbite after we parachute into the Apennine Mountains by mistake," Fabbio explained. "Supposed to be a field in Germany. But I come through portal, and they are not waiting for me. I no understand. My men would follow me anywhere."

Beatrice gave May a meaningful glance, patting Fabbio's back underneath where his parachute lay.

"Isn't that heavy?" May asked, pointing to the chute, remembering a book she'd read about paratroopers in France.

"A soldier must always be prepared," he answered, thrusting his chest out. Beatrice and May grinned at each other, and Beatrice rolled her eyes.

"What were you planning to do?" Beatrice asked. "If you weren't going to the Edifice, where were you headed?"

"I don't know." May thought for a moment. "To hide somewhere, I guess." She squeezed her knapsack close to her and listened to the crumple of her letter inside. "I heard there's a train north, but . . ."

May's voice trailed off. But what? But she was too scared to go. But she was too small to help anyone. But the Lady might not want her anymore.

"I know that train—it runs just outside the city. I've thought for a long time that my mother might have gone north," Beatrice said. "She always liked the mountains and the cold." May nodded. "I've thought many times about just taking it up there," Beatrice continued, "and looking for her. But of course, the North is vast. And I've read that many ghosts that go there don't return. It would be foolish."

They moved along in silence for a while.

"Beatrice, what's your mom like?" May asked finally.

Beatrice sighed gently. "Pretty. Kind. She has a nice singing voice."

"Sounds like my mom," May said softly.

Beatrice gently took May's hand, and the girls stared at each other, tears in their eyes.

"You should call me Bea. That's what all my friends call me." May squeezed Beatrice's fingers with a flush of embarrassment, but didn't pull away.

It was strange. She'd been around the girls at school her entire life. But within these few minutes she began to feel like she had known this one for a million years.

꙳ ꙳ ꙳

"When do you think we should go?" Beatrice asked. She and Fabbio both looked at May expectantly, as if she might have the answer. But May did have the feeling in her gut that they should go as soon as possible. The longer they waited in Ether, the more dangerous it was.

"I think tonight?" she said with a slight nod of her chin. To her surprise Beatrice and Fabbio didn't question her.

"We take the sewers last time," Fabbio said. "There is secret way, but we get lost, eh?" Fabbio rubbed his nose and thrust his chin in the air. "Well, we try that twice, and both times entrance is . . . not where it is supposed to be."

Beatrice gave May a glance, and May began to think she might have an inkling of why the captain and his men had gotten lost in the Apennines.

"I have a map," Beatrice said. "I got it at the E. P. L., from an ancient map of the underground of the city." She pulled a folded piece of paper from a pocket in her dress and laid it out on her lap.

"E. P. L.?"

"Ether Public Library," Beatrice said nonchalantly. "I did a few days of research." She pointed to the map, which showed the sewers that crisscrossed the city in motion, a few specks wandering around the page. "It's funny. Nobody goes into the library. The door is very hard to find and very small, and the shelves are a dusty mess. It's as if nobody bothers." Beatrice wrinkled her nose as she said this. Clearly she thought it was very wrong not to bother.

"Beatrice and I use this way last time." Fabbio tugged his mustache. "We come up right under the Eternal Edifice." He thrust his finger at a tiny square on the map. "This is old door that spirits use thousands of years ago. Only a few still know it. It is our only way in."

"What are those?" May pointed to the moving specks.

"Ghouls." Beatrice's lashes fluttered. "Unfortunately they love to bathe in the sewers."

May gulped. "Do you have any maps for once we get *inside* the entrance?"

Beatrice shook her head, her eyebrows descending deeply. "Those pages had been ripped out. But believe me it's bad enough just getting there. The sewers are endless and go all over the city." She added, "And if you get lost, you may end up outside the city gates—or worse, you may never find your way up again."

"Fortunately I memorize map. I have much experience in these things," Fabbio said. "It is no good to use light in sewers. Ghouls will see. It must be all up here." He tapped his forehead.

The dangers gathered in May's head, like a murder of crows, flocking to a tree. The bravery she had felt a few minutes ago had slunk into a corner of her mind, replaced by fear and the crushing feeling that the three of them were just too small for such a great task. She wished they had John. She wished that she could be back in Briery Swamp, safe and protected in her tiny, comfy life. But wishing was not enough.

"We should leave at rush hour," May said finally.

"Midnight," Beatrice and Fabbio agreed.

Huddling close together in the gazebo, they waited for dusk to turn into night.

The basket containing Somber Kitty was carried to the city by one of the many streams that came together to form one giant river.

This river was made completely of ectoplasmic sewage, and flowed directly under the city wall into Sewerside.

When Somber Kitty saw that his vessel was fast approaching a dark drainage pipe beside the west gate of the city, he leaped out, gingerly bouncing along the wet sand until he was on solid, dry ground. Here he licked himself in disgust, shaking the wet drops from his tongue and peering up at the gigantic creature standing about a hundred yards away at the city wall.

Startled he hissed, then scurried into the shadow of the wall itself, far from where the giant creature stood.

His instinctual fear of the city had increased as he'd gotten closer to it, and now he stood very uneasy in the dark, wondering what to do. He sniffed at the air.

Since he was standing upwind of the river, he no longer breathed the scent of sewage. And since spirits have no smell, he failed to scent the three boatfuls of Egyptian souls who had tracked his progress downstream and were now sending for backup.

But since he was standing *downwind* of the city, he did get one particular scent that was familiar. Somber Kitty's tail jolted up. His ears did their satellite turn.

All at once he turned to the wall, placed his paws upon it, sank down, gazed at the giant figure by the gate, then at the pipe on his opposite side. He meowed; he growled; his slitty eyes rolled; his whiskers waggled with wild abandon. Deciding he had no other choice, he began to dig.

After thousands of miles of searching, Somber Kitty had finally scented May.

CHAPTER TWENTY-SIX

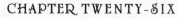

The Eternal Edifice

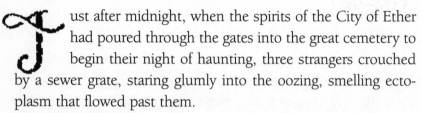

ust after midnight, when the spirits of the City of Ether had poured through the gates into the great cemetery to begin their night of haunting, three strangers crouched by a sewer grate, staring glumly into the oozing, smelling ectoplasm that flowed past them.

"The ghouls always swim in pairs," Beatrice advised, "and you may have noticed they love to chatter, so we'll hear them if they're there."

"You stay behind me," Fabbio added, thumping his chest once with his fist. "And do not fear." May and Beatrice looked at each other.

"Bravely we go." Fabbio slid into the water, and May and Beatrice slid in behind him, the coolness and sliminess of the ectoplasm making them suck in their breath.

They moved along the short stretch of canal with the current, which wasn't too strong here, and then got to the place where the road overhung the water, where they would go into darkness. Carefully they continued to move forward, till the last of the stars snuffed out of sight. They twisted and turned in the dark, Fabbio leading the way.

"I'm actually getting used to the smell," May whispered.

Beatrice squeezed her hand.

"Yes," Fabbio answered. "Any smell, if you are around it long enough, will become invisible to your nose. For instance—"

"Shhhhhh," Beatrice hissed, coming to a stop so hard that May slammed into her. They all stood with ears perked for a moment, and then May heard it.

Hbbbblelllllleeehhhh. Gbbbleh heh bleh heh.

Down the tunnel ahead of them, the water splashed.

Beatrice's hand clutched May's. There was nowhere to hide.

Hbbbbllllbubbbllllllllbleh.

A sound like laughter came out of the darkness, getting closer and closer.

Glubbebbbbbwb. The voices grew steadily louder. May held her breath.

And then the voices began to get lower. It was hard to tell at first, but then it was clear—they were moving away.

The three waited several minutes, listening carefully to hear if the ghouls would come back. They didn't.

"We go," Fabbio whispered, moving again. After that, they all kept their mouths shut.

They wound through the sewers for what seemed like hours. May had stopped feeling the coldness of the water.

"I not sure, but I think we a little bit lost," Fabbio finally whispered.

"Oh, my," Beatrice said.

"I think this map, it is wrong. But it's okay, I fix."

They took several more turns. Fabbio went slower and slower, which made May feel more and more doubtful. Soon they heard a sound up ahead—a series of loud splashes.

They pushed up against the walls of the sewer, the splashing getting louder and louder, moving toward them. This time it kept coming until it was suddenly upon them. Whatever it was it seemed to see them, because it came to a dead stop inches away. May could hear breathing and began to make out two shapes.

"Die!" In the darkness Captain Fabbio leaped forward, tackling one of the creatures and dragging it under the water.

The other creature let out a high-pitched scream. But it wasn't the scream of a ghoul. It was the scream of . . .

"Pumpkin?!" May gasped.

"May?"

There was a giant splash, and Fabbio and the other shape emerged from the water.

"Let go of me, ye idiot! Let go."

This voice was familiar too. May, forgetting for a moment the danger, pulled her starlight out of her sack, and suddenly the tunnel was cast in the bright white glow. Standing before her, looking like drowned dogs, were Pumpkin, Fabbio, and—his neck hooked inside Fabbio's elbow—John the Jibber.

"John!" May leaped forward and threw her arms around his neck, knocking him backward.

John caught himself and straightened up. He laughed. "Well, eh, ahem. Hi there, lassie."

"But . . . but . . ." May was speechless. She didn't know what to say first. "You went into the incarnerator! How did you get away? We saw you!"

John didn't answer for a second or two. He tugged at his collar awkwardly. "Eh, the Jibber's always got a few tricks up his sleeves. Didn't I tell ye I was the wiliest knave there was?"

"You did." May hugged him again. "How? How is it possible? How'd you two find each other?"

"Why, at the Final Rest, of course," John said, skipping over the first question. "I waited in room nine thousand nine hundred ninety-nine, but ye never showed. And then I found Pumpkin wandering up and down the hall, cryin' 'is eyes out, looking fer ye. We've looked fer ye everywhere." John swiped a ragged sleeve along his brow. "I was sure in trouble if I'd lost ye."

"In trouble?" May squinted, confused.

John tugged at his collar again. "Well, I woulda felt terrible for the rest of Eternity, of course. That's trouble, ain't it?"

John's eyes darted away from hers.

"Ahem."

May turned to see Pumpkin, standing with his arms crossed over his chest and his droopy eyes slitted angrily.

"Pumpkin, I—"

"You left me."

"I thought it'd be safer for you if . . ."

Pumpkin turned and showed her his back.

"I thought it would be safer for you."

No response. May reached to touch his back, but he stepped farther away.

"And what do we have here?" John asked, eyeing Beatrice and Fabbio darkly.

"Oh." May grinned. "They're coming to the Edifice with me. With us. Oh, but I knew we'd be lost without you!"

John waved his cracked, callused hands sharply. "Ah, now hold on just a moment. Nobody extra's coming to the Edifice. It's hard enough having blasted Pumpkin along."

Behind him Pumpkin lifted his shoulders dramatically and huffed.

May glanced at Beatrice and Fabbio. Fabbio was staring at John indignantly. "But I told them they could come."

"M'girl, I won't have it."

May gazed down at the water, making patterns in it with her fingers. She stared around the group for a few moments. Then she crossed her arms over herself decisively. "I'm not going without them, Mr. Jibber." Then she added, less surely, "And if that means you won't take us, that's, um, fine." The truth was it wasn't fine. May held her breath, waiting for John to explode at her.

He looked shocked. He gazed back and forth among the three helplessly, then growled.

"Er, have it your way. Let's go in."

May's body went slack. *Thank goodness.* "Are we close?" she asked, once she'd recovered.

John laughed. "Close?" He took the starlight from her hand and held it up toward the wall. "It's right here."

May let out a small scream. Before them, carved into the gray rock of the tunnel wall, was an old woman's face, surrounded by leaves. It was covered in cobwebs and flecks of ectoplasm.

"I *knew* we are close," Fabbio asserted.

May, her eyes huge, hunched her shoulders and reached out to touch the face ever so gently. The Lady . . .

"Ahh!"

The mouth flew open wide and snatched for her hand. May leaped back, yanking her arm away.

The mouth immediately recoiled. May had time to glimpse a tiny hole in the back of its stone throat before it closed.

Pumpkin had already started flailing a path down the sewer. He stopped a few feet away, watching fearfully.

"Ah, ye wouldn't get far without me, ye see? Ye've got to be careful with these doors. They're ancient and tricky, meant to protect the Edifice from more than the likes of us. Here, hold this." John dug into a hidden pocket in his pants and thrust a white key into May's hand. May took it, confused.

"It's me skeleton key, made out of the bone of a master locksmith. I stole it off Harry Houdini last year on the Sea of Tranquillity while he was tubin'." John winked, but his smile stayed hard. "When this mouth opens again, I want you to stick the key in the hole, all right?"

"I'll lose my arm!"

"Trust me." John smiled again, without the smile reaching his eyes.

May nodded. "Okay."

With his left hand John reached out and pinched the lady's nose. Nothing happened for several seconds. And then the face's eyes began to bulge. Its mouth began to twitch. *I'm sorry,* May thought, grimacing.

A few more seconds and the mouth flew open, panting hard. John thrust his hands against the top and bottom lips, prying them farther apart. "Now!"

May hesitated, holding up the key, her eyes locked on the powerful stone teeth.

"Do it, lass!"

"It's going to eat you!" Pumpkin moaned in the background. But May set her jaw and thrust the key back into the throat, fumbling it against the hole, until it slid in with a click. Nothing happened for a moment, and John gave a grunt. And then the mouth opened wider and wider, all the way up to the ceiling, until finally it split right down the middle. Both sides slid apart like an elevator door. A skinny stone stairway waited on the other side.

"C'mon," John whispered, rescuing the key from the rubble.

He floated up the stone stairs first. May followed, then Beatrice and Fabbio, who had to stand sideways and jam himself through the door.

"Captain, why don't you leave your parachute here."

"I do nothing of that sort," Fabbio snapped, jamming himself in harder. "A soldier, always prepared."

"Captain, really . . ."

Beatrice looked at May for support, and Fabbio followed her eyes, both of them looking to May to resolve the conflict. She nibbled on her pinkie. *Poor Fabbio,* she thought. Specters didn't change.

"Well, I suppose if it's really important to you . . ." Together she and Beatrice helped yank the pack so that both Fabbio and the parachute came through. John the Jibber stood a few stairs above them, shaking his head in disgust.

Pumpkin reluctantly brought up the rear, and the doors slammed closed behind him, making them all jump.

At the top of the stairs was an impossibly long hallway, so long that the end was nowhere in sight. It was paved all around with tiny mirrors.

"Don't touch anything, ye hear me?" John whispered. As he did, Pumpkin reached his arm to the side.

"But it's so shiny!" He thrust a hand forward. As soon as his long fingers connected with glass, a great sucking sound was heard, and Pumpkin's hand disappeared through the wall. "Ahhhhhhhhhhh!"

"Pumpkin!"

May leaped forward and wrapped her arms around Pumpkin's waist just as Beatrice wrapped him in her arms from the other side. Pumpkin's body sucked up tight against the wall, and everywhere he touched seemed to dissolve and go black, sucking harder and harder.

May felt someone else's arms around her from behind, and then she was toppling backward, down the stairs. Pumpkin and Beatrice came tumbling down on top of her, and May felt herself land on something soft that groaned, *"Ay, Dio mio!"*

After a few moments of confusion Fabbio pushed May off him, and they all stood up, making sure they were in one piece, and looking at one another wide-eyed.

John stood at the top of the stairs, "Ye idiot!" he hissed at Pumpkin, then looked over his shoulder. "We'll be lucky if we're not caught by the time we reach the ground floor!"

Up at the landing, the blackness that had spread on the mirror began to turn opaque again, until it was back to its previous shiny surface, appearing as harmless as before.

John fished in his sack and brought out a bolt of silk, muttering out of the side of his lips. "The mirrors will trap your soul unless they're covered up." Morosely he flung the bolt into the air, and it went rolling down the hall, like a red carpet, disappearing into the darkness.

"Stay on the silk path, ye got it?" he threw back over his shoulder, shoving May out in front of him and not waiting for the others to reply.

Meanwhile, he counted.

"Seventeen paces, eighteen paces, nineteen paces . . ."

This went on for a good hour. Every once in a while they came to the end of the silk bolt, and John pulled another one out of his sack, throwing it out in front of them, where it spread itself out evenly. Fabbio let out a deep sigh, making it clear that he was getting impatient.

"Goodness, does this hall ever end?" Beatrice asked, rubbing Fabbio's shoulder soothingly.

"Nope," John said, bewildering all of them, then went back to muttering. "One thousand, three hundred eleven paces . . ."

They were at one thousand, seven hundred ten when he came to a stop. "It should be here." He took a long stick out of his bag and poked it forward. To May's amazement it didn't disappear into the mirror. "Ah."

John stepped forward too, right into the wall. And he didn't disappear. He took several steps, and then turned to face the others. "C'mon, then." He looked to his left, then walked in that direction, disappearing completely behind a ledge that blended in so well with the rest of the mirrored wall that it was practically invisible. May and Fabbio gasped.

"Ay!" Fabbio breathed.

A moment later John's head reappeared. "Soft spot. C'mon. I ain't got all night."

To May's surprise Pumpkin was the first to follow, smiling in wonder. Everyone else trailed after him, holding their palms forward and grinning in awe when they didn't bump into anything.

"It took me a week and a half to find that last time," John whispered, leading them into the dark stone hallway ahead. "I hear the hall loops around on itself eventually, so ye never get to the end. Spirits end up trapped, walking the hall forever. Lots of things like that in the Eternal Edifice. Powerful architecture, it is." He stopped and looked forward, then behind them, as if to make sure no one was following them, then he continued. "The upstairs is much more modern. That's where all the guards are, and that's where we get on the floaterator. But word is Cleevil doesn't even know this way exists. In any case, he's left it alone. Now"—he yanked on his beard—"where was that service entrance?"

As he ran his fingers along the wall, a white, sparkling light began to glimmer farther down the tunnel.

"Mr. Jibber," Beatrice whispered. "What's that?"

"What?" John looked up, jolted, and cursed. "Hurry," he whispered. "Find the door!"

As they all fanned out, feeling along the wall, the beautiful light continued to grow. Watching it, May began to feel warm inside.

"Here!" she heard someone say, but it was like she heard it in a dream, and then someone yanked on the back of her bathing suit, and she was pulled backward, into the deep arch of a doorway. Fabbio shifted stiffly, his elbows jarring everyone else.

"Have ye ever seen a North Farm spirit?" John whispered, his body trembling against the others. Everyone shook their heads.

"Well, yer about to."

They squeezed hard up against the door as the light grew to a blinding white, and moments later a form drifted past them— long and white, and as filmy and soft as a cloud. May held her breath, mesmerized, and held the hand that Pumpkin slipped into hers. The spirit had a round head that tapered down to a long, gently pointed tail, like a comet, but its light was too blinding to make out any features. It floated slowly by until its light became dimmer and dimmer, and then it disappeared.

Behind May, John began to fiddle with his skeleton key, and then there was a loud crack as the door opened onto the stairs.

"Follow me."

John crouched lower and lower as he climbed the stairs, until finally he knelt down and crawled the last two on his hands and knees, peering around the corner of the landing. He ducked back just as two pairs of slimy, clawed feet appeared and passed by.

Slowly and silently he crouch-walked back down the stairs, mopping his forehead with a rotted handkerchief and looking around nervously, up and down the stairs.

"There's a couple ways we can get to the floaterator from here. One's through the Aurora Atrium, which has lots of nooks and crannies to hide in, but is guarded by at least twenty ghouls. Or we have the recreation hallway. That's where the guards have their Holo-Visions and arcade games and such, to use on their time off. We're less likely to meet ghouls that way, but we'll have to pass the goblins' lounge, and there's no place to hide that way—just a straight shot to the lobby. I'm thinkin' the atrium—"

"But . . . ," May interrupted, without meaning to. Her gut told her to use the hallway. When John paused and looked at her, she stammered. "What are the goblins like? Surely they're not as bad as the ghouls?"

May was surprised when John actually seemed to consider her

question. "They're faster. And they have bigger teeth. But they *are* a lot more likely to be fallin' down on the job. Lazy little things, and vain, too. When they're haunting down on Earth, they're either sleeping under people's beds or hiding in their closets, looking fer things to wear." He seemed to catch himself rattling on nervously. He thought for another minute. "All right, lass. We'll do it yer way."

May swallowed.

"Yes. That is also the way I would suggest," Fabbio interjected.

"Do ye lasses have any baubles on ye? Jewelry or a nice handkerchief, perhaps?"

May and Beatrice both shook their heads. "Why?" May asked.

"Something we can throw at them if they see us. They'd be mighty distracted by a fine bauble. I'm kickin' meself fer not bringin' any."

May thrust her hands into her pockets. She pulled out the quartz rock she'd brought from her shelf at home. "What about this?" She hated to give it up. It was the only thing she had from the woods back home.

"It might work. Keep it handy, and I'll let ye know if we need it."

May tucked the rock back into her right pocket. As she did, her hand brushed against something else. It felt like a tube of lipstick. She pulled it out and held it up—a glass vial full of black liquid. She whimpered.

John squinted. "Gwenneth! Of all the stinking knaves! That's Gwenneth's handiwork, I'll swear it. A sea capsule. Breaks when it's squeezed. She's probably taken out two hundred knaves that way."

May's mind leaped to all the times the capsule could have

broken in her pocket, and shuddered. Then she thought back to Gwenneth on the dock at the grotto, hugging and patting her.

"She likes to get 'em when she's nowhere around," John spat. "Gets a satisfaction out of it. A poor soul'll sit down on his bed, and . . ." John ran his hand across his throat. "Sick. Put it there, girl, down in that corner."

"But what if somebody steps on it?" May asked.

"Lay it down, child. I'll not debate with ye. We're on a schedule."

May gazed at him, confused. "What schedule?"

John blinked for a moment, then shook his head, as if shaking off a bee. "Stop askin' so many questions and lay that vial down."

May considered. In a place like this, surrounded by enemies, a vial of deadly water seemed like a good thing to have. As John watched, she scooped down and laid the vial in a corner of the stairs, but when he turned around, she picked it up again and very gently slipped it into her pocket.

When she stood back up, she met eyes with Beatrice, who'd been the only one watching her. She let May know with her eyes that she'd seen and understood. She reached out and squeezed May's hand. "Careful," she whispered, then leaned closer. "I'm not sure I trust your friend."

May had no time to answer before they all gathered, crouching, behind John at the top of the stairs. "When I give the signal, we float . . . or, er, tiptoe . . . forward, fast as we can into the hall across the way. Ye got it?"

"Of course we *get* it," Fabbio whispered, thrusting his nose in the air.

Beatrice nodded, but Pumpkin merely bit his fingers. May held tight to his sleeve, prepared to pull him into action. Beatrice's words tickled at her brain.

John held one arm outstretched in front of him, and then waggled his fingers slightly. May tugged Pumpkin hard, and they all moved forward, gazing around them as they scurried across a wide, gleaming marble floor under a vaulted glass skylight that reached several stories above them. May sucked in her breath as she saw a pair of ghouls talking a short distance away, but in another moment they'd arrived in the small hall John had told them about, hidden from view.

John came to a halt and held his arms wide to hold May and the others back as they all bumped into him. There was an open doorway on the right up ahead. John gave them a significant look to let them know this was the goblins' lounge he'd talked about. Then, quick as a flash, he levitated past it. Fabbio, Beatrice, and Pumpkin did the same. May hesitated, knowing she'd have to tiptoe.

She crept up to the edge of the door, peered around the corner, and sucked in her breath again. The room was full of hundreds of little goblins, shin height, with huge fangs and floppy ears. They hung off shelves, chairs, and the Holo-Vision set. Some were sprawled on a long orange couch watching *The Sound of Music* and singing along loudly, but most were sleeping in various positions all over the room. A few were looking in mirrors, doing their makeup. One pair had a pile of tiny shopping bags lying in between them, and they were pulling out outfits to show each other.

May tilted her chin down bravely and darted past, catching up with the others and looking behind her. The hall remained empty.

John grinned his black-toothed smile and patted her back. "Right. Now we—"

A great rattling sound shook the walls of the hallway, interrupting before John could finish. Everyone froze.

Snoooooooore. Snooooooore.

"That is what, please?" Fabbio whispered, crossing his arms and looking at John severely.

John clearly didn't know. He yanked out his handkerchief and wiped at his forehead, though May couldn't see an ounce of sweat. "Let's hope we don't find out."

They moved warily down the hall toward the sound, watching in awe as the walls rattled around them. The ceiling had been built on a rise here, tilting steadily upward. At the end of the hall it disappeared completely where it met an enormous walled circle that rose for as far as the eye could see, with not a roof in sight. In the center of the circle, the floaterator shaft stretched its glowing way upward—a walled circle within a circle.

The gold doors stretched at least two stories high, and at the foot of them, its massive teeth poking out from underneath its enormous black jowls, a silver tag inscribed MAMA dangling from its neck, was a dog the size of a small house. A Black Shuck. Its eyelids, slightly open, revealed bloodred eyeballs.

"Somebody go ahead and push the button for the floaterator," John whispered after a minute, indicating the glowing blue Up button. It was very small and at a normal height beside the doors.

Everyone looked at one another.

"I am allergic to dogs," Fabbio said. He faked a soft cough, way down in his throat.

"N-N-Not me," Pumpkin stuttered.

"Oh, my," said Beatrice, fluttering her perfect eyelashes. "I don't think I'm brave enough either. What about you, John?"

John shook his head. "Not on yer life."

Finally everyone looked at May. "Oh, um." She could think of no reason why it shouldn't be her, when she'd gotten everyone here in the first place. But she didn't want to go.

She began to tiptoe forward. John reached out and grabbed her arm. "Watch fer ghouls," he said, nodding his head to either side to indicate that the area around the floaterator shaft might be guarded by other things than Mama. A ghoul could come around the curved hall at any moment.

May nodded, clenched her jaw tight, and tiptoed forward again.

She wrinkled her nose as she approached the sleeping beast, covering her mouth and nose with one hand and making sure that the coast was clear of ghouls, then looking back at the dog. Her red eyes, seeming to stare at May between the cracks in her eyelids, sent goose bumps racing up and down May's skin and set her knees to trembling.

You can do this, May thought. She stepped wide over the beast's back leg, gently climbing over it and going very still when it twitched, then settled back. She slid down the other side of the leg and pushed the button, then stood back and watched the numbers along the top of the doors come alight one by one, from 800,000 to 700,000 to 600,000 and down to 1,000, then through the hundreds until it reached a star symbol.

The doors slid open, a bell dinging gently. May watched Mama the whole time. She stirred, but did not wake. Behind May the doors started to slide closed.

"Oh." May turned and leaped forward, punched the button

again, and held it, then turned toward the others and waved them forward.

One by one they levitated toward her, floating over Mama's legs and past her into the empty space of the floaterator, until only Pumpkin remained across the hall.

The others waved him forward frantically. With his right index finger resting on his lip, he shook his head.

"Come on," May mouthed, waggling her free hand at him and peering left and right. "Hurry."

Pumpkin stood there for a few more seconds, nibbling his fingers, his body quivering, and everyone scowling at him. Finally he started forward.

"Gbblllllgghh!"

May and Pumpkin both looked in the direction of the sound. A ghoul had just come into sight. Seeing them, he let out a howl, then thrust back his arm to throw his spear.

"Ahhhh!" Pumpkin screamed, sailing forward, but not fast enough to dodge the spear, which stabbed right through his arm. "Ahhhhhh!"

At the same time Mama's giant head shot up, her red eyes burning with life. There was only a moment of confusion before she saw Pumpkin and yelped in rage, leaping toward him. Pumpkin dodged left, then right as, far above, a bone-rattling alarm screamed to life.

"Let's go, lassie!" John called from behind May, but May kept her finger jammed in the button, dodging Mama's back legs as Pumpkin looped around her and zipped in May's direction.

He sailed into the floaterator, followed by May, who didn't realize until she was in that she was standing on what looked to be pure air. Beatrice was pressing another button just by the doors, over and over again, to get them to close. Finally they did, but not before Mama thrust her jaws inside. The doors slammed on the sides of her muzzle, making her yelp. Her bloodred tongue lashed out hard, smacking Fabbio backward.

Acting on instinct alone, May grabbed the spear sticking out of Pumpkin's arm, yanked it out, and jammed it into the beast's nose. Pumpkin's scream and Mama's howl sounded in unison. Beatrice, Fabbio, and Pumpkin flew toward the nose and slammed on it with their fists, until finally Mama yanked her head back. The sound of ghouls running and yelling could be heard as the doors slammed shut.

John floated forward and pressed the top button: floor 1,007,869. The floaterator gave a loud whine. And then May found herself zipping upward so fast that everything became a blur. *We're going so high,* May thought, and her stomach did a sick little flip.

Looking up, she saw a ball of light, like the sun, directly above her. She started feeling hotter and hotter. It felt like they were all hurtling right into the sun. A moment later the whiteness divided itself into a prism of light, shooting rainbows down and all around them. It looked like they would crash right through it.

May closed her eyes.

That morning all eyes in Ether were turned to the Eternal Edifice, where, it was said, three specters, a ghost, and a Live One had managed to sneak in. Not one spirit, not even the sniffing phantom, had its eyes turned to the area outside the west wall. Anyone who had been looking would have noticed an unusual sight. A group of more than a thousand ancient Egyptian spirits had gathered in a giant rolling wooden mouse, a hundred yards or so across the sand—a trick they had learned from a group of spirits in tunics they'd run into in the Nothing Platte. They were waiting for instructions from their spies within the city who were trailing Big Ears.

After a lengthy discussion, the spirits had decided not to make a move on the cat within the city, for fear it would surely duck into a building or a gutter and lose them again. No, with the help of the spies, they all agreed it would be better to wait for the cat to leave the city, which he surely would, as he seemed to be a nomadic type of god. And then, when he was in the open with nowhere to hide, they would catch him and take him back to his pyramid, to be honored the way a sacred cat should be.

Which included being sacrificed to Ra on the thirteenth of the month.

Tucked within the darkness of the mouse, and peering through the cracks, the Egyptians watched and waited. From their spot they could see the little tunnel Big Ears had dug into the city.

CHAPTER TWENTY-SEVEN

The Book of the Dead

The floaterator came to a screeching halt and the two doors opened, spilling May and the others onto the top floor of the Eternal Edifice.

The group looked at one another, smiling weakly with relief. The wail of the sirens drifted up to them, but only faintly.

"Ohh," Pumpkin moaned, holding up his arm, which had a spear-sized hole running right through the middle of it.

John, who was sweating profusely, immediately dug into his knapsack, pulled out an ancient nutcracker, and went to work on the button of the floaterator, yanking it out, and then digging at the wires inside. The others gathered around Pumpkin.

"Does it hurt?" May asked.

Pumpkin shook his head.

"We're in trouble," John grunted over his shoulder. "But this'll hold 'em fer a bit. Ghouls and bogeys can't fly, after all."

Nobody was quite listening to him, though. Beatrice, Fabbio,

Pumpkin, and May had turned their backs, and were staring down a long hallway filled with light, which fell in colored stripes across a crystal blue floor. On either side the walls were made of stained glass, of the richest hues May had ever seen—far deeper and more vivid than anything she'd seen on Earth, in shades she'd never dreamed might exist. In several places the glass had shattered, leaving shards scattered across the floor ahead. A revolving door spun at the end of the hall.

The group drifted slowly down the hall in silent awe. The hallway felt so far above everything happening in the city, and it was so breathtaking, that for the moment the danger below seemed a distant memory.

The glass, once May looked at it more closely, appeared to depict different scenes. The first, on her left, she knew well. And she was no longer surprised. It was of a giant tree growing out of the snow, but lush and full of green leaves and giant magnolia flowers. The eyes that peered out from behind the leaves were the deepest sky blue. Were they hunting her? Welcoming her? Chiding her? The eyes were too mysterious to tell.

May moved on. The next scene showed a vast black ocean, giving a view of the depths, where at the very bottom, waiting on the murky ground underwater, were several horrible-looking creatures—ghouls and goblins and others.

"That must be South Place," Pumpkin whispered behind her, his voice shaky.

The next scene was one May recognized—it was a view of Earth, but divided into four corners, with a tiny star marking a spot in each corner. "The portals?" May whispered. Surrounding the Earth was a large border, also divided into four parts. In each there was a scene from Earth: monkeys gathered around a steaming pool with Mount Fuji in the distance, an old airplane flying above an aqua blue sea dotted with islands, a stone well in the middle of a desert—

"May!" Pumpkin gasped, thrusting his white finger toward the last scene. But May had already seen it. The picture was of a small, swampy lake, nestled into a blanket of trees. Far off in the hills beyond it, a white house could be seen.

Tears quivered on May's eyelids.

She felt an arm around her, and Pumpkin leaned his big round head against hers.

"We're close," he whispered.

May accepted his cold hug gratefully. She hoped he was right.

Her feet crunched on shattered glass as they moved forward again, this time to a scene that showed a dark figure cloaked in black, with glowing red eyes and long skeletal fingers. He held up his hand while a group of four eight-legged creatures bowed to him. "The water demons," Beatrice said, floating up behind them with Fabbio at her side.

"Do you think these pictures are telling a story?" May asked.

Nobody answered.

The next few windows were broken, offering a sliver of a view outside, of the zipping stars and below, the city, which looked tiny. May's fear of heights sent her knees wobbling and her stomach churning. She could see where Ether ended and the desert began. It seemed to stretch forever.

A heavy thud fell on her back. "What are ye all standing around fer?" John the Jibber's face was contorted in anger and fear. "The Book!"

He dragged May forward by the back of her bathing suit, but

as he did, her eyes caught on the second-to-last pane of glass, and she pulled out of his grasp. The panel depicted a city—not at all like the one they were in. It was nestled on the side of a great mountain. Many of its buildings had fallen, with plumes of smoke rising from the ruins. Spirits crouched in fear on the streets, many of their faces filled with terror as others—ghouls, goblins, demons—ran rampant everywhere, hauling spirits around in sacks. Enormous winged creatures flew through the air, ridden by ghastly skeletons.

"Have you ever seen a city like this?" May asked John. He had come to a stop, and now he stared, pale faced, as mesmerized by the scene as she was. He licked his lips nervously and shook his head.

A castle at the edge of the city loomed up into the sky. Spirits stared out through its windows, fearful and terrified, looking like they were crying to get out. Thousands of others dotted the hills, tied in chains. And there in the lower corner of the picture, tucked between a few shadowy, chained figures, were two spirits who looked very much like Beatrice and Fabbio. And beside them was a spirit with short black hair, big brown eyes, and knobby knees.

May glanced at the others to see if they'd noticed, but their eyes were elsewhere.

May looked back at the girl again. It was her, May. And it *wasn't*.

She seemed to be wearing the death shroud she wore now, but looking closely, one could see she had a quiver of gleaming silver arrows strapped to her back. Her face was striped with white and black paint, making her look like a skeleton.

It was the face that was different. The girl in the picture had the face of a warrior. Her mouth was set in a grim, determined line. Her eyes were shining with anger and despair. She looked full of darkness. And it was hard to tell, truly, if she was alive or dead.

That's not me, she told herself, shaking her head. She didn't want the others to see such a horrible scene. And where was Pumpkin? Quickly she glanced toward the final panel, but it was shattered beyond recognition.

"What happens?" She reached down and sifted frantically through the shards of glass on the floor beneath her. "What happens to everyone? . . . Ouch!"

She lifted up her hand to watch the stream of blood trickle down from where she'd sliced her skin. At the same time she heard the faint barking of dogs.

May felt all the blood drain to her feet.

"Ooooohhh," Pumpkin moaned.

Again John grabbed the back of her bathing suit and lifted her up, pushing her toward the arched doorway at the end of the hall. "There's no time, girl. Come on now." A great clanking rang up the floaterator shaft behind them.

They gathered in front of the revolving door, which was spinning all on its own. May looked up at John.

"Go on, lassie," he said, nudging her forward. May squared her shoulders and stepped forward, keeping in sync with the movement of the door. It spat her into a cylindrical room with no windows. In the middle was a podium. And on the podium sat a small black book.

The others followed. John came through last, and hurriedly jammed his sack into the door to keep it from rotating.

Everyone looked at May expectantly.

"You are going first," Fabbio said, tapping her shoulder lightly. "Go on, May."

May looked at Pumpkin and Beatrice for approval, then stepped up to the podium and reached her hands gently toward the Book. As soon as her fingers touched the cover, it began to glow and buzz. Wincing slightly, she pulled it open. Behind her, everyone gasped.

"Ye've got it, lass!"

May's heart raced with excitement. The page that opened before her was filled with thousands of words, and the lines twitched slightly. It took a moment for May to realize the words were changing, shifting, and rearranging themselves.

She was in the *As*. She read the first passage her eyes came to:

> **Abraham Lincoln**: *Former president, killed by shooting, retired in the southern town of Gaunt, enjoys golf and long floats along the sand.*

"I guess it's alphabetized by first name," May said.

"Then look fer Sheba, girly. Remember, yer looking up the treasure first."

"But . . ." May was inches from finding out how to get home. And Beatrice needed her mother. It all seemed much too important to—

John reached out for the top of her bathing suit and squeezed it in his fist, his face forming itself into a mask of grim, seething anger. "Do it, lass!"

May flipped through to the *S* section, looking for Sheba. There was nothing. She shook her head. "There's nothing here on Sheba."

"Check again."

She did. And shook her head.

John leaped forward as if to throttle her, but Fabbio stepped in front of him stiffly.

"She say there is nothing there," he boomed, readjusting the parachute on his back. "I am suggesting you back up."

Just then a loud whine from down the hall announced that the floaterator had roared back into life. Pumpkin whimpered and pressed himself against the part of the wall farthest from the door. Fabbio wrapped his arms tightly around Beatrice, whose eyelashes fluttered madly.

"Look up John the Jibber, then," John cried desperately. "Hurry. Find out how I make me riches."

May nodded, biting her lip, her pulse thumping in her ears, and flipped through again. "John the Jibber. John the Jibber."

Ding. They all looked at the door. Down the hall the muffled sounds of barking were followed by the sound of the floaterator door sliding open with a creak.

"Go on!" John cried.

May looked down at the Book. "Here it is!" She stabbed at the entry with her finger. "Here it is! 'John the Jibber, born 1805. Betrayed his fellow smugglers to the king of England and led them into a trap, from which they escaped. Was later found by same smugglers and murdered. Resided in Nine Knaves Grotto for more than two hundred years until' . . ."

May paused. The barking was no longer muffled. It sounded like it was right outside the revolving door, accompanied by the sound of ghouls. Fabbio drew a dagger from a hilt on his belt. John braced himself against his sack to keep the door from revolving.

"Go on, go on . . ."

May swallowed. "No, I—"

"Read it!"

May let out a long deep breath. "'Met his second death on the top floor of the Eternal Edifice, where he was sucked into nothingness.'"

John cried out and backed up harder against the door.

At the same time, in front of May, the pages began flipping on their own. She gazed down in amazement. They flipped to the Ms, then to the Mas, and then there was her name:

> **May Bird**: *A type of bug found in the West Indies, which mates in May.*

> **May Mary Bird**: *Irish, born 1863, died 1923 when her buggy went over a cliff. Lives in the Western Territories in town of Flat Canyon.*

> **May Mary Bird**: *Irish, named after her great-grandmother [see above], born 1940, resides in Pluckville, Iowa.*

May's breath caught when she landed on the next name.

> **May Ellen Bird**: *Born in the portal town of Briery Swamp, West Virginia. Currently standing in the tower of the Eternal Edifice.*

May's throat went dry and cold. There was a loud crash, but she didn't look up. She felt as if she'd entered a deep trance.

The words of the entry kept changing, arranging themselves into different lines. May tried to read each one before it changed.

Little, known visitor to the Ever After, who returned home to Briery Swamp, West Virginia, after a brief and ineffective sojourn in the Ever After.

Known far and wide as the girl who destroyed Evil Bo Cleevil's reign of terror. Resides in Briery Swamp, West Virginia.

Little known visitor to the Ever After, was sucked into nothingness on the north edge of the City of Ether.

May was gripping the paper so hard that it ripped in her hands, the sheet with her name on it remaining between her fingers. She didn't notice the barking had gone quiet. "It doesn't say how I get . . ."

She looked up, and at the same time, her whole body went numb. The door was no longer where it had been—it was lying shattered in the hallway. Pumpkin, Beatrice, and Fabbio were in the arms of a group of ghouls.

And beside them, his black top hat resting perfectly on his head, his white eyeballs trained on May, and his sharp pointed teeth revealed in a wide grin, stood the Bogeyman, holding a leash full of panting, sitting Black Shuck dogs. He tilted his hat at her, his white eyeballs glinting.

He drifted forward and took the slip of paper out of May's hands, then ran his fingers along the words and nodded. His face then contorted into a fearful grimace, and he smiled again, shook his head at her, and waggled one finger in a no-no-no gesture. There was a tiny suction cup on the tip of the finger, just as John had said.

The Bogey then turned to John the Jibber, who cowered against the wall. Slowly he raised the same finger toward him. John squirmed.

"Sir, heh heh, I know what this must look like. Ye see, it's like this. I promised the phantom I'd bring her to the front hall, but ye see"—John swallowed loudly—"er, the little rascal gave me the slip. Run up here to get at the Book. I was just trying to stop her when—"

The Bogey pulled his hand back and placed his finger against his chin, as if he was listening thoughtfully. He kept smiling. His smile sent deep chills through May, who took in what John was saying slowly, flabbergasted.

"Now, ye all promised me my freedom, ye know, if I brought her in. She's got the letter, ye know, from the Northern Spirits. On their side, she is. I found it meself—just go on and look in her knapsack, and I'll just be on me way. . . ." John let out a nervous laugh and took a few steps sideways, toward the floaterator at the end of the hall.

The Bogeyman smiled extra wide and chucked his chin up and down a few times as if he was joining the Jibber in a joke. Then he shot out his hand again, pointing his fingers toward John. John's eyes widened in terror. "No, oh please, no!"

Strange things began to happen to John's body. It began to unravel in a long rope of vapor—first his feet, then his ankles and his legs, and on up—the vapor disappearing into the Bogeyman's

fingers. "Ahhhhhhh!" he screamed, more and more of him twisting in a long thread of vapor until his mouth, too, had vanished.
And then, with a sucking sound, the last of his greasy, mud-caked
hair disappeared completely.

"Ooooh," Pumpkin moaned as the Bogeyman looked around
at them all.

He made a fast motion with his hands. The ghouls sprang forward.

Somber Kitty knew something had gone horribly wrong. The little
bit of fuzz covering his body stood up on end, along with his tail.
Crouching in a duct across from the Eternal Edifice, he was bewildered by the chaos surrounding him. But his gut told him that
May, so close, was in trouble. He had picked up her tracks in front
of a bakery and followed them here, where, curiously, they had
doubled back. Another scent, rising up from far below the street,
told him that she had returned this way, right into the great building before him.

He had searched the building from all sides, sniffing along
the bottom of its wall, and that had taken more than an hour.
Now he watched the front stairs—the only entrance he could
find—and tried to gauge his chances of darting fast enough to
make it through the ranks of horrible creatures staggered along
its stairs.

Somber Kitty could think of no other strategy. If he was going
in, he was going like a warrior.

After a deep growl, he leaped forward.

He took the stairs two at a time. For a moment the creatures
were too shocked to do anything, and then they began lunging
for him, jabbing toward him with their spears and swiping at

him with their claws. Ahead of him the golden doors stayed res-
olutely closed. Somber Kitty slammed into them, turned with
his back against them, and hissed, swiping forward with his tiny
right paw.

A few of the creatures made a sound like laughter. They
swooped down to claim him.

CHAPTER TWENTY-EIGHT

Nothingness

"Hello?" May was crouching at the bottom of a dark pit, her arms wrapped around herself, shivering. "Is anyone there?"

"May?" Pumpkin's voice echoed back to her.

"Pumpkin! I thought they'd taken you! Where are you?"

"I don't know. I'm in some kind of pit."

"Me too!"

Another voice rose out in the darkness. "Hey, are you two all right?"

"Beatrice!" Fabbio called. "You okay?"

"I think so."

"I'm okay," May called. Everyone voiced agreement. But May knew none of them were okay. John the Jibber was gone. And there was no one who knew how to help them. They were caught. May rubbed at her elbows and knees where they'd been scraped a few moments before, when she'd been dropped into the pit.

Then she began feeling along the walls. And then, with a gasp, she felt her shoulders. Her knapsack was gone. It must have been torn off in the struggle.

Suddenly a blue glow illuminated the area, and May looked toward a giant Holo-Vision screen mounted in the wall.

"You all have this HV?" Fabbio called. Again everyone voiced agreement.

The blue screen dissolved into a scene of a specter—the same one who had been in the movie at the Spectroplex—with a knife in his chest. He smiled at the camera, seeming to smile directly at May.

"Hello, and welcome to the uppermost dungeons of the Eternal Edifice. On behalf of the great Bo Cleevil, we would like to extend our regrets that your stay is under such unfortunate circumstances."

"What circumstances? What's going to happen to us?" May asked as if the man could hear her, but he went on talking.

"Because you are being detained for questioning, you may at this time enjoy a few extra minutes or hours of the afterlife before you are destroyed completely. To prepare for your execution, you may like to empty your pockets of all valuables at this time. You may also wish to say a silent good-bye to all of those that you have ever loved. Remember to remain in your pit patiently until the ghouls come to get you. Though of course"—the man chuckled softly—"you have little choice."

He turned serious again, his big dark eyes focused on the camera. "Remember, execution is, quite literally, *nothing* to be scared of. Once you have vanished from existence completely, you won't know the difference."

He gave a chilling smile. "Have a pleasant stay!" Suddenly the HV blinked off, and the pit was enveloped in pitch-blackness once again.

"Ohhhh," Pumpkin moaned.

"We've got to get out of here," Beatrice moaned.

"No worry, Beatrice, I will find a way." The grunts of Captain Fabbio leaping and jumping and trying to climb carried into May's pit. But May had gone numb. She crouched down against the wall and hugged herself tight, staring toward the darkness of the ceiling. At any moment the boulder covering the pit would be pushed aside, and she would be dragged out. She would never see her cat, or her mom, or her woods, or anyone again.

"Pumpkin," she finally called. "I'm so sorry. You'd be back in Belle Morte if it weren't for me."

There was a long silence, and then, "I really didn't have anything else to do."

"Hush, you two," Beatrice called. "You sound like you're giving up! We just have to think."

May was thinking a lot. She was thinking of how she had thought once that if she could go somewhere else, she could *be* someone else. But she had come here, clear across the universe, and her life had not amounted to much of anything. She was thinking how much she had let everyone down.

They waited in silence for a long time. But for all their thinking, nobody came up with a way out of the pits. Occasionally May heard the muffled sound of ghouls jabbering above, and then the scrape of a boulder being moved from its place, and terrible screams as a spirit was dragged out of its pit and away.

"I just hope it's not the Bogey who does it," Beatrice said heavily, her earlier note of hopefulness gone. "I couldn't take that. I'd rather be . . . destroyed by the ghouls." Then came the sound of her softly crying, and the weight of May's guilt hung more heavily on her shoulders than ever.

She reached out toward the dirt in front of her and began to trace a picture of Somber Kitty, to make up for all the ones she hadn't drawn of him at home. She sank back and placed her hands against her hips, missing him. Her fingers skimmed the tops of her shorts.

And then, like a spark of lightning, she remembered the vial of seawater in her pocket.

It must have been hours before a scraping sound came from above May, and the boulder covering her pit was moved, letting light spill in and admitting two ghoul faces who jabbered at May. May's heart threatened to pound its way out of her chest as she watched them throw down a ladder made of chains and climb toward her. They dragged her back out of the hole, where she quickly looked around the room, a great gray cell filled with boulders to mark each pit. She was careful not to scream or call out, though she wanted to. She knew Pumpkin was scared enough as it was.

"May, is that you?" Beatrice called.

"Be brave," May called back. The ghouls pulled her into a long hallway and up a set of stairs, through two gleaming steel doors into a huge room made completely of glass. The doors slid shut behind her.

The room was enormous and gave a complete view of the dusky sky, as well as the city beneath their feet. In the middle of the floor was a large circle, sliced into parts. And beyond that a gold and purple chair that looked a lot like a throne.

Through the window May could see the buildings of Ether stretched out below, and then farther, the barren outskirts—a vast field of gravestones—and beyond that, the desert. A tiny stripe curved its way outward from the great cemetery, curling around the northern outskirts of the city, and then shooting farther north. May realized with an extra thud in her chest that that must be the northern railroad. And then the height made her so wobbly she had to move away from the window.

A sliding sound behind her made the hairs on her neck and arms stand up. Without turning around, she knew by the silence the Bogey had entered the room. Slowly, her body feeling numb, she turned around.

The Bogey smiled his horrible smile at her and waved his fingers in a long, lazy movement. He sat in his throne and continued to smile.

Behind him were two ghouls who, at his silent command, scurried forward and grabbed onto her arms, holding her tight.

She squirmed as the Bogey drifted up again and over to her, stroking his hands along his long pointy chin before running them gently through her hair, his empty white eyes shining. May stayed perfectly still.

When the Bogey finally spoke, his voice came out of a set of speakers at the top of the room. It was a hoarse whisper.

"You were very fortunate in opening the Book. It is a great honor. My master, long ago, was able to open it too. Can you guess what it told him?"

May swallowed, and shook her head just slightly.

"The Book told him that a Live One would come to destroy him." The Bogey patted her head. "But it didn't tell him who."

May clenched her teeth and tried to stand completely still.

"So he set guards at each portal to protect our world from those like you. It seems you got through anyway."

Now the Bogey pulled his hands together and cracked his knuckles one by one. Behind him May could see the southern part of the city. A tiny plume of smoke, she noticed absently, had risen up in the distance where the train tracks met the horizon.

"You have led us to the answer, to your name in the Book. Now you must tell me, how were you planning to do it?"

May tried to move her arms slightly, but they were pinned solidly by the two ghouls. She was still trying to take in what the Bogey was saying. "I . . . I wasn't planning anything. You have the wrong person."

The Bogey's hand shot out and grabbed her at the top of her bathing suit, his frigid knuckles grazing her collarbone. "The Book doesn't lie. Tell me how."

"I don't know." May scrunched her shoulders up against the deadly fingers digging into her throat.

The voice, though still hoarse and whispery, came through the speakers so loudly that the glass all around them began to vibrate. "What kind of weapon is it you have that you think can destroy a power as great as Bo Cleevil?"

May shook her head. "I don't have a weapon."

The Bogey's eyes glinted at her for a long moment. Finally he nodded. "It doesn't matter anymore. You will never get a chance to use it.

"Search her," he said to the ghouls, still talking through the speakers. "Bring me anything you find. Then dispose of her."

He tilted his top hat at her, then turned and drifted toward the doors. With the push of a button they slid open. But before he went out completely, the Bogey pushed another button. He floated through the doorway a moment before the circle in the floor opened up, full of blackness and gaping at May. She stared at it, petrified. She knew instantly that that blackness was what nothing looked like. She tried to scrabble backward, thrusting her hand toward her pocket.

"Hbbblgglglg," one ghoul said to the other.

While the one took both of May's flailing arms tightly in his hands, the other stuck his slimy claws into her pockets, pulling out her quartz rock. He let out a squeal when he saw it, and the other ghoul swiped at it with one hand while holding May's wrists with the other, fighting for the rock. It went flying across the room.

In a flash the first ghoul had his claws back in her pockets again, digging for more treasures. Grunting, he jerked out the sea capsule and held it up high.

This time the second ghoul let go of May completely. The creatures tackled each other, their hands closing over the capsule. May held her breath. She took a step back.

Smack! Both ghouls looked straight at her the split second before they vanished completely.

May swooped to grab her quartz rock before she sprinted out the doors and back to the room of the pits.

"Pumpkin! Bea! Fabbio!"

"May!"

She followed Pumpkin's voice to the nearest pit and lunged against the stone. "I can't move it!"

May tackled the stone again, pushing with all her might. It gave a little bit, then a little bit more, until there was room for May to throw the chain ladder down into the open space. A moment later a pair of long fingers appeared on the ledge of the pit, and Pumpkin squeezed his way out, shaking all the way.

He and May peered around.

"Beatrice, Fabbio!"

They followed their voices to two other pits and, with great effort, rolled the boulders out of the way.

Once the group was all on level ground, they sprinted for the door opposite the one May had been dragged through before. They ran out into a long passageway.

"The floaterator!" Pumpkin pointed.

They sprinted down the hall. Beatrice jammed her finger into the Down button. At that moment, the light said it was at floor 3,987.

"Ay, Dio mio," Fabbio muttered, shifting his parachute on his back.

Slowly the floaterator made its way up. While they waited, the group looked frantically over their shoulders. Finally, there was a ding in front of them—and a chorus of chatter came from behind the floaterator doors.

"Run!"

With Beatrice, Pumpkin, and Fabbio speeding along in front of her, May pounded away from the floaterator. The floaterator door had opened behind them and a chorus of ghoul voices rang out as the ghouls gave chase. The group zipped through the dungeon area littered by boulders and turned right, stopping only when they'd zoomed straight into the glass room and realized they were trapped.

May dove for the button that would close the doors. Beatrice searched for a way to lock them and finally slammed her small white fist into every button there was until they heard a great magnetized sound. The doors seemed to have locked.

Outside, a heavy thud announced the arrival of the ghouls and that they were trying to break the doors down.

"What'll we do?" Everybody looked at May.

"My guts!" Pumpkin cried, darting behind May and holding her shoulders, gazing at the doors.

May stared out the window at that curious puff of smoke in the distance. Suddenly she realized what it was.

"There's the train north," Beatrice said sadly at the same time May thought it. Beatrice was breathing hard, sticking her finger against the glass and pointing beyond the northern gate of the city. "That's the station I read about," she said, glancing over her shoulder at the door. May could make out a little dot that marked the station.

"I wish we were on that train," Beatrice said, "headed out of the city."

"I always wanted to see snow," Pumpkin warbled.

The ghouls outside the doors slammed into them harder and harder.

May watched the puff of smoke. If there was one fast way out of Ether, it was by train. Not that it mattered.

Or did it?

May racked her brain. She remembered tying herself to those balloons last year and trying to fly off her mother's car. There was an idea buzzing just out of her reach, like one of Arista's bees.

"Would you really get on that train?" Everyone looked at May.

"I would go with you, if we were going," Beatrice said gently. "Why?"

"Ah, I go where Beatrice goes," said Fabbio. "It is a nice dream."

"I always wanted to see snow," Pumpkin repeated.

May stared at him for a long while, the buzzing in her head getting louder.

The thuds on the door produced a great creaking sound, and ghoul-shaped indents appeared in the metal. A slit appeared between the doors.

And then, in a flash, May had it. The idea sent a shock through her that was half hope, half fear.

"Fabbio," she said, her voice rushing out in one long breath. "Do you think your parachute can hold us?"

Fabbio blinked at her for a second, and then smiled with trembling lips. "Yes, I am already thinking this," he recovered. "Is great idea I have, no?"

His Adam's apple bobbed up and down, and his smile dropped. He gazed through the glass at the distance to the ground below, then looked back at her, his brown eyes fearful. "Do we have choice?"

May swallowed, remembering how—it seemed like a million years ago—her balloons had failed, and she'd crashed to the ground, hurt and embarrassed. She looked behind her at the wall of glass, so far above the ground. This wouldn't be like a plunge from the top of her mom's car. If it didn't work . . .

May gazed at the rest of the group. Her stomach flopped. "We can choose to try."

In one movement they lifted the Bogey's throne and slammed it through the glass, which shattered into a thousand pieces and went flying toward the city below. May, Beatrice, Fabbio, and Pumpkin stood on the ledge. Everyone hugged Fabbio tightly.

He leaped forward.

Far below, Somber Kitty had managed to run the ghouls around in circles for several minutes, dodging their spears and their swooping hands, unwilling to leave the stairs that were his only way of getting to May. His energy, though, was beginning to give out. His tongue hung out of his mouth in an unsightly, embarrassing way; his small rib cage heaved. And it was becoming increasingly difficult to dart up and down the stairs, ducking and diving out of harm's reach.

Panting and bleary-eyed, Somber Kitty finally did the unthinkable. He slipped. Rolling lopsidedly down the stairs, his chin thudding on each step, he had a horrifying moment to wonder which was worse—the pain and fear, or the humiliation.

A slimy arm scooped him into the air, squeezing him against a slimy body with a tight grip. Somber Kitty was too tired to fight very well, and the creature hung on to him easily. And then something happened that was, if possible, even more disturbing.

Glass fell out of the sky. All of the slimy creatures suddenly froze, mumbling to one another and looking up. Somber Kitty looked too. There, sailing across the air and headed farther and farther away from him, was a tiny speck. Somber Kitty's nose twitched and sniffed, his eyes narrowed, and he let out a howl.

"Mmmmmeeaaayyyyyyyy!"

With breathtaking strength, he twisted like a corkscrew, sliding right out of the slimy grip that held him. He landed on wobbly legs.

Shaking his ears, he shot like an arrow toward the west gate of Ether, keeping his eye on the object in the sky above, and running with all his force for the desert.

CHAPTER TWENTY-NINE

The Station

Pumpkin, May, Beatrice, and Fabbio careened across the sand, kicking up dust in their wake, each of them falling off Captain Fabbio like ticks falling off a dog after a flea bath.

May landed with her mouth in the sand, which she spit and spluttered out as she sat up. Her bones ached.

"Are you all okay?"

Pumpkin was moaning. Beatrice and Fabbio were slowly levitating back up to sitting. The parachute lay tattered and flat behind them. They were several hundred yards from the walls of Ether.

They all stood up, stared at one another groggily for a few moments, and then they started to smile.

"Whoop!"

"Yahoo!"

"We did it!"

"Mama mia, it is too good to be true!"

May thrust her hands in the air, jumping up and down and clenching her fists in triumph. "We did it!" she yelled again. "We did it we did it we did it!"

They all hollered and hooted and hugged one another.

When they had all calmed down, they peered around them.

"What do we do now?" Pumpkin asked.

May spoke quickly, with authority. "The train station. Which way is it?"

Beatrice stretched a long pale arm ahead of her. "The train was on its way. We'd better go fast. Unless we've missed it already."

The travelers hurried across the desert as swiftly as they could in the direction of the station they had seen from the air. It rose up before them, small at first, but getting larger and larger.

May had just made out the roof when a massive sound came from behind them. They all turned to look. As they watched, the huge gates of the city slowly swung open. And then what looked like hundreds of black dots swarmed out through the gates.

"Oh, my gosh," May said.

Beatrice threw her small hand over her heart. "Shuck dogs."

No one needed a second look. They started zooming now, and soon not only the roof but the whole of the train station was clear and vivid in front of them. They arrived at top speed, slamming to a halt right in front of the platform.

"Do you see the train? Do you see it?" Beatrice asked, scanning the horizon. "How close is it?"

May scanned the sand in both directions, hoping that if she saw the train, it would be heading toward them and not away. For a heart-stopping moment there was nothing to be seen on the desert but the Black Shucks in the distance. And also, strangely, a giant wooden mouse rolling along to the far left. May shook her head, befuddled. And then, there it was, a tiny plume of smoke in the distance.

"Look," May pointed.

"That's it!" Beatrice said. "Is it getting closer or farther away?"

They all strained their eyes to see.

"Closer!"

Everyone cheered except Pumpkin. He stood with his fingers jammed in his mouth, frowning. "Ohhhhh."

"It's good news, Pumpkin!" May assured him.

Pumpkin groaned again. "It would be"—he pointed to the growing black blobs in the distance—"but I think the dogs are moving faster."

If May had been paying attention while she was flying through the sky, she may have seen a tiny speck, smaller than any ghost, trekking across the ground below, moving more and more slowly, like a car running out of gas. She also would have seen that the giant mouse, with hundreds of feet poking out from the bottom, was closing the distance between itself and the speck.

Somber Kitty had known he was being followed for several minutes. The fact that it was by a giant wooden mouse did not faze him. There were all sorts of things in this world to confuse him, and he was too close to May to think of any of them anymore. He had seen her, with his keen eyes, land on the sand, and now she was running away. He had noticed, from the corner of his eye, the fast-moving train in the distance. And he had also seen the gates of the city open and a cluster of strange black specks pour out onto the landscape, moving at lightning speed.

Those didn't faze him either.

Somber Kitty set his course and tried to push his tired legs faster.

CHAPTER THIRTY

The Black Shucks

They could see the train clearly now—a long black snake curling its way toward them. It seemed to go on endlessly.

May, Pumpkin, Beatrice, and Captain Fabbio watched it, willing it to go faster, looking back over their shoulders every few seconds, frantic. Both the Black Shucks and the giant mouse were getting closer and closer.

The crack of a whip sent a sickening dread into May's heart. Behind the dogs, the shape of the Bogey became clear, riding on his sled, his top hat secure despite the wind.

Oh, please. Please please please, May thought. *Please.*

"The train's not going to make it in time," Beatrice said, saying what they all, in the past few seconds, had begun to realize. "We can't outrun them."

"Right." May turned to them, pushing the fear way down into her gut and trying to pull out courage instead. "We need to look for weapons. Anything you can find. We're going to have to fight them."

They ran around the station looking for things they could break apart to use as clubs. Fabbio pulled out his dagger. Beatrice held a length of pipe dug from the sand. May reached into her pocket and clutched the quartz rock. They all looked at one another, and May could see in everyone's eyes that they all knew weapons wouldn't help them. And there was no place to go.

"I don't have a weapon," Pumpkin said.

May's lip began to tremble. Pumpkin stared at her hopefully with his fingers tugging at his wrinkled lips, trusting and innocent and helpless.

"That's okay," she said, trying to sound brave. "You just stay behind me. If something happens, something bad, I want you to close your eyes and wait till it's over." May felt like that was all she could offer him.

Tears began to fall from Pumpkin's eyes. And that made them fall from May's too.

She reached out and hugged him. Everybody hugged one another one last time.

For a moment May remembered her picture, the one of her in the woods, dressed as a warrior with Somber Kitty at her side. *You are that girl,* the Undertaker had said.

May tried.

"Everyone get ready," she said, cocking her arm back behind her shoulder.

They readied their weapons and waited for the Bogey and his dogs to arrive.

Somber Kitty could smell tears on the air. He could see the shape of May clearly now, and the others she was with—though she hadn't yet seen him with her inferior human eyes. The smell of fear—of May's fear—was also in the air, and Somber Kitty, confused, looked in the direction that May and the others were looking, toward the black specks that were growing larger on the horizon. Suddenly Somber Kitty's nose twitched madly. His skin began to tremble on his bones. The specks weren't specks anymore. They were dogs.

Somber Kitty stopped in his tracks. A low growl began deep in his belly, and he stayed frozen, torn, distraught.

With the very last of his strength, he ran.

CHAPTER THIRTY-ONE

A Figure in the Distance

They could hear the dogs' breath now, could even smell it. They were almost upon them.

Pumpkin, May, Beatrice, and Fabbio looked at one another, then back across the sand. The train was close now; they could see a skeleton wearing an engineer's cap at the front window. But it was too late. In another moment the dogs were there, yelping and screeching, pouring around them. Beatrice and Pumpkin crouched and held up their hands to defend themselves. Fabbio and May stood before them bravely. Fabbio waved his sword at the dogs uselessly. "Not another step!"

One dog was lunging for his throat when a high sharp whistle pierced the air, causing the dog to snap its jaws shut just inches from Fabbio's face. All of the dogs sat, but only just. Their teeth dripped bloodthirsty drool. They whimpered at being so close to their prey and unable to attack.

And then, from behind them, floated the Bogeyman.

He was smiling as he made his way around this dog and that one, his pointy teeth bared, his eyes crinkled up in what looked like a laugh.

May winced. Behind her she could hear the train squealing to a stop, and then the doors sliding open. She wanted to tear her eyes away to look back at the train, gauging their chances for making it, but she couldn't get herself to move an inch. She rolled her eyes to the side.

"Don't even try . . . ," the Bogeyman rasped, his voice—without the speakers—coming out low and whispery. He seemed to know what she was thinking. "You take one step, and a hundred Shuck dogs will tear you apart."

He floated up to May and ran his fingers along her chin. "There'll be nothing to help you now, May Bird." He looked around at the others. "Now is your time to die."

The Bogeyman held his fingers up to May's face and placed the suction cups on her cheeks. May felt her vision going black.

Suddenly there was a squeal on her left. A shape shot forward and tackled the Bogey around the waist. It took a moment for May to realize who it was.

"Pumpkin, no!"

The Bogeyman, though thin and gaunt, did not even sway. He seemed amused as he plucked Pumpkin off him and tossed him onto the ground, stepping on him with one black-clad foot. "I'll save you for Mama. She loves house ghosts."

A whimper came from behind him, and then Mama padded up beside the Bogey, a full three times bigger than the other dogs.

Behind May a voice called, "All aboard."

May jerked her head to see a skeleton conductor standing on the top step of the train door, seemingly oblivious to all that was going on. In another moment he disappeared into the car, and with a sickening thud, the doors closed. The train chugged into life and began to pull away.

May felt the last hope die within her. Beside her, Beatrice began to cry. The Bogeyman once again stretched his fingers toward May. Her skin went tingly, and then it began to stretch.

At that moment Mama let out a huge snuff, loud enough to make the Bogeyman look down at her. "Don't be jealous, Mama. You'll have your turn with the others."

But Mama wasn't listening to him. She had begun to whimper. And then a strange thing began happening with the other dogs. They all lifted up their heads and sniffed at the air, curiously at first. Then a few tails became ramrod straight, a few ears pricked up, and every one of them began sniffing and huffing hard, standing up and looking all around them.

The Bogeyman let go of May for just a second.

"Run!"

It had been Captain Fabbio that yelled it. And it was a hopeless cause. But they all started running, not toward the train but away from it, away from the Bogeyman, taking the dogs by surprise just enough so that they got a minuscule head start as they rushed across the sand.

It wasn't enough.

They ran toward a slight rise in the sand, the dogs just on their heels. May waited for the first set of fangs to sink into her back. She crested the rise and then, at the sight of a figure before her, stumbled forward.

May landed hard on the sand, dazed and blinking. She forgot about the dogs behind her. She forgot about the train.

A tiny figure was running toward her in the sand, with high pointy ears and a skinny tail. As it got close to her, it slowed down, as if unsure of itself. And then it let out a plaintive, melancholy sound.

"Meay?"

May lost her breath. She blinked madly and tried to get her voice to come out. "Kitty?"

A loud yelp sounded behind her, making May look over her shoulder. The dogs had all come to a dead stop. They were all staring at the figure in the sand.

She looked back ahead. "Kitty?" she whispered again, her eyes filling with tears.

At that moment every dog let out a petrified howl, turned tail, and began to run. But May didn't see them. She climbed to her feet and ran the last few yards that separated her and her cat, falling onto the sand beside him and swooping him into her arms, then holding him out to look at him, to make sure it was really him.

Somber Kitty's legs dangled beneath him. "Meay. Meay. Meay."

May rained kisses all over Somber Kitty's head, squeezing him so hard that he finally let out a small mew to let her know he was getting smushed. By the time Beatrice, Fabbio, and Pumpkin caught up, she and Kitty were rocking back and forth. The others watched in amazement, flabbergasted.

May leaped to her feet, cradling Somber Kitty tightly in her arms.

When she lowered him to look at him, the Bogeyman was staring her in the face.

May drew Somber Kitty back to her chest with a groan. "Leave him alone." The Bogey chuckled soft and low. Before May could move in either direction, he reached out and grabbed her by the shoulder, the suction cups at the edges of his fingers digging into her skin.

"Please, just leave him alone," May whispered. She felt her skin, where his fingers touched, start to tingle and pull.

The Bogey tilted his head sideways for a moment. He looked her up and down, squinting. "Him? Him who?" he rasped.

At that moment, with a loud meow, Somber Kitty leaped out of May's arms onto the Bogey's face, digging cat claws into his cheeks before leaping onto the ground.

And then, with Somber Kitty leading the way, they ran. This time, they ran for the train.

May's arms and legs pumped as she trailed the others and tried to drag Pumpkin along in step. The train was still picking up speed and had not yet curled the last of its empty train cars past the station.

The Bogeyman, screeching in pain, caught up quickly and zipped up behind them, slower without his sled but still deadly fast. When May looked over her shoulder, the Bogey was inches from Pumpkin, who was bringing up the rear. His hands latched onto Pumpkin's ragged shirt. At the same moment, May reached into her pocket and hurled her quartz rock at him with all her might. It hit the Bogey between the eyes and sent him reeling backward, just enough to free Pumpkin.

At that moment May saw the great wooden mouse lying on its side on the rise. And in front of it thousands of spirits, tan, with white sheets draped around their waists and chests, poured out of it and ran toward them. They let out a collective cry. "Raaaaa!"

May's group let out a cry too. "Ahhhhhhhhhhhhhhh!" They

sprinted alongside the train, nearing the open platform of the last car.

Somber Kitty was the first to jump on, which he did with ease. He was followed by Fabbio, who hoisted Beatrice into his arms and with truly astonishing strength, and then brought himself onto the floor of the car. Pumpkin went next, using his long legs to vault forward and grab the others' hands, which then pulled him on. They all reached out their arms and waved May on. She leaped once and fell.

They waggled their arms frantically. "Hurry!"

May quickly got up and started running again, her legs carrying her faster than she ever knew they could, faster than dead fast. She threw herself forward, and this time several hands grabbed her and pulled her up.

Behind her the Bogeyman had almost caught up. But so had the Egyptians. Desperately trying to reach Somber Kitty, they didn't stop for the Bogey, and trampled right over him, their cries drowning out his screams of terror as he was flattened beneath their feet.

But it was too late for them to catch their sacred cat. A few of the faster spirits kept up with the train for a few seconds, only a few feet behind the car, and then even they collapsed, holding their bellies and panting.

Somber Kitty gazed at them from his safe spot on the train, flapping his tail tauntingly like a victory flag. And then he retreated into the circle of May's arms.

Beatrice, Fabbio, Pumpkin, and May were all piled together, ghostly and living limbs overlapping one another. Beatrice reached out and grabbed May's hand.

"May, that's a cat."

"My cat," May said, beaming.

Beatrice beamed back. "They were outlawed, you know. Shuck dogs are deathly afraid of cats."

May couldn't help but shake her head. The crowd in the sand, and indeed the City of Ether, became smaller and smaller in the distance.

CHAPTER THIRTY-TWO

The Train Headed North

That night May scratched under Somber Kitty's chin, his favorite spot, and watched the stars zoom above as the long black train sped its way across the desert. Already May could feel just the slightest coolness in the air, as if the North had breathed a colder breath onto the sand. The landscape had begun to change—the elevation had gotten higher, and a few tiny, skinny trees had popped up here and there. May had never been so glad to see a few scrawny bushes. They reminded her of home. May hugged Kitty closer to her heart, feeling his warmth.

The others had gone to sleep hours ago, and behind her, Captain Fabbio let out a loud snore. Beatrice had snuggled into the crook of his arm. Even Somber Kitty purred dreamily.

"Hi," Pumpkin said, crawling up beside her and sitting cross-legged.

"Hi," May said, feeling a lump rise in her throat at the thought of Pumpkin's bravery. He had risked his life to save her. And he was here now. On this train.

"So I wonder what it's like up there," Pumpkin said, nibbling lightly on a finger.

They both knew the North was unknown and dangerous. They didn't have to say it.

"I wonder what she wants from you." Pumpkin pulled his knees in tight.

May shrugged. She had told Bea and Fabbio about the Lady of North Farm. It had just seemed right. She wondered too.

"Do you think she'll be angry with you?"

"I don't know. I don't know anything about her, really. But I guess it doesn't matter. I don't seem to have a choice." She breathed in the night air. "The Undertaker said I wouldn't."

Pumpkin surveyed May with his droopy eyes. "You look worried."

May smiled, brushing a small tear from her eye.

"Nah. Not about that. I was thinking of my mom. She doesn't have me *or* Kitty now."

Pumpkin thought for a few moments. "You'll find your way back. We'll make sure."

Actually, May had been thinking of something her mom had said. About how you didn't make friends, but let them happen. May wanted to repeat this to Pumpkin, who had happened to her most of all, but she was too shy. Instead she said, "I know we will."

Pumpkin smiled. They looked back at Beatrice and Fabbio. May stroked Somber Kitty, who didn't look somber at all at the moment. "He is pure goodness, you know."

They didn't say any more. And for hours they were content to watch the Ever After go by in the dark.

The text of this book was set in Berkeley Oldstyle.
The illustrations were rendered in pastels.
Editor: Jennifer Weiss
Production editor: Jeannie Ng
Designer: Debra Sfetsios
Production manager: Melisa Idelson